Murder at an

Carlene O'Connor comes from a long line of Irish storytellers. Her great-grandmother emigrated from Ireland to America during the Troubles, and the stories have been flowing ever since. Of all the places across the pond she's wandered, she fell most in love with a walled town in County Limerick and was inspired to create the town of Kilbane, County Cork. Carlene currently divides her time between New York and the Emerald Isle.

Also by Carlene O'Connor

An Irish Village Mystery

Murder
AT AN
Irish Wedding

CARLENE O'CONNOR

🔟 CANELO

First published in the USA in 2017 by Kensington Publishing Corporation

This edition published in the United Kingdom in 2022 by

Canelo
Unit 9, 5th Floor
Cargo Works, 1–2 Hatfields
London, SE1 9PG
United Kingdom

A CIP catalogue record for this book is available from the British Library.

Print ISBN 978 1 80032 691 0
Ebook ISBN 978 1 80032 690 3

Look for more great books at www.canelo.co

Printed and bound in Great Britain by Clays Ltd, Elcograf S.p.A.

This is for James and Annmarie—may your Irish wedding be free of murder (but let's leave room for a little mayhem). Here's to you, love you both, loads!

Chapter 1

As the sun rose over Kilbane Castle, it struck the stained-glass window in the highest turret, casting the grounds below in an unearthly glow. A breeze whispered through the grass, rippling the wedding tents, making them shiver down to their stakes. Neighboring hills shook off the morning mist, and wooly apparitions began to dot their peaks, grazing and bleating into the damp fall air. From a room high up in the castle, Kevin Gallagher lay in bed, battling the terrors. Pre-wedding celebrations were in full swing and a bit of drink the night before had loosened his tongue. Upon his stumbling return to the castle, he may have upset a few heads in the Cahill/Donnelly wedding party. He blinked at the ceiling and tried for the life of him to remember the carnage.

He'd told Paul Donnelly, the groom-to-be, that only an eejit would marry a beautiful woman. And Alice Cahill wasn't just beautiful, she was downright gorgeous. A proper fashion model to boot. She was *way* out of Paul Donnelly's league, and if his best man couldn't tell him, then who could?

"You always have to watch your back with a beautiful woman," Kevin slurred on the way home from the pubs. They tripped along on the cobblestone streets of Kilbane as the morning birds began to trill, with the rhythm of the fella playing the spoons in O'Rourke's still thrumming in his chest. "An ugly woman, that's the way to go. Never have to be afraid of losing her. And that father-in-law! Who in his right mind would want to be related to Colm Cahill? If I were you, I'd do a runner and save m'self a life of misery, lad!"

"Shut your gob," Paul said. "You're bollixed."

"Would Alice still marry you if she knew all your secrets?" Kevin clapped Paul hard on the back, causing him to stumble.

When he recovered, Paul's eyes burned with rage. "What secrets are you on about?"

"I could tell Alice a thing or t'ree about her groom-to-be, now couldn't I?" Kevin joked. He and Paul had known each other since they were grasshoppers.

"I can't believe I chose you as my best man." Paul was practically roaring down the streets, his handsome face creased with rage. Kevin had never seen him so furious. He was only messing. Was Paul really worried about his secrets? Why, Paul Donnelly's secrets couldn't shock a virgin on her first day at the nunnery. If you couldn't take a bit of ribbing before snapping on the old ball and chain, then when could ye?

Kevin had had a falling out with Colm Cahill too. The father of the bride was having a cigar around the back of the castle, and the trail of sweet smoke drew Kevin directly to him. Colm was planted between a maze of shrubs, with his cigar in one hand and a glass of Jameson in the other. Ice cubes clinked and crickets chirped. The fat yellow moon hung low, and stars dotted the sky like diamonds. Reminded Kevin of the rock on Alice's hand. She'd better be careful flashing that yoke around.

Colm Cahill made his fortune on a start-up technology company called Swipe-It. An app that allowed you to pay for things with the swipe of a finger. Made himself a pile of money. Can ye imagine that? Making money off taking people's money? The world was upside-down, it was. Kevin had tried to talk a little business with Mr. Moneybags—had a great idea for a new app called Alibi. If the wife was out of town and a man wanted to do a bit of sneaking around, he could send the missus a phony selfie showing himself doing the washing. Of course, she'd expect the washing to be done when she returned, but every new idea had a few bits and bobs to work out.

It wasn't until Kevin was nearly on him that he saw Mr. Moneybags was talking on his mobile. "Just do it. Send the confirmation to the castle."

"How nice to be bossing people around at this hour of the mornin'. Business never sleeps, does it?" Kevin called out.

The old tyrant whirled around. "What is the matter with you? Sneaking up on a person like that."

"I'm having a stroll. Just like you."

"Listening in on me conversation, were you?"

"Your conversation intruded on me, not the other way around."

Colm's face was scrunched with rage. He shook his fist. "Pack your bags and go home."

Kevin shook his head and glanced at the moon. A full one sure did bring out the strange in folk. Especially this crew. "I have another business proposition for ye," Kevin started in.

"Who do you think you are?" Colm approached Kevin, his large frame towering over him.

Did he really not know who he was? Why, the old man was completely off his head. He was starting to think the sooner this wedding was done and dusted, the better. Kevin pointed to himself. "I'm the best man."

"Not anymore. You're not needed anymore." Colm threw a look over Kevin's shoulder, and Kevin whirled around to see Paul lurking behind him. Ear-wagging. Colm pointed at Paul. "Did ye hear that? Was I good and clear?" Colm stormed off. Paul stood staring after his future father-in-law, mouth agape. When he recovered, he turned on Kevin.

"What did you do?"

Kevin threw open his arms. "I am an innocent lad. Didn't even get a chance to pitch me idea."

"You're making things worse," Paul said. "For the love of God, just stay out of it." Then he whirled around and stormed off. Kevin didn't know what to make of it, but it made him feel a bit dirty.

Speaking of dirty, he might have made a pass at the mother of the bride. Susan Cahill was descending the steps to the guest rooms just as Kevin was sloshing up. He must have startled her for she cried out when she saw him. She had the look of a woman caught sneaking out. Kevin gave her a pinch on the arse and may have even planted a kiss on her middle-aged lips. Ah but sure, a woman Susan Cahill's age should be thanking him for the attention, she should. And he could see where Alice Cahill got her looks. Susan was a bit ripe, but you could still see the vestiges of beauty about her. Tall, the Cahill women, mighty tall.

There was at least one other person he had had a run-in with last night—who was it? Ah, Jaysus, for the life of him he couldn't remember. Alice, gorgeous Alice? He hadn't upset her, had he? No, she hadn't even joined the fun. Said she needed her beauty sleep, which was out and out ridiculous.

4

Brian? That whiny little wedding planner? Could be. Anyone who went around wearing little colored squares in their jacket deserved a bit of hassling. Ah, wait. The wedding photographer. Mr. Fancy Artist with a show coming up in Dublin. Eejit. The lad was in everyone's face with his fancy camera snapping and flashing away. It's a wonder he hadn't blinded anyone. Kevin had knocked the yoke flat out of his hands. The lens smashed to pieces on the cobblestone street. Lad should have had better reflexes. He went a bit mental from what Kevin could recall. Wailed like a woman. Said Kevin owed him five thousand euros. What a wanker!

Who else? He was forgetting someone.

Kevin sunk his sore head back into his pillow and stared at the elaborate crown molding rimming the ceiling. Such fine craftsmanship. Not like the shoddy estates going up today.

Kevin drank in the crystal chandelier, rose wallpaper, and arched limestone windows. His head throbbed, and he was damp right down to the bones in his toes.

The pints. The shots. A few pills. Oh, Jaysus. His head began to pound like a drum. Where were they exactly? Kilbane, was it? The walled town. Luckily the castle was outside the proper walls. Kevin couldn't imagine being so closed in, like.

A wave of panic hit him. Was the wedding today? It couldn't be today. He'd be puking down the aisle. No, no. T'anks be to God. The wedding was on Saturday, and today, why it was only Thursday. Lucky for him, weddings in Ireland were often three-day affairs.

Speaking of affairs—did he hear last night that someone was having one? A shocker, it was. Who was it? It was all a bit of a blur.

Something stirred next to him, and he nearly jumped out of his birthday suit. Slowly, he turned his head, and what a fright. Beside him, long blond hair fanned out over the pillow like a den of snakes. Medusa was in bed with him. Her face and body were hidden, burrowed under blankets. There was a colleen in his bed. Or was he in her bed? Perhaps every guest room looked alike.

"If I'm going to ravage anyone tonight, it'll be the maid of dishonor," Kevin suddenly remembered saying. She'd batted her eyelids and wiggled her full hips at him all night. He glanced over at the snoring beauty. What was her name? *Ah, right. Brenna.* Too bad she was nowhere nearly as gorgeous as Alice. Then again, who was?

How cliché. The maid of honor and the best man knocking boots. His eyes landed on the nightstand. His wallet. Keys. A folded-up piece of paper. He snatched it up. The message was typed and centered:

> More when the deed is done. Meet me at
> sunrise. Top of the hill.

Deed? What deed? More what when the deed was done? Once more he glanced at the nightstand, where his eyes landed on the answer, and it came as quite a delight. A thick stack of euros tied up with a little red string. He swiped it up and fanned through it. Why, there were at least a thousand euros here. He read the note again. The hill. The one behind the castle?

Kevin ran his fingers through his hair and plucked his packet of fags off the nightstand. He started to light up, then thought better of it. He might wake the bird. The last thing he needed was Brenna clucking around his business. It was almost sunrise. The note sounded a bit desperate.

6

Parting desperate folks from their money was well within Kevin Gallagher's skill set.

He sat up, fighting the throbbing in his skull, and reached for the blue tracksuit hanging on the chair. Every member of the wedding party had been given the silly tracksuits. Alice had insisted on a group photo in front of the castle before breakfast. He'd have to hurry to the hill if he wanted to be back in time for the photo. Only thing worse than marrying a beautiful woman was riling one up. Especially one about to get married. He dressed, donned his trusty watch and gold chain, then shoved the money and note into his tracksuit pocket and crept out of the room.

He began to whistle a little tune as he wondered who would be waiting atop the hill. He couldn't shake the feeling that he was about to strike a killer of a deal.

Chapter 2

Siobhán O'Sullivan clutched her platter of brown bread and met the steely gaze of the castle security guard head-on. A beefy lad, for sure, but a baby was all he was, no more than eighteen years of age, if she had to guess.

"I'm tellin' ye, I'm a guest of Macdara Flannery. *Garda* Flannery." Usually her auburn locks and bright smile were enough to disarm a young man, but this one seemed immune.

"And I'm tellin' ye. You're not on the list." He stared at his clipboard as if it contained all the mysteries of Ireland. As security guards went, he was as intimidating as their new Jack Russell pup, Trigger.

"There's been an emergency." Siobhán hoisted the platter of bread. "Seems the chef here is French—which is all well and good for the tourists, but as you know, the bride and groom are Irish."

"I know, yeah," he said. "I'm a Limerick man myself." Pride rang through his voice. Well then, why wasn't he letting Siobhán pass? Imagine, seconds from now she was actually going to get to meet Alice Cahill. Tucked underneath the platter was the most recent fashion magazine that sported the gorgeous Alice on the cover. Siobhán had promised her sisters she'd try to get Alice to sign it. Gráinne and Ann, two blossoming beauties themselves, were most definitely starstruck.

8

The security guard glanced at her pink Vespa parked a few feet away. In addition to her prized cappuccino machine back at the bistro, the scooter was near and dear to her heart. She'd been riding it so often it was starting to feel like an extra appendage. It was the one thing she had that was just for her. When she was on it, the breeze in her face, the thrum of the machine through her body, it was like a little escape. A momentary break in her responsibilities when she could imagine there was nothing between her and the rest of her life but an open road and the Irish countryside. The security guard's lip twitched. Apparently he'd never seen a guest ride up on a pink scooter.

"You'll mind it, won't ye?" she asked him. "It's very dear." He looked startled as if she'd just asked him to wash her delicates. Just when Siobhán thought she was either going to have to kiss him or kick him, a heavenly voice rang out.

"Siobhán O'Sullivan?" Alice Cahill was floating toward them in a plain blue tracksuit, yet despite the casual attire, she was just as glamorous as her magazine covers. Long, ebony hair that flowed out in perfect waves, sky-blue eyes with thick eyelashes, and at six feet tall, she was just a few inches taller than Siobhán. "She's with me, Val," Alice said, lightly touching his arm.

Val's face flamed up, and he stepped back from the gate. "By all means." He waved Siobhán through as if puzzled that she was still standing on the outside.

"Thanks, luv," Alice winked. Val straightened himself up, and if Siobhán had had a handkerchief she'd have been wiping the drool off his double chin. There was a definite power that came with beauty and, unlike Siobhán, Alice seemed completely at ease with it. Siobhán could learn a thing or three from the fashion model.

Alice linked arms with Siobhán and began to escort her up the winding drive to the castle. "Your hair is gorgeous. Like the sun lit it on fire. You probably get sick of hearing that."

She was sick of hearing it, but not from the likes of Alice Cahill. "It's an honor to meet you," Siobhán stammered. In the distance, white tents dotted the sweeping, lush grounds.

"Any friend of Garda Macdara Flannery is a friend of mine. Paul just adores him. The two of them are thick as thieves. You'd never know they haven't seen each other since university."

At the mention of Macdara Flannery, Siobhán felt the top of her head lift off and soar toward the Ballyhoura Mountains. She wondered where he was, then forcefully put the top of her head back on and pushed all such thoughts away. He hadn't invited her to the wedding nor offered a word of explanation as to why not.

On the bright side—which Siobhán always tried to look on—thanks to him she was here now. Nice ruse, hinting that Alice should try Siobhán's brown bread. There were worse ways to spend a morning than at a castle with a gorgeous fashion model. Not to mention how nice it was to be near another tall woman. At five feet nine Siobhán usually towered over everyone. She loved standing next to Alice.

The castle and grounds were gorgeously framed by the Irish sky, the Ballyhoura Mountains, and a wooded hillside. The air smelled of lavender and heather, and the promise of an earthy rain.

Within the castle grounds, wealth and beauty flirted in equal measure. Interspersed amongst expanses of green lawn were manicured gardens delineated by polished black stones. The gardens were arranged into distinct sections: blossoming flowers of nearly every color in the rainbow, manicured hedges, and sculpted topiary. Wild heather grew in patches along the stone wall surrounding the grounds. Several fountains were strategically placed in the middle of the gardens, sculptures of angels spouting water. There was even a small moat, complete with a stone bridge crossing over a creek.

The castle, a fifteenth-century structure, was a grand affair. It boasted two turrets and a stunning stained-glass window. Stone lions flanked the massive front entrance. Siobhán was dying to have more of a walkabout, but Alice headed straight for the tents, where three women dressed in identical blue tracksuits were huddled in a clump. The eldest two were gripping mugs of tea like they were miniature lifeboats, while the younger one, a blonde, was examining her fingernails. When they neared, the blonde broke out of the group and practically lunged for Alice.

Her eyes were bloodshot and her skin splotchy, and her hair looked like it could conduct electricity. Like Alice and Siobhán, she appeared to be in her early twenties. Probably pretty if she had a bit of sleep and a bit of sense. She raised her arms as if waving in an aeroplane. "Thanks be to God, the brown bread is here." Alice's lips tightened, and she shook her head in admonishment. The blonde just laughed and flicked her eyes to Siobhán. "Alice has been losing the plot." Her voice was raspy, as if she'd spent the night screaming. "We've got a French chef making hot, buttery croissants, and herself wants brown bread!"

Alice blinked her disapproval. "Macdara said Siobhán's brown bread is the best he's ever tasted." She flashed a smile. "The best in County Cork."

The best in all of Ireland, Siobhán thought with pride.

"It had better be," the blonde replied with a pointed look. "You'd think Saint Peter himself had blessed it."

Alice elbowed Siobhán. "This is Brenna. My maid of *honor*. As you can see from the state of her, your little town has quite the nightlife."

Brenna crossed her arms, accentuating her ample cleavage. Everyone else had their tracksuits zipped well up past the cleavage zone. "It was a wonderful hen night."

Siobhán turned to Alice. "You had your hen night, so?"

Alice sighed.

"You would t'ink, wouldn't ye?" Brenna cut in. "Alice didn't want a hen night. What's the purpose of having a bloody wedding if you aren't going to have a hen night? I had to put the tiara and boa to other uses, if you know what I mean." A smile spread across Brenna's splotchy face as she fluttered her eyelashes.

Alice pursed her lips. "Unfortunately, we always know what you mean."

Siobhán had yet to go to a hen night, but she'd seen plenty of ladies out, tripping around in tiaras and boas, celebrating the bride's last days of freedom with bottom-less pints and penis-shaped pastries. Part of Siobhán thought hen nights were immature and silly, but another part of her was dying to experience one. She admired Alice for not giving in to pressure.

Alice offered a tight smile. "I refuse to have a sore head and splotchy skin for my wedding."

Brenna groaned. "You would have been sorted by then." She began to count off on her fingers. "The wedding is Saturday, it's only Thursday. Last night was Wednesday."

"Thank you for the lesson on the days of the week. You had plenty of fun without me, didn't ye?" Alice snapped.

Brenna shrugged and then scanned the horizon, where the blue skies were being painted by angry purple streaks. The weather was in turmoil. A light wind started to blow. "You forced me to have a session with the lads instead. The craic was mighty."

"I heard you were quite the flirt." There was an angry edge to Alice's voice.

Brenna shrugged. "It's your own fault. Leaving me at the mercy of Kevin Gallagher!"

Alice groaned, and all the women exchanged looks. Alice must have noticed the curious expression on Siobhán's face for she turned and filled her in on the story. "Kevin got absolutely blotto and ruined everyone's evening."

"Kevin?" Siobhán couldn't help but ask.

"The best man," Alice said.

"Not anymore," a tall woman said, breaking out of the group and stepping into their semicircle. "Your father told him to pack his things and leave. Did I mention he accosted me on the stairs?"

A chorus of "yes" rang out from the others.

So this must be the mother of the bride. She was almost as tall as Alice and appeared to be in her early fifties. Her hair was pulled in a tight bun, and it was apparent that a pricey plastic surgeon had done the same to her face.

Alice shook her head. "Sorry to ambush you with our drama."

"It wouldn't be an Irish wedding without drama," Siobhán said with a laugh.

"It won't be an Irish wedding without traditions either," an older woman standing near the tents piped up.

"Where are my manners?" Alice said. "This is my mother, Susan, and this is Paul's mother, Mrs. Faye Donnelly." Faye Donnelly, the woman who had made the comment about traditions, turned at the mention of her name. She was about the same age as Susan, but not nearly as tall. Salt-and-pepper hair framed her soft face.

"Paul's mother thinks I'm a bit too modern," Alice explained.

Faye held up her hand. "I've already made my peace that there will be no bagpipes or harps at the wedding, but your groom should be wearing a kilt."

"Paul will look handsome in a suit," Alice said. "And he won't have to worry about which way the wind is blowing." She winked and lifted her head to the heavens as the wind blew her hair back.

"If only you would postpone this until next month," Faye wailed.

"Why is that?" Siobhán couldn't help but ask.

"Whoever marry in August be, many a change are sure to see," Faye recited. "Marry in September's shine, your living will be rich and fine."

"Useless superstitions," Alice said. "Besides, I'm already rich, and my life could stand a few changes. So that's me sorted."

"At least make sure the sun shines on you on your wedding morning," Faye said. "And try to spot three magpies or a cuckoo."

"I've already spotted a cuckoo," Alice said with a mischievous twinkle in her eye.

"On your wedding day," Faye emphasized.

Alice's eyes sparkled. "You'll be there, won't you?"

"I'm passing out bells at your wedding, and you can't stop me," Faye said.

Alice turned to Siobhán. "Did you know that ringing a bell helps keep evil spirits at bay?"

Siobhán laughed. "Oh, I love all the old superstitions. I take it you won't be having your hands tied to your groom's?" Hand fasting was an old Irish tradition in which the bride and groom's hands would literally be tied together during the ceremony. It's where *tying the knot* came from. Siobhán did love tradition and history, although she wasn't superstitious. "If you really wanted to be traditional, you'd wear a blue wedding gown and carry wildflowers," she added.

"The bride wore blue," Alice said. She shook her head. "I prefer my lovely white gown. But I adore wildflowers." She turned to Faye with a grin. "If I carry wildflowers, will it bring me luck?"

"It's a start. You'll also want a magic hanky, a braid in your hair, and whatever you do, on the day of your wedding do not wash your hands in the same sink as Paul. Disaster!"

Alice sighed. "Disaster indeed." She touched Faye on the arm. "I'm so happy you'll be going back to work."

"Work either keeps you young or takes you young," Siobhán sang. All heads turned to her, and every face looked quizzical. "Sorry. Me da always used to say it."

"Wonderful," Alice said, clapping her hands, but still looking confused.

Siobhán turned to Faye. "What is it that you do?" she asked politely.

Faye reached into her handbag, pulled out a business card, and handed it Siobhán.

FAYE DONNELLY, ESQ.
SOLICITOR

"Just in case you're in the market."

Siobhán wasn't in the market, but she politely dropped the card into her handbag and thanked her.

Susan Cahill's eyes flicked to the platter of brown bread, and then she stared at Siobhán's forehead as if it would blind her to look her in the eye. "Why are we spending so much time chatting with the help?"

Alice's musical laughter rang out. "She's not the help. Siobhán O'Sullivan is a dear friend of Garda Flannery and, as such, a dear friend of mine."

Dear friend. Was that what he said? Was that what they were? Normally Siobhán liked things orderly. Uncomplicated. Her relationship with Macdara was neither. *Dear Friend.*

Susan raked an icy gaze over Siobhán. Her eyebrows looked like they'd been drawn in by a thin black marker, arched in perpetual surprise. *Nod and smile,* her mam would have said. *Nod and smile.*

Alice gestured to their outfits. "You're probably wondering why we're all dressed alike."

Siobhán nodded. "It did cross me mind." And here she'd been worried that her trousers and black top weren't dressy enough. It wasn't practical to ride a scooter in a dress or a skirt.

"Compliments of the castle. I thought it would make a great group photo."

"Ah, lovely," Siobhán nodded in approval. "It will indeed."

"It's not to be." Alice's hands curled into fists. "The men have vanished into thin air. Ronan is fit to be tied."

She gestured toward the mote, where a lanky man with a large camera paced back and forth over the small bridge, cigarette smoke hovering above him like a miniature storm cloud. "Kevin smashed Ronan's favorite camera last night, and even a pile of money hasn't calmed him down."

Siobhán imagined if someone slipped her a pile of money she'd have no problem calming herself down.

"I don't understand why you insisted on brown bread," Susan Cahill said. "The chef here is *French*." Brenna sauntered over and took the platter out of Siobhán's hands. The fashion magazine dropped to the ground, and Alice stared down at her own face.

Susan Cahill shook her finger at Siobhán. "No autographs. This is a private affair. You should be ashamed of yourself."

"Mother!" Alice said. "You've got the wrong end of the stick. She's my guest."

Siobhán quickly retrieved the magazine and tucked it under her arm. "I'm sorry. My sisters asked if I would try and get you to sign it. I didn't mean to overstep."

"Not at all!" Alice pulled it out and looked at it. "I'm airbrushed, and that dress took me nearly two hours to squeeze into." It was a tight silver dress that indeed looked like it had been painted on. "I'd be honored to sign it." She looked around. "Does anyone have a biro?"

Sheepishly, Siobhán produced a pen. Alice signed it with a flourish and even drew a little smiley face on the page.

"Thank you." Siobhán tucked the magazine into her handbag and followed Alice to a table under the tent. Just as they were about to sample the brown bread, a young man wearing a pinstriped gray suit and thick black glasses ran up, holding his iPad out like a shield. A hot-pink pocket square protruded from his suit pocket. What a sharp dresser. Siobhán admired a man who wasn't afraid to wear pink. She had an urge to introduce him to her scooter.

"Ronan is steaming," he said. "Maybe we should have a photograph of you lovely ladies first."

Brenna shook her head. "I told you not to hire someone who considers himself an *artist*."

"He *is* an artist," Alice said. "That's why he's so temperamental."

"Ah," Siobhán said. She was temperamental too. Maybe she was secretly an artist.

"Who, may I ask, is this?" The sharp dresser had penetrating dark eyes, and his chestnut hair was slicked to a point atop his head. He had the appearance of an intense, young hawk.

"There I go again," Alice said. "This is Siobhán O'Sullivan, owner of Naomi's Bistro." Siobhán felt a familiar pang, as she'd always thought of it as her parents' bistro. Since their death in a tragic car accident a year and several months back, it now belonged to her and her siblings. The man was studying her like she was an exam he had to pass.

"This is Brian, my wedding sergeant," she said in a staged whisper. "He's forcing us to stay on task."

Brian's dark eyes stayed pinned on Siobhán even as he swiped away on his iPad. "She's not on the guest list."

"I'd better do something about that," Alice said. "Siobhán O'Sullivan, would you like to be a guest at my wedding?"

"No!" Brian said.

"I'd be so honored," Siobhán said. Did she have anything to wear? Would Macdara be browned off with her?

Brian pursed his lips. "The photo delay is going to put us at least an hour behind. We'll take the Dominican Priory off the list. If you've seen one ruined abbey, you've seen them all."

"You mustn't miss our abbey," Siobhán said. "Why, it's the most beautiful thing you've ever seen." Along with the medieval walls and King John's Castle, Siobhán considered the ruined Dominican Priory to be one of Kilbane's dearest treasures.

"It's settled then," Alice said. "Keep it on the list."

"Your father was very clear," Brian said. "We're not supposed to get behind." A twinge of panic had entered his voice.

"Is this his wedding or mine?" A childish whine snuck into Alice's voice. "Besides, like the rest of the lads, my father hasn't even bothered to show up."

Brian looked around. "I saw him earlier." He looked around, then lowered his voice. "He was in a ferocious argument with the innkeeper."

Chapter 3

Worry lines appeared on Alice's forehead as she stared at the exterior of the castle. "An argument?"

A look of guilt crossed Brian's face, then he waved his hand as if it didn't matter. "Something about a missing fax."

Alice sighed. "He promised to leave work behind for a few days."

Brian swiped through his iPad. "Shortly after I saw him out for his morning walk." Brian flicked his eyes to the wooded hillside. Siobhán watched an orange and black butterfly land on a purple flower and unfold its wings.

"He's a man of routines," Alice said. "What about the rest of the lot? Did you see anyone else?"

Brian laughed. "I can't be sure. Everyone looks alike in their tracksuits."

Alice gazed out at the woods. "Maybe we should send out search parties," she said. "If we want to keep to our itinerary."

"I say we skip Kilbane altogether and go to Cork City." Brenna sauntered up, swaying her hips, dancing to music only she could hear. "Especially with all the robberies in Kilbane as of late."

"Robberies?" Siobhán said. "What are ye on about?"

Brenna seemed to relish delivering the news. "The castle keep warned us that if we went into Kilbane, we'd have to mind our wallets and handbags. Said people were being robbed right on the streets."

The castle keep. George and Carol Huntsman, an English couple. They bought it five years ago from the previous owner. They kept to themselves, and rumor was they did all their shopping in Limerick. Why were they spreading such rumors? "Why, that's an out-and-out lie!"

Brenna snorted. "Why would they lie?"

Alice stepped forward. "I'm afraid I mentioned that Naomi's Bistro would be catering most of our meals so that the chef could focus on our wedding banquet. Perhaps they were jealous. Chef Antoine is a bit sensitive."

"A bit sensitive?" Brenna said. "Chef Antoine is psychotic."

Alice shrugged. "He's definitely passionate about his culinary talents."

Siobhán knew there wasn't a bit of truth to the tale. "I assure you, nothing is amiss in Kilbane. The flower boxes are filled to the brim, everyone is donning their Sunday best, and the streets are so clean you could eat a ham and cheese toastie off them!"

Alice's eyes brightened. "Speaking of toasties—I'm dying to try your brown bread." They merged in front of the platter, hands darted in, and slices began to disappear. Alice took a bite and closed her eyes. When she opened them again, a feeling of bliss settled across her face. There wasn't much in life that couldn't be made better by a cup of Barry's tea and Siobhán's brown bread with butter. "Heavenly. The best I've ever tasted."

"The best, is it?" Brenna took an enormous bite, chewed as if she was a cow bored with her cud, and then swallowed as if it pained her to do so. Siobhán might have been insulted if not for the fact that Brenna was reaching for her second piece before she swallowed the last bite of her first. Just then a handsome man came striding across the lawn. Siobhán immediately recognized him as the groom, Paul Donnelly. He was well over six feet tall with sandy hair that was feathered back and blowing in the breeze. She could imagine the glamorous life that awaited the pair. Beautiful babies, and summers in Spain, and endless nights in Irish castles.

"Thank heavens," Alice called to him. "I thought you did a runner."

"I came close," Paul said. "But then I realized I'd rather die than live a single day without you." Paul swiped the plate out of her hands, passed it off to Brenna, and grabbed Alice. Then, in front of Ireland and God, he bent her over and kissed her like he was of breath and she was pure oxygen. From a few feet away came the snap, snap, snap of a camera. Ronan, the artist, was capturing the kiss.

When the two of them finally came up for air, Paul Donnelly turned to Siobhán without missing a beat. "You must be Macdara's missus," he said with a grin. "That fiery hair gives you away." Siobhán's cheeks were soon fiery as well. She was only Macdara's girlfriend, and it was a very new relationship to boot, but Irish men loved to tease, and Paul was well-versed in the art. She hated how easily she blushed. Paul treated her to a wink, then turned back to his bride. Her beautiful face was once again furrowed with worry. "What's wrong, luv?"

Alice threw her arms open. "Our first photo? In our tracksuits?"

"I'm so sorry I'm late. It's the strangest thing." Paul laughed then looked away.

"Well?" Alice said.

"Someone locked me in my room." His handsome face darkened. "And I have a good idea who."

Alice groaned. "Kevin." She turned to Faye. "Unless it was you?"

Faye's eyebrows shot up. "Me?"

"Isn't that an old tradition as well? Lock the groom up so he doesn't get cold feet?" Alice laughed.

"Why didn't ye just give someone a bell?" Faye asked.

Paul frowned. "There was no phone in me room, and my mobile was gone as well. I must have left it at one of the pubs."

"Should be easy to trace; you only visited twelve or so last night," Alice said with a smirk.

"And how would you know that?" Paul said, grabbing her by the waist. "You couldn't even bother to come."

"I think the celebrating should take place after the wedding," Alice said with a seductive smile.

"I don't like all these shenanigans," Faye said. "And I don't understand why you couldn't open the door from the inside?"

Paul threw open his arms in frustration. "I don't know. I just know that I was locked in."

"It's an old castle," Alice said.

"Your point?" Faye said.

Alice sighed. "Maybe it was stuck?"

"No," Paul said. "It was locked."

"Locking you in your room," Faye said, shaking her head. "What if there was a fire?"

"Kevin having a laugh, no doubt," Paul said. He looked around as if Kevin might be hunkered behind a shrub, listening to his every word.

"How did you get out then?" Faye pressed.

"I was thinking I might have to climb out a window when the innkeeper finally heard me banging on the door." Paul took a step toward Ronan. "Let's get on with this photo."

"That's just it," Alice said, putting her hand on his arm. "We're also missing Kevin, your father—"

"Forget about Kevin. He'll be dead to the world."

"I hear he was quite the spectacle last night," Alice said. "My mam is rather upset."

"I've asked Macdara to be my best man," Paul said. "Kevin is too fond of the drink, and it doesn't suit him."

Alice began to count on her fingers. "Well, we're still missing my father, and Macdara, and your father. Is that all of us then?"

Paul laughed. "You insisted on a small wedding."

"Yet with this crowd it's still not small enough."

"You forgot Macdara's mammy," Paul added, looking around.

"Macdara's mam?" Siobhán blurted out. Was that why Macdara hadn't invited her to the wedding? His mam was his plus one? Nancy Flannery lived in Cork City, and Siobhán had yet to meet her.

Paul caught the look on her face and laughed. "Didn't know you'd be meeting the mother-in-law? Ah, she's a sweetheart." It was Paul's second reference to Siobhán and Macdara getting married someday, and even though he was only teasing, the very thought of it sent her pulse racing. *His mam was his plus one.*

Alice turned her pretty head toward the swath of blue sky. In the distance, gray clouds gathered in an angry swirl. "Ronan wanted to catch the morning sun. Why, the clouds are going to swallow it whole any minute now."

Paul turned. "Here they are now." Sure enough, a group of tracksuit-bedecked people were headed their way. Leading the group was a very tall man with broad shoulders. Even from a distance, he exuded power. That must be the infamous Colm Cahill. And behind him was Macdara Flannery. He flashed her a private smile, and if Siobhán's heart was a hammer hitting a bell, it would be ringing by now. He looked very becoming in his navy tracksuit. His brown hair was slightly tousled, his blue eyes smiling. It was odd seeing him out of his garda uniform. She had to admit that, whenever he was wearing it, she always felt a little zing. Especially when he was wearing his garda cap with its golden shield: An Garda Síochána— Guardians of the Peace.

"Is that everyone then?" Paul asked.

"Oh! Oh! Oh!" Alice cried out. She clutched her stomach and doubled over.

"What's wrong?" Paul rushed to her side.

"Are you alright, pet?" Siobhán asked.

Alice began to heave and then sprinted toward the nearest bush, where she promptly got sick. Siobhán threw her hand over her mouth. Paul ran up to his bride and began to rub her back.

Susan Cahill headed for her daughter. "What on earth is going on?" From nearby, the camera began to click.

"No pictures," Paul said, holding up his hand. "That's quite rude." Ronan glowered but backed away. He caught Siobhán's stare, and his eyes bore into hers. Then, as she gawked at him, he snapped her picture.

Brenna pushed her way front and centre, bosom heaving. "Looks like the best brown bread in all of County Cork has been poisoned!"

Siobhán gasped. "I assure you, you've got the wrong end of the stick."

Brenna turned her back to Siobhán. "I'm not at all assured."

"We've all been eating the bread," Siobhán said. "No one else is sick."

"I didn't touch it," Susan Cahill said. "Thank God."

"The bread is fine," Siobhán said. "It was never out of me sight."

"Maybe Alice is in a family way," Brenna said. "Could explain why they decided to have such a small wedding instead of a grand affair."

"You had better hold your tongue," Susan snapped.

Brenna pursed her lips. "I was only messing."

"I'm fine," Alice said, making her way back to the group with Paul at her side. "It's just me nerves." Her pretty face looked as if all the color had drained out of it. Siobhán wished she has some rouge in her purse just so she could dab it on Alice and bring her back to life. There couldn't possibly be anything wrong with the brown bread. It was quite possible that Brenna, as crude as she was, had inadvertently stumbled on a secret. Was Alice pregnant? It would certainly explain her preternatural glow.

The smell of cigar smoke infiltrated the air. Colm was puffing away and talking on his mobile while pacing. "Father?" Alice approached her father, and he held up an index finger. Siobhán caught the look on Alice's face: hopeful and rejected at the same time. She was obviously used to coming second to his business dealings. At least Paul seemed like the type of man who was going to put her first.

"We should get you up to your room so you can have a lie-down," Paul said to Alice.

"I'm fine," she answered. "A sup of water, please." She sunk into a chair near the tents and gently placed her hand over her stomach. Paul hurried to fetch the water.

"Siobhán?" Siobhán turned to find Macdara standing next to a petite woman with a large frown. Her brown curls matched Macdara's, only hers were most likely helped along by the hair salon. She was dressed in a sensible brown dress and flat shoes. She wore a matching brown hat and white gloves. She clutched her handbag as if expecting any minute now someone would try to rip it away from her. Macdara cleared his throat. "I'd like you to meet my mam, Nancy."

Siobhán stuck out her hand. "It's so nice to meet you."

Nancy looked Siobhán up and down. "She'll do, so." She shifted her gaze to the distance as if they'd just concluded a business deal. Macdara laughed and shook his head. His mother didn't break a smile.

Just as Siobhán was trying to suss out how to gracefully slip away, a man's voice rang out from direction of the woods. "Help! Help! Help!"

"What in heaven's name?" Siobhán said. Macdara looked as if he wanted to bolt toward the woods, but his mother gripped his arm fiercely.

Soon a blur of white was sprinting in their direction across the expanse of green. Every so often the man jumped a hedge like a horse at a hurdle competition.

"Why is the French chef exercising in his uniform?" Susan cried out. He was fast and nimble, despite his hefty frame, and by the time he approached, his face was covered in a sheen of sweat. Instinctively, half the group took a step back as he stood panting and sweating in front of them.

Apart from the exercising, Antoine indeed looked the part of a French chef with his dark mustache and round belly. A look of absolute horror was stamped on his face.

"Chef," Paul called. "What's wrong with ye?"

When he didn't answer, just blinked and gulped for air, Macdara stepped forward. "What's the story?"

"The woods," Antoine said, pointing, gasping for breath. "A man." The wedding guests closed in now, eager to hear.

"Is someone hurt?" Macdara said.

"He no longer hurts," Antoine said with a flip of his hand.

Macdara shifted, and a worried look crossed his face. "A drunk then?"

"No, no, no. There is a man. Hard attack."

"Heart attack?" Siobhán said.

"Ring the paramedics!" Macdara shouted. "A man is having a heart attack." Mobiles appeared and blinked from tracksuit pockets like fireflies.

The French chef waggled his index finger back and forth. "Non, non. Not heart attack."

"*Not* a heart attack?" Macdara was clearly flustered.

The French chef held his hands apart about a foot wide. "Big rock." He mimed throwing it.

"*Hard attack*," Siobhán said. Macdara and the rest of the guests looked to the chef as if waiting for him to correct Siobhán's sinister interpretation.

Instead, he nodded. "Oui. Very hard attack." He leaned in and uttered the one French word that needed no interpretation. "Meurtre."

Chapter 4

Macdara was the first to fly into action. He used his mobile to call the police, then turned and addressed the crowd. "The guards are on their way. Everyone stay exactly where you are until they arrive." He instructed Chef Antoine to show him the crime scene, and the pair made a beeline for the woods. It wasn't normal, and she'd hardly admit it outright, but Siobhán was dying to go with them. Instead, she focused on the collage of shocked faces in front of her.

"Someone needs to alert the Huntsmans." Siobhán gestured to the castle.

"I'll do it," Susan Cahill said. "They will have to answer to this." Susan strode to the castle, her long legs taking purposeful strides. Oh, Jaysus. Siobhán hoped Susan wasn't going to start accusing them of wrongdoing straightaway. Personally, she thought it best to warm up to damning accusations.

"It's Kevin," Brenna cried. "Oh my God. It has to be Kevin." She threw a desperate look to the woods.

"Keep calm," Paul said. "We don't know anything."

"Who else could it be?" Brenna's distress seemed genuine.

Faye Donnelly cried out. "Martin." She grabbed Paul's arm. "Where's your father?"

Paul's eyes widened. "Oh heavens."

29

"Don't worry," Alice said. "I saw him early this morning when I went out for a walk, and he said he was headed into town." She threw a weighted glance at Paul.

Paul slapped his forehead. "Our early-morning walk. I completely forgot."

Alice touched Paul's arm. "It hardly matters now. Even if you had awoken in time, you were locked in your room."

Paul sighed.

"Please, about Martin," Faye said.

Alice gestured toward the road. "He was standing by the castle gate. I didn't see him until he stepped out of the shadows. Nearly put the heart in me crossways."

"Are you sure he didn't go into the woods?" Faye was growing impatient.

"As I said, he was headed into Kilbane," Alice repeated. "Said he wanted to have a look at the medieval walls."

"That's nowhere near the woods," Siobhán added, hoping to reassure Faye. She admired this Martin's appreciation of history.

"But he should have been back by now," Faye cried. "What if he came back and went into the woods?"

Paul put his hand around his mother's shoulders. "You know Father. It's more likely that he's chatting up folks in town, dropping a word or two about his lorries."

Alice turned to Siobhán. "Martin runs a transport company." Siobhán nodded politely, although at the moment she didn't really care.

Carol and George Hunstman soon emerged from the castle. Carol was a striking woman from Jamaica, and her husband George was a pale man from Manchester. His mother was Irish born, but he seemed to identify more with his English heritage. They headed straight to Val, who was pacing near the gate. No doubt as the castle's only security guard, he was afraid he was going to catch some of the blame. Siobhán couldn't help but stare at the couple as they strode by without so much as a glance in anyone's direction. Had it been Siobhán, she would have stopped to soothe her guests and assure them that everything was going to be alright.

Carol paced and George gesticulated wildly, no doubt berating Val. Siobhán found herself drifting closer and closer to their conversation. She stopped when she was close enough to hear Carol talking. "How do they know the dead man is with the wedding party?"

"I assume he's wearing one of the blue tracksuits," Siobhán said before she could stop herself. The three heads snapped her way.

Carol put her hands on her hips and stared at Siobhán. She was wearing bold colors and bright red lipstick that looked gorgeous with her dark skin. "Who are you?"

"Siobhán O'Sullivan. A friend of Garda Flannery." In times like these it never hurt to toss around the name of a guard.

"You're with the guards?" George said. Unlike his striking wife, he was dressed in neutral tans. He was wearing a vest and a jacket and had binoculars sticking out of one of his pockets. He looked like a man about to go on safari. She could imagine him posing in pictures next to dead lions. The Irish countryside was as gorgeous as any place on earth, but he certainly wouldn't be encountering big game. Perhaps George Huntsman would have been better suited to prehistoric times, when giant Irish deer roamed the countryside. Their enormous skeletons had been found in Irish bogs. Thank heavens for extinction.

"I'm in with the guards," Siobhán said. It wasn't exactly a lie. Whatever got them talking.

"We don't want any trouble," Carol said. Gold bracelets jangled on her wrist. "We don't patrol the woods."

"Who did it?" George asked. "A drunk from Kilbane?"

The disdain in his voice was obvious. Siobhán did her best to ignore it. "Were either of you awake early this morning?"

"Carol is always at the front desk by eight," George said. Carol nodded.

"Not earlier?" Siobhán asked. Brian had stated that he had seen Colm Cahill arguing with the innkeeper this morning over a missing fax.

"I was up rather early this morning," Carol said. "The Cahills are very important guests." She threw a worried look toward the woods.

"What time?" Siobhán asked.

Carol shook her head. "I'm not sure."

George held up his hand. "My fault. The clock above the desk needs a new battery. I keep forgetting." Carol smiled and patted his hand.

So much for that line of questioning. It was now half nine. Siobhán had no idea how long the body had been in the woods. And it had already been established that several wedding guests had risen early for morning walks. Alice and Martin, for two, and Brian had mentioned seeing Colm go for his morning walk. Which meant Brian was out and about as well. This was definitely a group of early risers. Siobhán imagined if she were rich she would lie in bed until noon watching telly and eating biscuits. She looked at Carol and tried to keep her voice light. "Did you see or hear anything unusual?"

"Not a thing."

Siobhán didn't like how quickly Carol answered. Wouldn't she want to stop and reflect for a moment? "Anything at all?" Siobhán pressed. "I heard one of your guests was upset about a missing fax?"

Carol gasped. "What on earth does that have to do with the dead man in the woods?"

"Maybe nothing," Siobhán said. "Is there a reason you won't answer my question?"

"I put the fax on the basket on the desk. I turned around for two seconds. I don't know who took it."

"Surely they can send another fax," George said.

Siobhán was dying to ask if she knew who the fax was from, but their defenses were already up, and of course she didn't have the authority to press for such personal information. "Brenna said you warned the guests about robberies in the village as of late?" Siobhán resisted the urge to call them dirty liars.

"Robberies?" Carol said. "What robberies?" She sounded genuinely curious.

"I knew it!" George said. "That's your man then." He gripped his vest and stood taller.

"Who?" Siobhán asked.

"Whoever has been robbing the folks in the village."

"There are no robberies," Siobhán said.

George furled his bushy eyebrows. "You just said there were."

"I heard it too," Val spoke up.

This was how vicious rumors started. "I didn't say there had been robberies—I said that Brenna said that the Huntsmans"—she turned to George and Carol—"started the rumor."

Carol shook her finger. "We did no such thing."

"No such thing," George echoed, right down to the wagging of his finger.

Had Brenna lied? If so—why? "You're denying you said anything about robberies in the village?"

"Why is a bistro owner asking so many questions?" Val asked, stepping between Siobhán and the Huntsmans.

"Bistro owner?" Carol asked. Her tone of voice suggested the profession was right up there with serial killer.

"You said you were with the guards," George said.

"I have to check on the others," Siobhán said. "You can always stop into Naomi's Bistro if you think of anything else. Or if you want to try our famous brown bread."

Carol crinkled her nose. "Our chef is French."

Right. Chef Antoine. *The man who discovered the body.* Now there's someone she'd like to have a word with. Siobhán turned and hurried away, leaving the three of them staring after her. In the distance, the first of the sirens began to wail. The guards would be here soon.

Would anyone notice if Siobhán happened to sneak into the woods?

Having a peek wasn't a crime, was it? It wasn't that she wanted to see another dead body, and she crossed herself just thinking of it. But she had sharp eyes; Macdara had said so himself.

She had just resigned herself to being sensible and staying put when she spotted a man, clothed in black, hunched over and running in the direction of the woods. Did he really think all he had to do was crouch down and he would be invisible? She looked closer and caught sight of a camera in his hands. It was Ronan, the photographer. He was headed for the crime scene to take pictures.

How morbid. Someone had to stop him. This was the perfect excuse. Siobhán could say she had seen Ronan run into the woods and had followed him as protection, like.

Or to warn him not to disturb a crime scene. Yes, that sounded like a much better reason to be inserting herself into the crime scene.

Chapter 5

Due to the country's violent past, most of Ireland's woodlands had been viciously stripped, and now Ireland was the least wooded country in all of Europe. Siobhán was grateful for their patch of woods, although truth be told, the hillside was mostly formed with craggy rocks, thick hedges, and flowering shrubs. But there were enough trees in the mix to still call it the woods, and that's exactly how everyone in Kilbane referred to the steep hillside with sweeping panoramic views.

The minute Siobhán stepped foot into the woods, something dark and fuzzy darted across her path, and she nearly died with fright. Her head whipped to the left just as a squirrel scurried up a tree. She wanted to laugh at herself, but this was no moment for gaiety. She placed her hand over her thundering heart. *Jaysus.* She'd better keep her wits about her. There was a marked dip in temperature, and an earthy scent hugged the air. Ronan was at least twenty feet ahead of her, crackling leaves and snapping twigs as he plowed ahead. Macdara would hear him a mile away. She looked down and spied a packet of Newton cigarettes tossed to the right of the path. She froze. They could belong to the killer.

Or the victim.

Or any random person who had ever wandered into these woods.

But just in case they were evidence, she resisted the urge to pick them up. She'd make a mental note to point them out to the guards.

The path continued straight for another fifteen feet, then rose sharply, beginning the uphill slope to the peak of the hill. Male voices floated down, raised in anger. As she suspected, Macdara didn't sound happy about the intrusion into the crime scene. She'd better hurry up if she wanted her excuse to hold water. She began to run and, thanks to her daily jogging practice, managed the hill with only a little heavy breathing. She stopped at the crest to catch her breath. Macdara, Chef Antoine, and Ronan were facing each other in defensive stances.

And although it was hardly the time to appreciate the view, she'd have to be dead not to. The panorama from the top of the hill was stunning. Ireland's hills undulated below them like emerald waves. Medieval walls encircled her village like a protective maze. The steeple of Saint Mary's Cathedral rose high in the air, offering a bit of stoic comfort, and the gentle mounds of the Ballyhoura Mountains completed the postcard-perfect picture.

Siobhán was purposefully not looking at the body, although she could see a human form on the ground just past where the men were standing. She would work up to it, but for now she wanted to examine the immediate area. Had the victim come here to have a smoke? Sadly, the underbrush was probably full of cigarette butts. She'd have to let the guards sort that out. For now she continued the train of thought. He had had a smoke, stood, and looked at the view. He had finished his smoke. Tossed the butt to the ground. And then what?

"Ah, for the love of God," Macdara suddenly called out. Siobhán's head snapped up. Macdara was looking right at her.

Siobhán pointed at Ronan. "I saw him run into the woods, and I wanted to warn him not to disturb the crime scene."

"Did you now?" Macdara said, reaching into his pocket and pulling out his mobile. "Couldn't have just given me a bell?"

"I left mine at the bistro," Siobhán said, as she subtly scanned the perimeter. As a child, she had always been honest to a fault. As she grew older, she saw the need for little white lies. She took a deep breath and finally looked past Macdara and at the victim. The man was dressed in a blue tracksuit and was lying facedown in the dirt. His right arm was out at a slight angle, and his hand was still clutching his blue cap. There was no odor that she could detect; he couldn't have been dead long. Still, the crisp Irish air was at once a welcome relief. "Is it the best man? Kevin?" From what she could see, he had broad shoulders and short dark hair. He had a long body—tall if he was standing up.

"I believe so," Macdara said. "But we won't know for sure until he's turned over."

"Am I free to leave?" Antoine asked. He was drenched in sweat. He reached into his pocket and pulled out a pack of cigarettes. Marlboro Reds.

"You can't smoke near the crime scene," Madcara said.

"But of course," Antoine said. "May I go?"

"Go on," Macdara said. "Don't leave the castle grounds."

Chef Antoine looked stunned. "What do you mean?"

"The guards will want to question you."

"Moi? C'est moi?" He seemed to speak in his native tongue whenever he was stressed.

"Because you found the body," Siobhán interjected. Antoine turned and looked at her as if noticing her for the first time.

He shook his finger at Siobhán, and his belly shook in unison. "I was only coming to have a smoke and get a bit of exercise." He patted his belly.

"What time was this?" Siobhán asked. She could already feel Macdara's glare.

"Just now," he said slowly, as if Siobhán were incapable of understanding any language.

Siobhán didn't let her irritation show. "Tell me everything that happened moment by moment."

"What are you doing?" Macdara asked.

"I come." Antoine gestured to the spot. "I light." He mimed flicking a lighter. "I see." He pointed at the body. "I run!" He pumped his arms and pointed down the hill. He'd be killer in a game of Gestures.

"You're lucky you didn't witness his murder," Siobhán said. *Unless he was the one who killed him.*

"What do you think you're doing?" Macdara asked again. If he were a kettle, he'd be boiling. A little distraction was in order.

"What did you do with your cigarette butt?" She emphasized her point by scanning the grounds.

Chef Antoine shook his head. "I no smoke. I no smoke. I see. I run!" Once again he pointed to the body, then pumped his arms.

"Very well." She turned to Macdara. "The guards will want to search the grounds for cigarette butts, bag them as evidence, and check all of it for DNA."

"DNA?" Antoine said.

"Ah, sure," Siobhán said. "There will be DNA all over every cigarette butt found in the vicinity. Would you like to change your story?"

"I no smoke. I swear." He held both his hands out as if protecting himself from an onslaught. Siobhán took a deep breath in through her nose. This time she swore she could smell a trace of cigar smoke. "Is there a cigar butt anywhere around?"

Macdara sighed. "Just on the other side of Kevin." He caught himself. "I mean the body. The name of the victim has not been officially released." He directed the last bit at Siobhán.

"Not a bother," Siobhán said. "Can you manage to point out the cigar butt to the guards, or does it have to be officially identified as well, like?" She didn't mean to actually say that out loud, but it was too late, already out of her gob. She smiled, hoping to soften the sting.

Macdara folded his arms across his chest. "I'll make sure to point it out to the guards." He gave her a pointed look. "So they can check it out for DNA."

Siobhán continued. "There's also an empty pack of Newton cigarettes to the right when you first come on the trail."

"Unbelievable," Macdara shook his head.

"They are not mine," Antoine said. "Not mine."

"I know," Siobhán said. "You smoke Marlboro Reds." He gasped as if she was a mind reader, then looked down at the pack in his hands and nodded. "Do you know if any of the castle employees or guests smoke Newtons?"

"Siobhán!" Macdara said. "You are not a detective!"

"Why aren't you writing this down?" she asked Macdara. She started counting off on her fingers. "The cigarette butt. The empty pack of Newtons by the entrance. The discarded cigar, and the fact that Chef Antoine smokes Marlboro Reds."

"I'm going to quit," Chef Antoine said. "But not today."

"Have you tried the patch?" Siobhán asked.

"I have to ask all of you to leave the crime scene," Macdara said.

"May I go?" Antoine asked, his eyes ping-ponging between Siobhán and Macdara.

"You will have to stay on the castle grounds until the guards have cleared you," Macdara said.

Antoine began to pace. A horrified look swept across his face. "Will they cancel the wedding?"

"One thing at a time," Macdara said.

"Of course they'll cancel," Siobhán said. She felt a quick pinch to the back of her arm and jumped. Macdara. She stopped talking.

Antoine shook his fist. "I'd better still get paid. If the wedding is off, I'd better still get paid!" He turned, wiped his brow with his chef's hat, and shot Siobhán such a searing look she took a step back. She was relieved when he stormed down the hill.

Siobhán's gaze was drawn back to the body. There was a large rock lying by the head of the corpse. The rock was washed in crimson. She leaned forward to see the same dark color red clumped on the back of Kevin's head and running into the earth. She crossed herself. "Oh. The poor fella." Instinctively, Siobhán moved forward.

"Don't come any closer." Macdara clamped down on her arm. Suddenly the click, click, click of a camera brought her attention back to Ronan. Siobhán had forgotten all about him. What was it about someone behind a camera that rendered one invisible? She looked at

Ronan, and he returned her stare as if she was challenging him to some kind of dare.

Macdara pointed at the camera. "Every single photograph is going to be the property of the gardai. Do you hear?"

"Yes sir," Ronan said. This was the first time Siobhán had seen him up close. She pegged him to be in his thirties, and he had olive skin, spikey black hair, and green eyes rimmed with black eyeliner. A silver hoop dangled out of his left nostril. Streaks of neon green dotted his hair, making it seem as if blades of grass were growing out of his skull. Very artsy. He was rail thin and jittery. He looked like a cat burglar at the end of a long hunger strike. She had the urge to shove him into a chair and feed him bacon and cabbage until he filled out a wee bit.

"If one of those photos shows up anywhere else, I'll arrest ye meself," Macdara added. In lieu of an answer, Ronan snapped a picture of Macdara.

"What if he's still alive?" Siobhán said, glancing once more at the body. "Hello?" The body did not move.

"He's definitely not alive," Macdara said. "You need to leave the crime scene."

Siobhán crossed herself. "Who did this to you?" she asked the dead man.

"For the love of God, off with ye," Macdara pleaded.

She didn't move. The killer could still be in the woods, watching them. What if he or she followed Siobhán? Or what if she left and the killer attacked Macdara? If they both ran for help, what if the killer tried to hide the rock? Or remove the cigar butt? There could be loads of evidence they could cover up.

"Obviously the rock is your murder weapon," Siobhán said.

"No," Macdara said.

"No?"

Macdara shifted. "It could be alright, and it probably is, but you can't say for sure. It's a mistake to draw conclusions before all the evidence is in."

Siobhán nodded but continued mulling it over. "If the rock is the murder weapon, then it was an impulsive kill."

"Not necessarily," Macdara said.

"Explain." Siobhán waited. Ronan stopped snapping his camera and watched them.

Macdara sighed. "On Wednesday morning and afternoon, all the wedding guests took strolls in the woods. The killer could have seen the rock, maybe even taken it then." Macdara looked around, as they imagined the scene unfolding. "They could have even hidden it up here, waiting for an opportunity to strike."

"Literally," Ronan chimed in.

"Premeditated," Siobhán whispered. "How did they know Kevin would be here?"

Macdara pointed at her. "You are not investigating this murder."

Siobhán folded her arms across her chest. "Don't get your knickers in a twist."

"What?" Macdara looked genuinely confused.

"If men can say it to me, I can say it back."

"I swear I'll never say it to ye again. Now would you get out of here before the guards arrive and you become a suspect?"

"Why would I become a suspect?"

"Because murderers often like to revisit the crime scene," Ronan said. He sounded very enthusiastic.

"You could be the murderer then," Siobhán said, eyeing him.

Ronan flashed a smile. "You're right," he said as if it pleased him. He took a selfie with his tongue sticking out.

"The two of you clear out now," Macdara ordered. He pointed at Ronan. "I want that camera card. Now."

"Chef Antoine discovered the body. Does that mean he's at the top of the suspect list?" Ronan asked as he snapped Siobhán's picture yet again.

"Why are you photographing me?" Siobhán asked.

"Because I like your fiery red hair and gorgeous face." This time he popped the flash, and for a second she saw nothing but spots.

"Stop that!" She had a sudden urge to smash his camera and instantly empathized with poor Kevin for doing exactly that the night before. Could that have been reason enough to kill him? Earlier Ronan had been pacing like a caged tiger. Now he seemed calm and happy. Hardly appropriate given the circumstances. Perhaps he'd just been waiting for them to discover the body? "That camera looks very dear." Siobhán kept her voice light.

Ronan's eyes darkened. "I had a better one." He glared at the corpse.

"Oh? What happened to it?" Siobhán resisted the urge to flutter her eyelashes.

"What business is it of yours?" he said. His face showed definite signs of rage. Siobhán could imagine that to an artist a camera might feel like a child. One he couldn't live without. She'd be out of her mind if anyone ever damaged her prized cappuccino machine at the bistro. Or her pink Vespa. She'd definitely come to blows if anyone tried to scooter-jack her ride.

Had Ronan followed Kevin up the hill this morning? Tried to get Kevin to apologize? Maybe Kevin taunted him. She could easily see Ronan smashing a rock into the back of his head—just like Kevin had smashed his camera. No. Not just his camera. His *baby*. An eye for an eye. Ronan whirled around, then darted down the hill without another word. Strange, Siobhán thought. Very, very strange.

Macdara threw his arms open. "He still has the camera card!"

"I'll get it for you."

"You'll do no such thing." He sighed. "What was that all about?"

Siobhán was thrilled to fill him in. "Kevin smashed Ronan's good camera last night."

Macdara crossed his arms and sighed. "Who is Ronan?"

"The photographer that was just here, visiting the crime scene, avoiding my questions, and looking strangely thrilled?"

"Thrilled?" Macdara said. "I saw sulking."

"Before the body was found, he was pacing and raging. Had Alice fretting up a storm. But just now he seemed completely thrilled that a man has been murdered."

"Why was Alice fretting?"

"Apparently he's some famous artist in Dublin, and he doesn't like to be kept waiting."

"Waiting for what?"

"You were all supposed to have a morning photo taken in your tracksuits!" Siobhán pointed to Macdara's track-suit.

"Right, so. I was detained by Mam. She wanted to have tea and biscuits before we joined the others."

"He could also stand a good feeding."

"Who?"

"Are you not listening to me? Ronan, that's who. He's a twig."

"And that makes him a murderer?"

"Did ye not hear the part about the murder victim smashing his prized camera?" He definitely wasn't listening to her. Typical. "I take it ye missed all the excitement?"

"I had to take my mam home early. When I left the craic was mighty."

Siobhán crossed herself and sent a silent apology to the body before speaking. "I heard Kevin made quite the scene." She found herself whispering it. "Colm Cahill had to pay Ronan five thousand euros for the smashed lens."

"If he was paid that much for it, then what would be the motive to kill Kevin?"

"Maybe he followed Kevin this morning to demand an apology. Or"—Siobhán started to pace—"maybe there was something on his camera, one of those camera cards, and maybe Kevin stole it."

"Now you're just making things up."

"It's possible, though, isn't it? He stole some kind of incriminating picture and was blackmailing the photographer." She pointed at the body. "We'll have to search his pockets."

"We?"

"It's a figure of speech. You. You should search him." Siobhán pointed.

Macdara didn't make a move. "First of all, no one is touching the body but the state pathologist. Second of all, if Kevin was murdered over a camera card or any other object, don't you think the murderer would have taken the object in question with him?"

"Or her," Siobhán said.

"What?"

"You said *him*. The murderer could be a her."

"You're so busy henpecking that ye missed my point." Macdara was starting to sound browned off.

"Sorry. Good point," Siobhán began to pace, then stopped. "You'll need to question Ronan, hint that you think he killed Kevin over a stolen photograph. Monitor his reaction very carefully."

Macdara shook his head. "You're going to be the death of me."

"You are going to question Ronan, aren't you?"

"The detective superintendent will appoint the detective sergeant, who will appoint a guard to question all the suspects. Including me."

That sounded like an awful lot of appointing, but Siobhán kept her gob shut on the rankings of the Irish guards. "Including you?"

Macdara threw open his arms. "I'm a wedding guest."

"I'm not," Siobhán said pointedly. There was no need to mention that Alice had invited her ipso facto.

"I had to invite my mam," Macdara said. "I had no idea she was into fashion models."

"Who isn't?" Siobhán said. "Of course you had to invite her." *You also should have mentioned it.*

Macdara sighed. "I should have told you. Are you browned off with me?"

A mind reader to boot. She was going to have to watch herself around Macdara Flannery. "No. I'm too distracted with other things." She glanced at the body. "Do you have a notebook?"

Macdara gestured to his tracksuit. "I'm not on duty."

"Do they have pockets?"

Macdrara sighed and showed her. There were pockets in both the jacket and the pants. Plenty of room for mysterious objects to hide. Kevin would have at least had his room key and cigarettes and a lighter on him. Siobhán wished they could turn him over and go through his pockets. She crossed herself again. "Bet you wish you had brought a notebook."

Macdara started counting on his fingers as he spoke. "Newton pack, cigar butt, Antoine smokes Marlboro Reds, Ronan's smashed camera, and check the pockets of the deceased."

Siobhán smiled. As guards went, he wasn't too bad. "Don't forget Chef Antoine found the body, and Ronan was inappropriately thrilled."

Macdara groaned. Siobhán stepped forward and touched his arm. Macdara stepped in closer. "I was so happy to see you this morning," he whispered as he placed his hand on her back. "And now I take it all back."

Siobhán laughed and gently shoved him away. "I'm happy to help."

"You want to help? Go back to the castle and keep the others calm."

"I'm not leaving you here. There's a killer on the loose!"

"I'd say the killer is long gone," Macdara said. "Or he's back at the castle."

He had a point. Now that she'd seen the crime scene, she wanted to take a close look at how all the guests were behaving. Maybe she'd spot something amiss. She started to leave and then turned back. "Have you heard anything about robberies in Kilbane as of late?"

"Robberies?" Macdara said. "Of course not."

"I thought so."

"Where is this coming from?"

"Brenna said that the Huntmans warned their guests about going into Kilbane. Told them people were being robbed right on the streets."

Siobhán was pleased to see a perplexed expression come over his handsome face. "I'll speak with them."

"I already did. They denied it. So either the Huntsmans are lying or the maid of honor is."

"You have to stop."

"Also, did you see the state of her this morning?"

Macdara frowned. "The state of who?"

"The maid of honor. Brenna. Looked like she was having a tussle in the sheets. Do you think it could be with our man there?" She nodded toward the body.

"You seriously have to go."

"I'm going." Siobhán glanced at the body again. "Should I tell them it's Kevin?"

Macdara shook his head. "Not until he's been positively identified."

"I'm sure Antoine and Ronan have already told them."

"You're right. But still. There's a procedure to follow."

"Of course. Do you want me to bring you a cup of tea and some brown bread?" She flushed as she remembered Brenna's accusation. Her brown bread couldn't have made Alice sick, could it?

"Yes. But not here. Now go."

Siobhán took one last look at poor Kevin. This was the moment the sun chose to peek out from beneath the clouds and shine down through the late-summer trees, directly upon Kevin's mortal coil. She might not have seen it otherwise. Something gold, something shining from underneath his hand. From his cap. "What's that?" Siobhán pointed.

"What?" Macdara didn't seem to cop on.

"His hat—it just lit up. Or there's something underneath it? See? It's a shiny piece of gold."

Macdara edged closer, then fell to his haunches and leaned in as close as he could without touching him. He then shot to his feet, startling Siobhán. "Jaysus," he said. "Mary, Joseph, and Jaysus."

She had never seen Macdara this rattled. It's true what they say: one's face can drain of all color, go white as a bedsheet. The little hairs on Siobhán's arm stood at attention. "What is it?"

"It's me cap," Macdara said. "It's the shield of me garda cap."

Mary, Joseph, and Jaysus. "How do you know it's yours?"

"I joined them in the pub last night after me shift. Kevin was yanking it off me head all night long. We had a bit of a row over it."

"Even so, couldn't it belong to another guard?"

Macdara shook his head. "Mine has a splotch of white paint at the tip from the time I had a run-in with a few wee spray-painters. The splotch is there. It's my cap alright."

Siobhán leaned forward until she could make out a splotch of white paint on the tip, just like he said. She tried to think through the implications. "So Kevin grabbed it off your head last night and you just let him keep it?"

"Of course not."

She waited for him to explain, and when he didn't, she jumped in again. "So why is it underneath his hand?"

Macdara sighed and ran his hand through his hair. "The final time Kevin snatched it, I might have hollered at him a bit. Mam put it in her handbag. We left early. I saw her to her room. Then I forgot all about it."

"Did she reach into her handbag for anything on the way home? Perhaps it fell out."

"That's the only possibility. If he snuck into me mam's room—God help me—I would've killed him myself."

"Don't repeat that."

Macdara stared at the cap, then looked back at Siobhán. "This is going to make me a top suspect," he said.

"Don't be ridiculous. They're going to know a guard wouldn't be dumb enough to leave his own cap with the murder victim."

"You're right," he said. "Of course you're right." He didn't sound convinced.

"You're not thinking of removing it, are ye?" Siobhán asked.

Macdara looked as if she'd slapped him. "Do ye or do ye not know me?"

"I'm sorry. Of course. I take it back."

Macdara ran his hand through his hair as if imagining his cap was back on. "It's going to look worse if they see I've let you all over the crime scene."

"I'm off," Siobhán said. "Don't stand with your back to the hill."

"What?"

"The killer could still be out here." She pointed at Kevin. "You don't want to turn your back like he did."

"Whichever way I turn my back is to the hill," Macdara pointed out. He was right. They were at a peak that had slopes in both directions.

"Ah, right so. Just keep turning in circles then," Siobhán said.

"Mighty helpful," Macdara quipped.

"Not a bother." Siobhán turned and hightailed it out of there while she still had the last word.

Chapter 6

Once the first set of guards arrived, Paul Donnelly was escorted up to the crime scene, and although they couldn't touch the body and get an official proclamation until the state pathologist arrived from Dublin, Paul confirmed that he believed the deceased was indeed Kevin Gallagher. Any further examinations would have to wait. Siobhán hoped the pathologist would hurry. It looked like a hard rain was coming. What if it washed away precious evidence? Upon her suggestion, the guards agreed to erect one of the tents from the castle yard around the crime scene, thus keeping it as dry as possible. Macdara didn't seem happy that she offered the suggestion, but she couldn't worry about that now.

While the detective superintendent was on his way from Cork City, he let it be known that he didn't want the wedding guests trampling all over the castle grounds, so they all agreed to be escorted to Naomi's Bistro. Macdara and the Huntsmans were asked to stay behind. The rest of the guests piled into a waiting limo, and Siobhán led the procession on her scooter. This wasn't exactly the way she had imagined their entrance into Kilbane. As her scooter and the limo passed through Ballygate, the first of the town's four original entrance gates, followed by the limo, curious folks peeked out their windows while others ran out to the footpath, for even getting mowed down by the

Cahills' limo would be a story they could tell in pubs for the rest of their lives.

Sheila Mahoney stood outside her hair salon smoking a cigarette. Her husband, Pio, poked his head out from the window above her. Mike Granger was sweeping the footpath in front of his fruit and veg market, but he stopped to wave. Peter Hennessy was carrying boxes into his hardware shop but still managed to nod his head. The smell of curried chips wafted out from the chipper. The early drinking crew gathered in clumps in front of O'Rourke's, just off their graveyard shifts and ready for pints. Siobhán took in all the shops, which were warmed up with colors: yellows, blues, greens, pinks, and the occasional spot of red; she was proud of her village, and the cheerful paint saw them through many a gray day. Add to it the cobblestone streets, gas lamps dotting Sarsfield Street, and the occasional cheerful mural, and Kilbane was a place where everyone was made to feel welcome.

Minutes later they had arrived at Naomi's Bistro, and just the sight of her mam's name scripted into the robin's-egg-blue sign above their door gave Siobhán a bit of peace. Parking was plentiful given that the entire town had conspired to leave spaces right in front of the bistro for the full weekend celebration. In no time, the wedding guests filed into the foyer of the building, and immediately the smell of a good Irish breakfast wafted their way. The entryway, normally stuffed with wellies and jackets, was now clear, and the floors were shining from a recent polish. Ahead of them was a set of stairs leading to the family's upstairs dwelling, and to the right, French doors led into the bistro. Siobhán stopped at the threshold, as if to relish the sight. It was a quaint bistro, with windows looking out onto Sarsfield Street, a fireplace in the front room, and more seating in the back adjacent to the yard and garden.

"How lovely," Alice said, taking in the room. Siobhán could only imagine the McMansion that Alice had grown up in and would probably continue to occupy, but the sentiment seemed genuine and was followed by a fresh flood of tears. She'd been hysterical since the discovery of the body. And in her grief, she'd seemed to regress. Instead of leaning on her groom-to-be, she was being propped up by her father. Siobhán had heard a lot of rumors about Colm Cahill and his ruthless business dealings, but at the moment all she saw he was a father trying to comfort his only daughter.

Everyone else was deathly quiet, even Brenna. They had been delivered a great shock, Siobhán knew, and it would take a while for the reality to sink in. Siobhán told herself she had better appreciate the curtain of silence while it lasted. For once they realized they were all suspects, hostilities would be aired and accusations would fly. And to think, this was supposed to be one of the happiest times of the young lovers' lives.

"Make yourselves at home," Siobhán said. "We were expecting you tomorrow, but we'll have breakfast out in no time at all."

"I couldn't imagine eating at a time like this," Brenna said. "Especially after Alice's reaction to your brown bread."

"That's enough," Alice snapped. "I told ye it was my nerves. You scarfed down two slices, and you're fine." Brenna seemed to shrink from her words. *Or maybe the hostilities would start right away, like.* Alice looked at Siobhán with a polite smile. "Your offer is much appreciated. But I dare say I don't think any of us have an appetite."

Heads began to nod around the room.

"Of course," Siobhán said. "We'll just have tea then."

The guests began to explore the bistro, distracting themselves by taking in all the little details. Every table was covered in delicate lace special-ordered from Waterford. The cost had been extravagant, but now that Siobhán saw it in all its glory, it had been well worth the extra cabbage. The bridal table, holding pride of place in the front room, was the most lavishly decorated of all. A Waterford Crystal vase was prominently displayed and filled to the brim with roses—a dozen white yokes with two red ones cozied up in the middle. Long tapered candles were ready to be lit, and their best china, a gorgeous pale blue, was set with the polished silver. And thanks to their friend and neighbor Bridie Sheedy, every linen napkin had been folded into an elegant swan and placed on top of the china.

"You went to such lengths to please us," Alice sobbed.

"You should have a lie-down," Colm said. He looked at Siobhán. "Do you have a bed upstairs?"

"Of course," Siobhán said, mentally trying to figure out when she had last washed the bedding. She had thought of everything but the wedding guests needing a nap.

"I'm fine." Alice wiped her tears with the handkerchief her father handed her.

Paul stepped up and took her arm. "I'll mind her." A look of disapproval flashed across Colm's face, but it quickly passed, and he nodded his consent. Siobhán couldn't imagine what it would feel like to be under that man's thumb. If anyone was up for the job, Paul Donnelly seemed to be the man. He had just lost his best man and presumably his best friend, yet he seemed to be holding it together. She had a feeling waters ran deep behind those calm brown eyes, but of course it was just a feeling.

Siobhán made a mental note to gather information about Paul and Kevin's friendship. She was definitely going to have to get hold of a notebook straightaway.

A shrill series of barks sounded from the back garden, and Siobhán practically jumped out of her skin.

"Jaysus, that nearly put me heart in me crossways!" Susan Cahill said, clutching her chest.

Siobhán flushed with embarrassment. "I'm sorry. He's a new pup." Trigger. That cheeky little yapper! He was costing them all precious hours of sleep, treating them to his nightly serenades. He had a perfectly good dog house and plenty of room to run and dig, yet his snout was constantly pushed up against the back window, begging to be let in. Truth be told, he was on her last nerve, and she got the distinct feeling the dislike was mutual. With the rest of The O'Sullivan Six (as they were known about town), he was a bundle of love, but for some reason he always flattened his ears and growled at Siobhán, actually bearing teeth, like. Ciarán figured he was afraid of her hair. James said he was afraid of her height, until she pointed out that he was taller and Trigger greeted him with licks. "You're just not a dog person," Gráinne offered. *I'm not a yappy little dog person*, she wanted to retort, but Ciarán was so in love with the mutt that she zipped her piehole.

She glanced at the window now, and sure enough, there he was, drooling all over the recently washed panes. She wished to heaven that Ciarán had never brought home that pup. But there was no taking him away from the lad now.

"He's adorable," Alice said. "May I fetch him?"

"Oh, you wouldn't want him in here," Siobhán said. "He's a holy terror."

"May I step into the garden then?"

"Of course," Siobhán said. "Apologies if it's a bit over-grown." *A bit*. You couldn't find Godzilla out there if he was dropped from the sky. Her father had always taken meticulous care of the garden, especially the herbs. She would have to make a point to tend to it soon.

"I love nature," Alice said. "Even when it's a bit on the wild side. You should speak with Carol Huntsman. She has the soil from her gardens imported. It's dark and silky."

"I love dark and silky," Paul said, running his fingers through her hair. He winked, and Alice blushed. The lovers slipped outside. Siobhán felt a pang for them and couldn't decipher if it was jealousy or worry. She turned back to the rest of the guests.

"The kettle is on the cooker. Tea will be out in no time. Please, make yourselves comfortable." A cozy fire would be in order. Siobhán set the kindling in for a quick light and hurried into the kitchen to greet her brood. When she pushed through swinging doors, Ciarán, Ann, and Gráinne stumbled back. Ear-wigging! She'd nearly wiped out the nosy trio.

James and Eoin were at the cooker, where black and white pudding sizzled on the grill alongside the rashers, and their neighbor Bridie stood holding a tray of teacups, ready to be served. They all stared at Siobhán with wide eyes.

"They won't be eating," Siobhán said. "Just tea for now."

"More for us," Eoin said with a grin. Fifteen and rail thin, Eoin had an appetite that was growing along with his limbs. He was wearing a Yankees cap backward and an apron that said CHI-TOWN RISING. Siobhán had no idea what Chi-town was or why it was rising. Eoin had never been out of Ireland, save a single trip to London, yet he loved ordering American items off eBay.

"You're like a divining rod for dead bodies," Gráinne piped up. She had just turned seventeen a fortnight ago and was a raven-haired stunner. Whom you constantly wanted to pummel.

"How on earth did ye hear so fast?" Siobhán asked.

"Bridie got a call," Eoin said.

Siobhán turned to Bridie. She was a petite woman with bouncy chestnut curls. Their neighbor and a dear friend, Bridie was also a whiz at crafting. She made scarves, hair accessories, and shawls that she sold in Courtney's Gift Shop. Since her husband, Seamus, had been arrested a few months back, she'd been working part-time at the bistro. "Who called ye?" Siobhán asked Bridie.

"Annmarie." Annmarie was Courtney's sister. She'd taken over the running of the gift shop, and apparently was also stepping into her late sister's role as the gossip queen as well.

"How on earth did Annmarie hear?"

"She heard it from Peter, who heard it from Pat, who ran into Mike—" Bridie's voice was picking up speed.

"You know yourself," James said. "The grapevine is alive and well."

Siobhán sighed. News did travel fast.

"How was he killed?" Ciarán asked. He was the youngest, and the only O'Sullivan besides herself with red hair. Ten years of age going on fifty.

"No such talk," Siobhán said. "We have guests to soothe."

"We heard it was the best man," Bridie said, stepping forward. "Is that true?" The teacups rattled on the tray.

She was getting a mighty workout holding the tray for so long, but she didn't seem able to let it down.

Siobhán sighed. If she didn't give them some details they would obsess on the murder all morning. "Yes, it was the best man, Kevin Gallagher." Everyone but Bridie crossed themselves. "Sadly, this morning he was found dead in the woods behind the castle." Ciarán was all ears and eyes. "He had a bump to the back of the head, and that's all I'll say." Her mind flashed to Macdara. She wondered how the guards had reacted to his cap being found clutched underneath Kevin's fingers.

"A bump?" Ciarán said. "What do you mean?"

"Who did it?" Gráinne demanded.

"We'll leave that to the guards this time," Siobhán said.

"Is the wedding off?" asked Ann, the youngest girl and the only blonde. She was caught between the desire to remain a child and the longing to be an adult. Siobhán didn't envy her; it was a tough time of life.

"I assume so, but please, no such talk. Especially not in front of the bride. Let's keep them calm."

"How did he get the bump to the head?" Ciarán asked again.

A large rock. He never saw it coming. Siobhán shuddered at the thought and kept her lips closed. The last thing she needed was to get Ciarán hyped up on another murder.

James stepped up. Her elder brother was so handsome, and he had been clean and sober for the past six months. "Bridie will go out with the teacups."

"About time," Bridie said like it was Siobhán's fault. "Me arms are about to fall off."

James continued. "Ann, you can follow with the kettle, and the rest of us will tend to the breakfast. Understand?" One by one they nodded their heads.

"I'll do it." Ciarán grabbed the teakettle and rushed toward the swinging doors leading into the bistro.

"Hold your horses," Siobhán said. He turned and waited. He looked like a traveler who had been sleeping on the streets. His hair was sticking up, and his T-shirt was wrinkled.

"The state of you," Siobhán licked her finger and then tried to calm down the stray hairs.

"After the shock they've had, I don't think they'll care about Ciarán's hair," James pointed out. Siobhán sighed and allowed Bridie and Ciarán to go out with the tea. She grabbed a platter and headed to the oven, where she had a batch of brown bread warming. Would anyone eat it after what Brenna said? Perceptions counted. Brenna was poisoning everyone's mind by accusing Siobhán of poisoning the brown bread. The nerve of that woman. Siobhán suddenly understood why Macdara had been so worried about his cap being found with Kevin. Even if a sensible person would see that in essence it should clear Macdara altogether, the association would still linger. Hopefully the guards wouldn't announce the findings to anyone else.

Siobhán set the tray of bread on the cooling rack and stepped into the dining room. Everyone now had a cup of tea, including Alice and Paul, who had been served in the back garden. Alice had her cup of tea in one hand and Trigger in the other. Siobhán stopped to gawk. Why, even the dog seemed smitten with Alice. Instead of squirming and scrambling to get down like he did with the young ones, or growling and bearing teeth like he did with Siobhán, the pup was cozied up to Alice's chest, his chin resting on her shoulder. Siobhán half expected the mutt to treat her to an evil wink.

Siobhán felt something move behind her and turned to see Colm Cahill standing directly behind her. He stared down at her with intense eyes. He smelled like cigars. "When can we return to the castle?"

"Were you at the hilltop this morning?" Siobhán asked.

Colm's eyes narrowed. "I don't answer to you."

Siobhán sighed. He was a man whose ego needed constant feeding. She placed her hand on her heart. "I didn't mean to sound like a guard. I was very impressed to hear that you had announced your intention to visit the hilltop every morning at sunrise. No wonder you're so successful; you're a man of good habits."

Colm blinked, and his shoulders relaxed. He thrust his chin up. "It nearly could have been me!"

"So you were headed that way?" His eyes narrowed again, and Siobhán smiled and fluttered her eyelashes.

"We would fall to chaos without our routines," Colm said. "It was dumb luck that I overslept." His eyes darted around as if he was expecting someone to jump out and call him a liar. Which he most definitely was.

Brian had stated that he'd seen Colm arguing with the innkeeper that morning over a missing fax. Didn't he know the guards were going to speak to everyone? Where did he go after he asked after the fax? And where had he been just before?

Siobhán decided to play along with his lie. "So if you hadn't overslept, you would have gone to the hilltop to smoke a cigar?"

"And to watch the sunrise," Colm said. "How did you know?" His eyebrow arched in surprise.

Darn it. Siobhán didn't want to bring up that she'd spotted the cigar butt at the crime scene. "The top of the hill has the loveliest view," she said. "I was told you had announced your intentions previously."

"I was hoping to start a trend. I don't approve of sloth. Earlier risers have the biggest bank accounts."

"And yet you slept in?"

"How did you know about the cigar?"

"You were smoking a cigar when I first met you."

Colm nodded. "Not bad for a bistro owner. I had planned to be up on the hill, but I had a late-night call with some overseas investors. By the time I awoke, I was late for Alice's photo."

"Your late-night investors," Siobhán said. "Was that the fax you were expecting?"

Confusion, then suspicion played out on Colm's face as it dawned on him that she'd just uncovered his lie. "Now you're crossing a line! You have no authority to interrogate me." Mentioning the fax had definitely hit a nerve. Who was it from? And if not Colm, who had taken it?

"The guards are going to ask you the same questions," Siobhán said. "You'd best be prepared to answer."

"I stumbled down to see if the fax had come in, then went right back to bed."

"You must have been angry that it was missing."

"Who told you that?"

"If the investors were important enough for you to be taking late-night calls from them, surely the fax was equally important."

"Now you see here—"

"And like me, I can see that when you're angry, you're actually quite energized. I just can't imagine why with all that angry energy, you didn't just storm up to the top of the hill and smoke a cigar."

"You insufferable servant. I had a sore head, that's why. And if you know what's good for you, you'll mind your own damn business." Steam was practically rising from him.

Now that she saw how easily he became enraged, she was quite clearly able to picture him bashing poor Kevin in the back of the head with a rock, then standing and smoking a cigar over his body. Jaysus. Murder was such a frightful business. And if he didn't go up to that hill, Siobhán would bet her life on one thing: he certainly did not go back to bed.

Colm crossed his arms. "When can I go back to the castle, get my things, and get out of this godforsaken village?" His tone was menacing; she was now persona non grata.

"I'm afraid it's going to be a while," Siobhán said.

Ciarán popped up next to Siobhán. He had to tilt his entire head back to look up at Colm. His freckles gleamed. "Investigations don't happen as quickly as they do on telly."

Startled, Colm stared down at Ciarán. He shook his head, then pointed at Siobhán. "I saw you run into the woods." He sounded like he was accusing her of something. "You were crouched down like a crab. Did you think we couldn't see you?"

"Ronan was headed to the crime scene with his fancy camera. I had to stop him from disturbing the crime scene." Something clicked in place as Siobhán spoke. Where was Ronan? She scanned the crowd. He was nowhere in sight. Neither was the wedding planner, Brian. Were they together? Was anyone else missing?

Colm leaned down. His breath could kill a racetrack full of horses. "Are you sure Kevin Gallagher didn't just pass out from the drink and hit his head on that damned rock?"

Siobhán gently scooted Ciarán toward Bridie and waited while Bridie scooped him up and steered him to the other side of the room. "Someone delivered a crushing blow to the back of his head," Siobhán said. "He was found facedown." She kept her eyes glued to his face, waiting for any kind of reaction.

"Who's to say he didn't pass out and fall backward onto the rock?"

"Then turned himself over?" Siobhán said, trying to keep the bite out of her voice.

Colm straightened up. "It was a local then." He wiped lint from his jacket.

Siobhán pretended to contemplate his theory. "How would this local have gained entrance to the castle grounds?" She thought of the security guard, Val. Why, anyone could have slipped past that inexperienced lad, but she wasn't going to offer him up as a scapegoat.

"I agree," Brenna said, stepping up. She twirled a strand of blond hair around her index finger. "It's definitely a local. One of the robbers." Her words were like little daggers she thrust at Siobhán.

"Speaking of the robbery rumor," Siobhán said in a cheerful voice, "I asked Carol and George Huntsman about it myself. Would you like to know what they said?"

Brenna narrowed her eyes and let go of the strand of hair. It un-twirled like a disoriented ballerina. "Go on then."

"They claimed they never said any such thing."

The porch door slammed, startling everyone inside. Alice and Paul were just in from the garden.

"Where's Father?" Paul said, his voice cutting above the din. Heads began to turn. "Mam?"

Faye's hand fluttered to her mouth. "In all the excitement, I'd forgotten all about him."

Forgotten all about a husband and father? Was that likely? Possibly. Murder did have a way of knocking all sense out of your head. But so much sense that you would forget all about your missing husband?

"Ronan and Brian aren't here either," Alice said, pointing from person to person as she silently tallied them.

"I saw Ronan stop to snap a picture of a wall," Susan said. "What kind of artist is enamored with a damp stone wall?"

"We're one of the few walled towns left in Ireland," Siobhán interjected. "They carry great historical significance." The medieval walls were erected at a turbulent time. Kilbane had once been a town of great strategic importance and as such was a frequent target during times of war. In Siobhán's opinion, anyone who couldn't understand or appreciate the walls didn't deserve to set foot within them.

Susan Cahill crossed her arms and glared in Siobhán's direction. Siobhán really disliked the woman. But that didn't necessarily make her a murderer. And her nails looked pristine. They were covered with a clear gloss. Too pristine to have picked up a large rock and lobbed it at the back of Kevin's head. Unless of course she wore gloves. Or had time to clean up. Or perhaps she'd hired someone to do the actual deed. Siobhán looked around the room again. "What about Brian?"

"I saw him dart inside the castle just before the guards arrived," Brenna said.

"Did anyone see him come out?" Siobhán asked. One by one, heads began to shake.

Paul held up his mobile. "I'm going to ask Macdara to fetch our missing guests." He hurried off to a private spot up front to make the call. Alice went to Faye's side and linked arms with her.

"I'm sure Martin's fine," she said. Faye smiled at Alice, but the expression never reached her eyes. She seemed extremely uncomfortable with Alice's touch. That was an Irish mam for you. Never liked the woman who wanted to marry her son. Even a woman like Alice.

"I want to go home," Nancy Flannery said. Speaking of Irish mams. Siobhán hadn't had a minute to spend with Macdara's mother. "Will someone take me to the train?" Her delicate voice shook. Siobhán wanted to take her hands and comfort her, but Nancy was holding them firmly against her stomach, still clutching her handbag as if one of them might snatch it at any moment. Did she know Macdara's cap was gone? Was that why she was clutching her handbag? Siobhán definitely wasn't going to mention it—she had too much of a knack for mucking things up.

"How do you feel about Dara being involved in this awful business?" Nancy asked.

"Involved?" Siobhán said.

"Being a guard."

"Oh," Siobhán said. "He's a terrific guard."

Nancy frowned. That's not what she wanted to hear. "It's too dangerous. He has many other talents. He needs to move to Cork City, find a nice lassie, and have children *of his own*." She glanced around the bistro, as if counting out her brood.

Nancy Flannery would be the luckiest woman in the world if her imaginary future grandchildren were half as wonderful as Siobhán's siblings. But she kept her gob shut. "Macdara will be here soon," Siobhán said. "Please, just have a cup of tea." Nancy drew a breath, but then nodded. Gráinne, who had sailed into the dining room, escorted her to a nearby chair and saw to the tea.

"I want to go home too," Brenna wailed.

"Nobody is going home," Alice cried out. "The wedding is Saturday."

"Wedding?" Susan Cahill chimed. Her voice, so far calm and authoritative, had gone shrill. "You can't possibly go on with the wedding."

"We are," Alice said. "We are going on with the wedding."

"The wedding"—Colm said, drawing up to his full height and sending his voice hurtling across the room—"has most definitely been called off."

Chapter 7

When Paul returned from his phone call to Macdara, he found his bride-to-be slumped in a chair, sobbing. "What now?" He immediately went to Alice's side and began rubbing her back. Siobhán watched in fascination. She'd never seen such a caring man. Paul lifted his head and looked at her. "Macdara rounded up all our stray ducks. Including Father. They're on their way."

Siobhán, embarrassed to be caught staring at him, nodded her head, then looked away.

Faye cried out with relief. "Where's Martin? Asleep all this time, was he?"

"You can ask him when they get here," Paul said. "Now why is my beautiful bride in tears?"

"We've canceled the wedding," Susan said. She sounded unusually chipper.

"You can't do that," Paul said.

"We just did," Colm said. "The matter is closed."

Paul gently let go of Alice and took a step toward Colm. "It's *our* wedding. Kevin was *my* best man. He'd want us to go on."

"It's our wedding," Alice repeated, standing and wiping her tears with the back of each hand. "Our decision."

"Why on earth would you carry on now?" Susan said.

Paul threw open his arms. "If nothing else, this proves how short life can be. I don't want to waste another second."

"What would they say about us?" Susan said.

"They?" Paul asked.

"Society. The papers. Kevin's mam." Susan gesticulated each with her hands.

Alice stepped forward. "We honor Kevin by going on."

"The decision has been made," Colm said. "The wedding is off."

"Love should win," Nancy Flannery said, startling everyone as she set her teacup down with a clink. "Love is the only thing can drive out such horror." For the first time, Siobhán could see where Macdara got his stoic kindness. Maybe she had been too quick to judge his mammy. She tried to give her a nod and a smile, but Nancy wouldn't look her way.

A murmur ran through the group as they considered Nancy Flannery's words.

"It's a private affair anyway," Alice said, her voice suddenly girlish and hopeful. "We'll tone down the celebrations."

"Is that how you want to marry, dear?" Susan Cahill said. "Under such macabre circumstances? Toned down? With tears in your eyes?"

Alice squared her shoulders. "There will be tears in our eyes either way. Shouldn't something good come of all this evil?"

Paul wrapped his arm around Alice's waist and pulled her close. Siobhán wasn't sure what to think. Oh, she loved the idea of love winning out. But to marry under such a dark cloud!

The front bell jangled, and seconds later Macdara appeared with Brian, Chef Antoine, and a silver-haired man she assumed was Martin Donnelly in tow. Siobhán had forgotten all about the chef. He was carrying a folded case. His chef knives, no doubt; he had stayed behind to collect them. Much like the knives, Siobhán would have to stay sharper. Where had he been all this time? Ronan was the last to slink in, clutching his camera to his chest. Martin immediately went to Faye's side and took her hand. He had a handsome face, but he was barely taller than his wife. Paul hadn't gotten his height from either of them. Genetics was a mysterious thing.

Colm turned to Macdara. "When can we return to the castle? We must pack and go home."

"Daddy!" Alice cried. "Please."

He turned on his daughter. "If you intend to go on with this circus, it will be without your mother and I. We're off as soon as we can toss our luggage into the limo."

"I'm afraid that will not be possible, sir," Macdara said. "The detective sergeant was quite clear. No one is to leave Kilbane until there's been a full investigation."

"Are we suspects?" Faye said.

"Yes," Macdara said. "We're all suspects."

"Ludicrous," Susan said.

"It's procedure." Macdara used his calming voice.

"You're definitely all suspects," Ciarán said. Siobhán hadn't noticed him lurking by the fireplace, gawking at everything and everyone.

"Cheeky lad," Susan said. "Why aren't you in school?"

"School starts next week," Siobhán said. The snobby wedding guests were now getting on her nerves. Siobhán had never mentally slapped so many people in her life.

"I can start taking alibis if ye like," Ciarán offered, thrusting up his index finger.

Macdara hid a smile and placed his hand on Ciarán's shoulder. Siobhán's heart gave a squeeze. "We're going to let the guards handle it," he said gently.

From across the room, Nancy Flannery studied the exchange with a definite look of disapproval. It was all too clear. She saw the O'Sullivan Six as an impediment to the future she wanted for her only son.

Was she right? But what about what he wanted?

Naomi and Liam O'Sullivan had had only two goals for their children: healthy and happy. They never would have foisted their ideas on a single one of them. It was only now sinking in what rare and special folks they were, how lucky they had all been to have been born to them. Siobhán would have taken the twenty-one years she had with her parents over a hundred years with any other. She just wished she could somehow give the young ones longer with them. Sharing her memories and stories was the only thing she could do now, and she intended to keep those stories coming as long as possible. In that sense, their presence in their lives was strong. Once in a while, Siobhán swore she could even smell her mam's soft perfume.

"If we're stuck here anyway, might as well go on with the wedding," Brenna said.

"It's certainly too late for refunds," Brian chimed in. Colm glared at him, and Brian buried himself in his iPad.

"That's the spirit," Alice said with strained enthusiasm.

"We won't force anyone who doesn't want to participate," Paul said. "But Alice and I are getting married. Who's in?" He looked to his father. "Dad?"

Martin nodded. "We need something to occupy our minds. I say on with the wedding."

"Thank you, Father," Paul said. "Mother?"

Faye rubbed her rosary beads. "If I thought delaying the wedding would bring Kevin back or offer anyone a bit of peace, I'd say postpone. But since we're stuck here anyway, perhaps it would be a wonderful way to honor to Kevin's memory."

"One of us is a killer," Ronan said. "Doesn't that worry any of you?" He had his camera poised and began snapping their horrified reactions.

"Stop it, or I'll knock that yoke out of your hands," Paul said. Ronan flashed Paul a searing look, but let the camera come to a thudding rest against his chest. Paul cleared his throat. "We must assume that someone had a personal motive to kill Kevin. As horrible as that is, I truly believe the rest of us will be safe." He looked around as if the killer might confess. "Be assured. The guards will be watching our every move. There will be no more violence." Siobhán couldn't tell if he was pleading with the killer or threatening him. Or her. Or creating a distraction if, in fact, he was the murderer.

Motive was the thing Siobhán needed to suss out. Who wanted Kevin dead, but most importantly, why? Certainly he'd shaken almost every single apple in the cart last night, but so far none of his shenanigans seemed to warrant such a merciless repercussion. A blow to the back of the head suggested two things: fury and cowardice. This was personal, and yet the killer didn't give Kevin a chance to see it coming. Thus the killer was a coward. Siobhán studied the pale Irish faces in the group and sighed. It hardly narrowed the field.

Alice must have been thinking along the same lines. "Kevin was harmless," she said. "I can't imagine anyone wanting him dead."

"You called him a nuisance," Brenna said.

Alice's beautiful eyes flashed with anger. "So that makes me a murderer?"

"Brides are supposed to be murderous on their wedding days," Brenna quipped.

"You have no sense of decorum." Alice turned her back on her maid of honor.

"Why did you choose me to be your maid of honor then?" A needy whine crept into Brenna's voice.

"You're my oldest friend," Alice said. Her shoulders sagged.

"But not your dearest?" Brenna fired back.

"Why are you always looking for a row?" Alice said. "Haven't we had enough drama?"

Brenna blinked and clamped her mouth shut. Siobhán sighed. All relationships ran deep. There was definitely a load of water under their bridge. But if Siobhán went diving into everyone else's pond, she was very likely to drown.

"We all thought Kevin Gallagher was a nuisance," Colm said, steering the conversation back to the murder. "Hardly clears up the mystery."

"I'm ashamed to say that my last words with him were quite angry," Paul said. "He's not himself when he drinks." Paul placed his hands over his eyes, and for a moment Siobhán thought he was having a good cry. But when he removed his hands a minute later, his eyes were dry.

"Where were you, Mr. Donnelly?" Brenna asked, staring at Martin.

Martin Donnelly began to brink rapidly. "When?"

"All morning," Brenna said, her voice turning stern.

"I was wandering around this quaint little town," Martin said. "Until I began to feel ill. At that point, I returned to my room and fell asleep."

"Did you eat any of Siobhán's brown bread?" Brenna asked straightaway.

"Who's Siobhán?" Martin asked.

Siobhán reluctantly raised her hand as everyone stared. Martin nodded and gave a slight bow. "Pleased to meet ye."

"You as well," Siobhán sang before whirling around on Brenna. "Martin wasn't anywhere near my brown bread. It must have been something both Alice and Martin ate last night."

"We both had lemon meringue pie," Alice said. "Chef Antoine made it."

"My lemon meringue is beyond reproach!" Chef Antoine shouted. He was draped in a chair by the fire, looking as if he was contemplating throwing himself into the flames. "I'm sick of cooking for rich people!"

"You can cook for us," Ciarán said.

The chef grimaced. "Not that sick."

"Your father and I had the pie, and we're fine," Susan said. A chorus of "Same as" rang out around the room. A satisfied smile crept over Chef Antoine's broad face.

"I'm sorry I wasn't here when the news came," Martin said. "It's a terrible, terrible shock. What time did this dastardly deed take place?"

"We don't know yet," Siobhán said gently. "What time do you think Kevin locked you in your room?"

Paul frowned.

"What's this?" Macdara asked.

Paul filled Macdara in. "I couldn't open me door this morning. Thought maybe Kevin was having a laugh."

"Interesting," Macdara said. "He would have needed a key for that, don't ye think?"

Paul shrugged. "I suppose so. I didn't think about it."

"Who let you out?" Siobhán asked. "Mr. or Mrs. Huntsman?"

"The missus," Paul said.

"If Kevin did lock you in, he may have done you a favor," Macdara said.

"A favor?" Alice asked.

"If we can prove Paul was locked in his room at the time of the murder, it's as good an alibi as any," Macdara said.

Paul gave a wry smile. "That's a bit of relief."

"You think we're going to need alibis?" Alice cried.

Siobhán placed her hand on Alice's arm. "Routine questions. Nothing to worry about." She wished Macdara hadn't just publicly cleared Paul. What if he was lying? They couldn't prove whether or not he was actually locked in. At the least, Macdara should have waited until Carol Huntsman corroborated his story.

"Kevin was killed somewhere between half one and half nine," Macdara said. "I'd like everyone to write down the time they came home last night, the time they awoke, where they went, and what they did."

Brenna dropped her jaw, and her eyes widened. Sweat dappled her forehead. She swallowed hard. Given the unruly sight of her when they'd first met, and her obvious nervousness now, Siobhán was convinced that Brenna had slept with Kevin. It was normal that she would be embarrassed, mortified even, but this was no time for lies. Paul was staring at Brenna too. Did he know? Siobhán would have to speak to Macdara about it when they had a minute alone together.

"This is getting us nowhere," Brenna said. She pointed at Macdara. "Even the guard argued with Kevin. You were furious with him, weren't ye? All because he was swiping your cap, having a laugh."

Paul stepped toward Brenna. "Just what are ye playing at?" he said. "Macdara is the most honest man I've ever met."

"It's alright," Macdara said. "Yes, I was annoyed with Kevin for swiping me cap. In fact, he had it with him."

Siobhán flinched. Why did he just announce that?

Because he wasn't in detective mode; he was in friendship mode. And all of the suspects were in his blind spot.

"I'm sorry, I'm sorry," Nancy cried out. "I thought it just fell out of me purse. Your man must have sneaked up on me and lifted it."

Macdara quickly tried to soothe her. "Not your fault," Macdara said. "I'm the one who should have made sure to keep it on me head."

"Wait," Brenna said. "Are you saying that your garda cap was found at the crime scene?"

Regret crept into Macdara's eyes. *Finally. Cop on. You shouldn't be giving away any information.* "A garda cap was found at the crime scene," he said. "And mine is missing."

"Wipe that smirk off your face," Alice said to Brenna. "We all know Kevin was taking the piss last night."

"We can't just ignore evidence," Brenna said.

Paul shook his head. "Macdara wouldn't be daft enough to kill a man and then leave his own cap behind."

"Unless that's exactly what he wants us to think," Brenna said.

Macdara came up to Siobhán from behind and nudged her. "Can I borrow a notebook?" he whispered.

"Nothing would make me happier," Siobhán said.

"I'll fetch it." Ciarán ran off to get Macdara a notebook.

Just then Bridie entered into the dining room in a tight black dress overplayed with a white frilly bib, black stockings, and high heels. All she was missing was a feather duster and a pimp. Even Chef Antoine sat up in his chair and dropped his jaw. All conversation screeched to a halt. Siobhán couldn't even remember what she'd just been thinking about. Siobhán heard her mam's voice in her head, clear as day: *Mother of God.*

"If anyone would like an Irish breakfast, it's ready," Bridie said, curtseying in front of Alice and Paul as if meeting a king and queen.

"Jaysus," Brenna said, her eyes raking over Bridie's outfit. "The killer definitely has to be one of them."

Chapter 8

Siobhán stood in the back garden, hoping the sight of it would calm her nerves. The summer lords-and-ladies were going to seed, but the violets and pansies and white clovers were in bloom, along with a plethora of others Siobhán couldn't name, and she took her time breathing in their sweet, warm scents. *This too shall pass.* The herb garden was choked with weeds. Siobhán would make it a point to organize it this year, and she would never let it get this overgrown again. It was healthy and calming to get one's hands in the dirt. Her da knew the name of every single leaf. Siobhán could tell mint from parsley, but that was as far as her green thumb reached. Bunches of herbs tied with string used to hang upside down from the ceiling of their kitchen. Once they were dry, her mam would chop them and place them in little glass jars, labeled with her beautiful handwriting, waiting for use. Siobhán wanted to keep up the tradition and silently added that to her to-do list. There just weren't enough hours in the day.

Trigger was digging in a patch of dirt by the fence. She approached, ready to scold. His back was to her. He froze when she was just a few feet away and began to snarl. He hadn't even bothered to turn around and look at her. If he wanted to dig a tunnel out of here, she might as well let him. She backed off and began to pace.

That Brenna was strumming her last nerve. If she made one more crack about Siobhán's brown bread or how the killer had to be one of them—why, Siobhán couldn't be responsible for her actions. A person could only take so much. Siobhán's head was so filled with noise she didn't even know someone had stepped outside until she felt a hand on her shoulder. She whirled around to find Macdara in front of her, holding out a cup of tea.

"Thank you." She smiled as she took the cup and failed to mention that she'd almost kneed him in the groin.

"Not a bother." Macdara gave her a smile, then shook his head. "Let's have it."

"Have what?"

"I can hear you thinking from in there." Trigger stopped digging, trotted over, and whined at Macdara's feet. He bent down and patted the dog's head. Siobhán could have sworn she heard him purr. Cheeky mutt.

"Brenna is my top suspect." Siobhán began to pace around the herb garden.

"Because she keeps slagging on your brown bread?"

"Amongst other things."

"Go on," Macdara said.

"I'm pretty sure Brenna and Kevin spent the night together last night."

"Did someone tell you they spent the night together?"

"I deduced it."

Macdara groaned. "In other words—no."

"Her tousled appearance, the smug look on her face, the way she announced how she'd seen Kevin go for a walk this morning, and the repeated knowing looks Paul kept giving her."

"You're saying Paul knows they spent the night together?" Macdara asked. Siobhán nodded. He didn't look too happy to find out Paul was keeping a secret from him. "Sleeping with a man is a far cry from killing him."

"True. But she's definitely covering it up. And that narrows down the time of death."

Macdara pulled a notebook out of his pocket and jotted something down. "Who else?"

Siobhán stopped pacing. "Colm Cahill. He and Kevin are almost identically built. Easy to sneak up and hit him from behind."

Macdara frowned. "What does build matter if the person snuck up on Kevin from behind?"

"Kevin was at the peak of the hill. The killer came up from behind, on the incline. So he or she would have already been at a lower position. Situated so, I think a short person would have had trouble striking and killing Kevin with one blow."

Macdara shook his head. "Not if he or she got lucky with the trajectory."

Siobhán sighed. "Anything's possible, but for now I'm trying to figure out what's likely. And that's not all. Remember, Colm had announced his intention to walk to the top of the hill every morning to watch the sunrise."

"But he didn't that morning."

"Suspicious, isn't it?"

"You think he's lying?"

"First he said he slept in. But Brian saw him arguing with Carol Huntsman over a missing fax. So then he changed his story. Said he got up, argued about the fax, then went back to bed." Macdara nodded and took another note. He was taking her seriously. "And I smelled cigar smoke in the woods."

"Motive?"

Siobhán stopped and looked to the sky as if the answers might be written there. The clouds were almost black now, but the rain had yet to hit. "Kevin groped Susan on the stairs last night. He was protecting his wife's honor."

Macdara rubbed his chin. "That's not enough."

Siobhán agreed. "I think it has something to do with the missing fax."

"I'll ask the guards to search for it."

"He seems rather eager to cancel the wedding," Siobhán added.

"That's an understatement."

"Why?" Siobhán said. "Paul seems wonderful."

"Does he now?" Macdara's voice was playful, but if she wasn't mistaken, he was covering up a touch of jealousy.

Siobhán laughed. "He's also madly in love with Alice. Anyone can see that. Doesn't Mr. Cahill want that for his only daughter?"

Macdara sighed. "He believes the Donnellys are beneath him."

"He believes everybody is beneath him."

"True. But everybody isn't marrying his only daughter."

"So he doesn't approve."

"He does not. But surely you're not suggesting that he staged a murder just to get out of a wedding?"

"I'm simply postulating theories," Siobhán said. "Now onto Martin."

"Paul's father?" Macdara sounded surprised. "He's a decent man."

"He was missing throughout the entire ordeal. You have to admit that's odd."

"I'll ask around town. If he was scouting about in Kilbane, as he claimed, then someone will have seen him."

Siobhán nodded. "Ronan is next. A temperamental artist. And from his jittery demeanor I would surmise he might even be a drug addict. He was obviously upset about the camera, and he was eager to photograph the body."

"I'm surprised Chef Antoine isn't at the top of your list," Macdara said.

"Chef Antoine," she repeated. "Just because he discovered the body?"

"As a guard, I'd have to look closely at him for that."

Siobhán tagged on. "And don't forget his reaction when you said he couldn't leave the castle grounds. We should check with Brian. If Chef Antoine had any wedding-related errands to run, he would be the person to ask. Maybe we should start there." Siobhán headed for the door.

Macdara stepped in front of her. "There's no we."

So much for wanting her advice. Siobhán took a deep breath. "You asked for my theories."

Macdara held up his hand. "You misunderstand. There's no we—there's just you."

Siobhán blinked. "What?"

"The detective sergeant made it clear. I'm barred from investigating."

An uneasy feeling ran through Siobhán. She hated the saying, but it fit: *like someone walked over her grave.* "The cap," she said.

Macdara nodded. "I would have been a suspect anyway. I'm a wedding guest."

"You told them about your row with Kevin?"

"Of course," Macdara said.

"They don't really think you're guilty?" She hoped he didn't pick up on the panic in her voice.

"If I were them, I wouldn't rule me out."

"They know you. You're one of them. Not to mention you're the best investigator they have." She meant it too.

Macdara accepted the compliment with a simple nod of his head. "Luckily we have the second best investigator to help us out."

Siobhán was about to ask who when she caught him staring at her. *Her*. He meant *her*. "*Second* best?" She held his gaze until he laughed.

"Don't push it. I mean it, though. You have a quick mind, a wicked memory, and you're good at reading people."

"That's the nicest thing you ever said to me." This time Siobhán wasn't teasing.

His eyes softened. "Then I'm going to have to work on that. Because I can think of a hundred nicer things right off the top of me head." He moved in as if to kiss her. Trigger growled and yipped from below. The door swung open. Paul poked his head out. "Macdara?"

Macdara jerked back. "Yes, boss?"

Paul held up a mobile phone. "The detective sergeant wants to speak with ye. He has some news."

Chapter 9

The wedding guests crowded around Macdara as he delivered the message from Detective Sergeant O'Brien. "Each of you must write down everything you've done since you've arrived at the castle."

"You've already asked us," Susan said.

"I asked you to write down everything you've done since last night. Sergeant O'Brien cast a wider net." Everyone just stared at him.

"Everything?" Ronan said. "Even the juicy bits?" He scanned the crowd as if he had something juicy on every one of them.

Macdara cut him off. "You heard the instruction."

"Washing our teeth?" Ronan persisted.

"If you'd like."

"That won't be a problem for Brian," Brenna said. "He already logs everything he does in that iPad."

"It's called organizational skills," Brian said. "And she's right. I do. Will they accept an electronic copy? I can e-mail it immediately." He was probably the type of lad who always raised his hand first in school. Poor thing. He had undoubtedly been beaten up a lot as a young one. Good on him that it didn't stop him.

"Why don't you just use pen and paper?" Macdara said.

Brian chewed his lip, but obediently nodded.

"Are they going to analyze our handwriting?" Ronan asked. "If we don't dot our i's and cross our t's, does it mean we're guilty?"

"Keep it simple," Macdara said, irritation cracking through his voice. He turned to Siobhán. "Do kids these days know how to use pen and paper?"

"Quite a waste of time to write down everything that's already perfectly typed," Brian said, sounding stressed.

"Just do it, please," Alice said.

Brian had the decency to look ashamed. "Of course."

"I'll round up some biros and notebooks," James said. "Siobhán has loads of them."

"Thank you," Siobhán said.

"Notebooks you'll be using for school any day now yourself, won't you?" James whispered to Siobhán as he ambled away to fetch them. Cheeky. She had been procrastinating picking an online university. James wasn't going to let her forget it.

"You're a suspect too," Brian said, pointing at Macdara.

Macdara nodded. "I'll be writing down my activities as well."

"We're supposed to just hand them over to you, another suspect?" Brian certainly seemed to enjoy calling Macdara a suspect.

Macdara's eyes flicked to Siobhán. She got the message. "I'll collect them." She hoped she didn't sound too eager.

"You're going to read them all," Brenna said. "That's not fair."

"We'll put them in a sealed envelope, and Siobhán will deliver them to the guards." Macdara looked at her long and hard until she nodded.

"I'll find an envelope large enough," Siobhán said. *And perhaps one that has some age to it so it wouldn't be difficult to peel it open with a bit of steam from the kettle.*

"You said a few bits of news," Paul said. "Is there more?"

Macdara nodded. "Kilbane Castle will be off-limits for the rest of your stay."

"The wedding," Alice cried.

Brian hit himself on the head with his iPad.

"That's it then," Colm said.

"What about my belongings?" Susan Cahill said. "If I don't get out of this tracksuit and into Armani tout de suite, you're going to have to cart me off to hospital."

Ciarán, who was lingering behind Siobhán, piped up. "Who's Armani Toot Sweet?"

Gráinne, who was lurking in the doorway, gawking, piped up. "He's a clothing designer, you eejit, and obviously he has a sweet tooth."

"Oh my God," Alice said, smiling at Ciarán. "I just want to eat you up."

"What about me?" Eoin said. "Do you want to eat me up as well, like?" He was leaning against the counter, grinning. Alice actually blushed. Where did the lad get the confidence? Siobhán had never even seen him smile at a girl, let alone flirt so shamelessly. It was an alarming revelation that she could love her siblings so much yet never really know them, and despite wishing otherwise, she certainly didn't have any control over them. James walked behind Eoin and knocked the baseball cap off his head.

"Morons," Gráinne said. "Can I go upstairs now?"

"Me too?" Ann said. Apparently adults were boring even when they were discussing murder.

"Of course," Siobhán said. "Thank you for the help."

Ann turned before she reached the stairs. "Are we still going school shopping with ye?" she asked Siobhán. Gráinne leaned on the bannister to listen.

Siobhán smoothed Ann's unruly blond hair away from her face and rubbed her back. "I'm sorry. I forgot all about it."

"Not a bother," James said. "I'll take them."

Ann shook her head and pulled away. "Mam always went to the shops with us before school." Ann's voice carried across the room. Siobhán could feel a dozen pair of eyes on her back.

"I know. I'm sorry."

"You promised."

"This is work."

"How is it work? You're not a detective."

"Your brothers and sisters are going with ye."

"I don't want to go," Eoin said. "I don't need new clothes."

"Me neither," Ciarán said.

"We'll get a few bits and bobs and then curried chips while we're waiting for the colleens," James said to his brothers.

"And we won't get curried chips?" Gráinne pouted.

"You'll get them after," James said.

Curried chips did sound good. If Ann wasn't so browned off with her, she would have asked that they bring her some as well.

"You said you'd go!" Ann pouted.

"You're going anyway, and after you're getting curry chips. There's no need for a pity party," Siobhán said.

"Indeed. Even if I threw one and invited ye, ye wouldn't come anyway." Ann stomped her foot, then whirled around and ran up the steps to her bedroom.

"She'll be fine," James said off Siobhán's pained look. Siobhán didn't admit the worst of it. Ann was right. Siobhán didn't have to investigate this murder. She could go to the shops like she'd promised. Watch them try on outfits and eat curried chips. She just couldn't shake the feeling inside her that was driving her to stay and investigate. She wanted to solve this mystery. She wanted to catch the killer. It wasn't her job, but somehow she felt as if it were. A calling of sorts.

"Don't worry," Gráinne said. She was still hanging on the staircase. "I have a better sense of fashion than you anyway." She winked at Siobhán and then thundered up the steps.

"She'd better not come home dressed like Britney Spears," Siobhán called after her.

"Who's dat?" Gráinne yelled back.

"Thank you," Siobhán said to James.

He nodded. Bridie came out of the kitchen and glided over to Siobhán. Thankfully, she'd changed out of her outfit and was back in dress pants and a modest top. "The Frenchman is snooping around the kitchen," she whispered. "My shift is finished. Unless you'll be needing anything else?"

"No, thank you," she said to Bridie. "See you tomorrow." What was the chef doing snooping around their kitchen?

"I'm on it," James said, passing out the last of the notebooks and biros. He headed for the kitchen as the guests chose seats in which to sit and write down their alibis. Siobhán refilled mugs of tea, her fingers tingling as she watched everyone begin to write.

"I'll speak with the sergeant about all of your belongings," Macdara announced to the group when they had all finished and their writings had been sealed in a large envelope. Macdara handed the envelope to Siobhán, who tucked it into her handbag as everyone watched. The detective sergeant would be paying her a visit to collect it. She only hoped she might have the opportunity to do a little peeking before that happened.

Brenna flopped down in a chair. "If there's no wedding, how on earth are we going to pass our time in this wasteland?"

"I know," Alice said turning on Brenna. "Let's spend it figuring out where I'm going to get married now that the castle is off-limits."

"I'll marry you anywhere," Paul said.

"You can have the wedding at Saint Mary's and the reception here," Siobhán said.

"Here?" Susan said in a tone that clearly conveyed her horror.

"Your place is so lovely," Alice said gently. "I was just so looking forward to an outdoor wedding."

"Just before sunset," Paul chimed in. They took a moment to drown in each other's eyes. Colm cleared his throat and rolled his eyes.

"The abbey," Siobhán said. "If the weather holds, you can have the reception at the abbey."

"And if it rains, you can have it here," Bridie added. "You can always go out to the back garden for a wee bit of the outdoor experience."

That meant Siobhán was definitely going to have to have it tended to. She sighed. It seemed sometimes that life was nothing but work.

Alice clasped her hands together and looked at Paul. "It sounds wonderful," Paul said.

"Wonderful," Alice repeated. She was smiling, but her voice was cracking like an egg. Siobhán admired her determination to have her day, no matter what. The vows hadn't even been taken, yet they were already taking them to heart—*through good times and in bad*. This was definitely bad. The bride was in need of a little help, and that's what friends were for. Even ones who had just met.

"I'll talk to Father Kearney," Siobhán said.

"I'll call Margaret at the inn," Bridie chimed in. Several minutes later, at least a few of their problems were sorted. Father Kearney would meet with the wedding party later this afternoon to render his decision, and Bridie had gotten through to Margaret. The Kilbane Inn had enough room to accommodate the guests. It wouldn't be as fancy as the castle, but it would do. Unfortunately, Margaret needed a few hours to make the rooms extra tidy. Another delay. The group was getting antsy.

"Let's take a stroll around Kilbane before it starts lashing rain," Alice said. "Siobhán, could you lead a tour?"

"Of course," Siobhán said. "Let me get something sorted first, and then we'll get our legs under us." She hurried into the kitchen. Chef Antoine was hunched over a large pot on the stove. James was directly behind him. They were laughing.

"Everything alright in here?" Siobhán asked.

"It's grand," James said. "We're making an Irish stew."

"Stew!" Antoine said. "I love this stew!" He held up a fat carrot in one hand and an onion in the other like they were trophies he had just won. He began talking to himself. "Guinness, Bailey's Irish Creme, Jameson. Roast beef carving station, but instead of potato soup for a starter, I am going to serve this stew. Sláinte!"

"Cheers," Siobhán said. "With that menu, no doubt all the wedding guests will be drunk."

"An Irishman is never drunk as long as he can hold onto one blade of grass and not fall off the face of the earth," James piped in. She shook her head. He winked. "Except me," he said. "I will be a sober Irishman."

"Good lad," Siobhán said. She turned back to the chef. "Did you hear that the wedding will be moved to Kilbane?"

Antoine's bushy eyebrows furled, and he whacked the carrot down on the counter. "I have to cook from here?" He gazed around the kitchen, no longer looking as charmed with their ways.

"We should have everything you need, and there's an herb garden out back," James said.

"We're going for a stroll," Siobhán said. "Would you like to join us?"

Chef Antoine shook his head. "Mais non. This kitchen is not equipped. I have too much to do."

"I'll help," James said. "If there's anything special you need, we can go to the shops."

The chef looked around again. "Can we go to Paris?"

"You're supposed to take the girls school shopping," Siobhán gently reminded James.

"Chef Antoine can go with us," James said. "Charleville will have everything he needs."

Siobhán thumped Chef Antoine on the back. "Charleville," she repeated. "At least it sounds French, non?"

91

"Named after King Charles the Second," Antoine said. "English. Not French."

"Can't have everything." Siobhán quickly backed out before he could retort. She met with the wedding guests on the footpath. "Are we ready?"

"Why are we going for a walk when it's obvious the rain is going to come lashing down?" Brenna barked as she cast an uneasy glance at the darkening sky.

"The fresh air will do us good," Alice said.

"Maybe it will wash away our sins," Ronan said with a grin. "But I doubt it."

"Plenty of places to duck for cover, if need be," Siobhán said, hoping everyone would ignore Ronan.

Paul held up his hands. "Before we start the tour, I have a request." Everyone stopped to listen. "After supper I'd like us all to meet at O'Rourke's to raise a pint for Kevin." A murmur went through the group. "It's the least we can do."

"It's the least we can do," Brenna repeated. After everyone agreed, they began their stroll.

"Welcome to Sarsfield Street." Siobhán was proud of the town's tidy streets. They passed the chipper, and the hardware store, and Butler's Undertaker, Lounge, and Pub, and the Kilbane Players, and Courtney's Gift Shop. They came to a stop in front of Chris Gorden's new shop, Gorden's Comics. Siobhán had been disappointed. She thought for a moment that he was going to open a proper bookstore; she would have been there all the time. Probably a good thing, as the Yank had a bit of a crush on her. And with his movie-star good looks and the newness of her relationship with Macdara, a girl didn't need any unnecessary distractions. Staring at the fangs and skeletons in the poster before her, she knew she had made the right choice. She wouldn't have imagined the Yank would do well with a comic book store, but the lads and even lasses in town seemed to love it. Vampires, and zombies, and heaven knew what else. Ciarán and Eoin were here every spare moment they could find. Especially now, standing in front of a window filled with blood and gore seemed altogether wrong, so Siobhán hurried them past it.

Soon they were approaching the town square, with King John's Castle rising proudly in the middle, and Saint Mary's Cathedral, with its spiral steeple, off to the left. In the fourteenth century the town square had been a bustling market filled with fruit and veg, and trinkets from far away. Now the gardai station was located in the square, Siobhán counted six guards gathered out front, their blue uniforms flashing.

They want the murderer to know they're watching, Siobhán thought. She held up in front of the castle and waited for the others to gather around. Unlike sprawling Kilbane Castle, King John's Castle was a four-story structure rising sixty feet above the active town square. A double set of wide-arched openings at ground level allowed visitors to freely pass underneath the impressive structure.

"King John's Castle was built in the fifteenth century," Siobhán said. "It's a good example of a peel tower. It was once used as an arsenal in the war with Cromwell, and later as a military hospital." An image of cots filled with bandaged soldiers filled her mind before she continued. "The nineteenth century brought the addition of the large windows," Siobhán said, pointing up. "And in its next incantation it was used as a blacksmith's forge." She could just imagine the horses lined up to get their new shoes, the blacksmith's hammer tapping away, the clack of wagon wheels. From the back of the group, Macdara was trying to suppress a smile. She supposed she sounded rather like a schoolgirl reciting a report. But she truly loved history. From the looks on everyone else's face, she was apparently the only one.

"Fascinating," Susan Cahill deadpanned.

Brenna yawned.

"It's lovely," Alice said.

"Charming," Paul said.

Siobhán got the distinct feeling they were all being polite. Castles were plentiful in Ireland, each with its own story; apparently theirs was old hat. Macdara caught her eye and winked.

As the first drops of rain began to fall, Paul turned to Alice with a gleam in his eye. "I'll race you underneath." The pair took off, their laughter ringing across the square. Some began to wander around, some seeking cover, others nonplussed by the rain. Ronan, she noticed, wasn't taking pictures for once. Instead he was chain-smoking. Brian hunkered underneath the passageway of King John's castle and buried himself in his iPad. Her siblings had been begging for iPads, and Siobhán had been starting to feel guilty for depriving them. But watching Brian attached to it as if it were a part of his body buoyed her confidence that she'd done the right thing by resisting. Siobhán glanced away from Brian, and that's when she saw Brenna hurry to take cover under the overhang of the tailor shop. The curtain was halfway open, and one could see starched shirts hanging from an overhead rack. The sign on the door said ON BREAK. They were free from prying eyes. This was her chance. Siobhán hurried up to Brenna and offered a warm smile. "How are you feeling?" she asked gently.

"I told ye it was going to rain," Brenna said.

"It would hardly be Ireland without the rain," Siobhán said in the cheeriest voice she could muster. "I'm very sorry for your loss," she added.

"My loss?" Brenna's hazel eyes narrowed.

"You were rather close to Kevin, weren't you?"

"What do you mean by that?"

"Why, you spent the last night of his life with him," Siobhán said. "I'd say that must be on your mind." Brenna silently moved her lips, as if working out what to say. Then she grabbed Siobhán's arm and dug her nails in.

"Who have you told?"

"Let go of me," Siobhán said in a harsh whisper. "Or I'll tell everyone." Brenna abruptly released her arm, but she held her index finger uncomfortably close to Siobhán's nose. Given that she was at least four inches shorter than Siobhán, it would have been comical if not for the look of hatred in Brenna's eyes.

"Who told you?" she demanded.

"You did," Siobhán said. "Just now."

Brenna dropped her hand and cried out. "That's a dirty trick!"

"Calm down. I saw the state of your hair this morning. And the look you exchanged with Paul this morning."

Brenna opened her mouth, then clamped it shut. "What do you want? Money?"

"Of course not. I'm not blackmailing you."

"You could have fooled me."

"Were you in your room or his?"

"You want all the dirty details, is that it?"

"No. Just anything that might help us figure out who killed him."

"My room," Brenna said. "We didn't even do the deed. Kevin was passed out by the time I got my knickers off."

95

Lovely. "Where in the castle is your room located?"

"What does that matter?"

"It might not. You never know."

"On the top floor. My window faced the woods."

"What time did he leave the room?"

"I have no idea. I woke up at half seven, and he was gone." Her eyes darted to and fro. She was mighty nervous.

This was getting Siobhán nowhere. She nodded and started to walk away. Brenna grabbed her again, but this time let go right away. "I'm not saying I'm glad he's dead. But Kevin Gallagher was a bleeding thief."

Chapter 10

The little hairs on the back of Siobhán's neck stood up as she digested the information. "A thief?" Was that why the Huntsmans had been speaking of robberies?

Brenna stared into the curtain of rain. "Kevin stole something from my room last night."

Siobhán took a step closer. "What did he steal?" *Had he also stolen Colm's fax?*

Brenna batted her eyes then looked away. "I won't say."

Siobhán nudged closer. "It might be important."

"I'll tell the guards before I'll tell you." For a moment the pair gazed at the gardai station, where the show of force had dwindled to two. They stood smoking and having a laugh.

"Like you told them about spending the night with Kevin?"

"How could I? They haven't questioned me yet."

Siobhán lifted the envelope from her handbag. "So if I were to open your alibi, I'd read the whole story?"

Brenna's eyes went wide with fear. "That's private!"

"There's no such thing as privacy in a murder investigation."

"That's not fair."

"Life's not fair." Siobhán couldn't believe she was having such a petty exchange. What could Kevin have stolen from her room, and why was she being so secretive about it? "Lies of omission are still lies," Siobhán continued. "The guards aren't going to like it one bit."

"Here." Brenna reached up and removed a small red ribbon she had tied in her mess of blond hair. She handed it to Siobhán. Siobhán held it in her fingers and waited for an explanation. Was she trying to buy her silence with a wee ribbon? Siobhán wasn't the type to be bought off, of course, but if she was the type, it would take more than a sliver of a ribbon, for feck's sake.

Brenna looked around, then lowered her voice. "I found it on the floor near my door. Kevin must have lifted it from the nightstand and then dropped it."

Siobhán held it up. It was too short to be a legitimate hair ribbon. "This is what he stole from you?"

"Is it a clue?" Brenna pressed.

"I don't see why a grown man would steal a wee little ribbon, and I don't see why you're making such a fuss out of it." Brenna was definitely leaving a figure out of the equation.

Brenna glared. "Maybe I should give it to the guards instead."

"What else did he take?" Siobhán asked, still holding the ribbon. No use handing it over until she knew whether or not it was a clue.

"Are ye going to tell your garda friend that I spent the night with Kevin?"

"Not now," Siobhán said. *Because she already had.* "But you might want to consider telling him yourself."

Brenna put her hands on her hips. "I didn't actually sleep with him. I just slept in the same bed."

"They're probably going to find his hair in your room."

"So? They're also going to find Macdara's cap at the crime scene."

"And then they're going to find out you lied about it," Siobhán added. It took everything in her not to rise to the bait. Macdara never should have blurted that out.

As if sensing the conversation had just turned to him, Macdara sidled up. "Everything alright?"

Brenna launched herself on Macdara, pressing her body full against him. "You have to help me," she said. "I need to tell you a secret about me and Kevin, and I don't want the guards taking it the wrong way." Siobhán tucked the red ribbon in her pocket and left Macdara to deal with the maid of dishonor.

There was more to the story about this ribbon; Siobhán just knew it. Brenna definitely had an on-again, off-again relationship with the truth. Siobhán hurried over to a nearby bench, took out the red ribbon, and laid it on the seat. Then she snapped a picture with her mobile. There. Now she could give it back if the guards wanted it, which she very much doubted. This was probably Brenna's idea of a red herring. But just in case she was wrong... if not a hair ribbon, then what had been its use? Did Kevin try to steal it? A memento, standing in for another notch on his belt?

Siobhán tucked the ribbon into her handbag. Across the way, Susan Cahill darted toward the passageway underneath the castle. She grabbed Brian along the way and towed him inside. What was that about? Curious, Siobhán crept forward until she was just outside the entrance. The rain had ceased, although if the sky was any indicator, the break wouldn't last very long. Siobhán flattened herself against the outside wall and strained to listen. The echo was grand underneath the structure, the acoustics fit for a band. Children loved to hide under it, stand at opposite corners and whisper to each other. Sure enough, she could make out strained voices.

"But it's already in motion." It was Brian, sounding panicked.

"I don't care. Make the change." Susan Cahill. No mistaking her.

"May I ask why?" His voice squeaked. It was obvious Brian wasn't comfortable talking back to Susan, so whatever they were talking about was worrisome enough to force him to stand up to her.

"Because I said so."

"It's too late."

"It's never too late."

"We will still have to pay."

"I don't care. Just make the change."

"But we're not allowed to leave. How can we possibly meet the shipment?"

"You figure it out."

The conversation abruptly ended. Shipment? Before Siobhán could move from her hiding spot, Brian barreled around the corner and nearly knocked her over. He was so flushed he didn't even acknowledge Siobhán. He reached into his pocket and pulled out his mobile, then hurried across the square. She was dying to follow him and eavesdrop on his conversation, but Alice and Paul were coming toward her. Susan must have exited from the other end of the passageway, for Siobhán hadn't seen her come out. She smiled at Alice and Paul, all the while making a mental note to mention the strange exchange to Macdara.

"How ya," Siobhán said as the couple approached hand in hand.

"We're dying to speak with Father Kearney," Paul said.

"Why?" Siobhán joked. "Do you have something to confess?" Alice flinched. Siobhán regretted her glibness immediately.

"Eager," Alice corrected. "Eager to speak with him."

Paul patted her hand. "Quite eager," he said.

"Of course," Siobhán said. "I was only joking. Let's make our way to the cathedral; he'll be expecting us."

—

Father Kearney stood in front of Saint Mary's Cathedral with his hands folded over his ample belly, waiting patiently as the entire wedding party approached. Siobhán loved the cathedral; gazing upon it always gave her comfort, reminded her she was home. Built in 1879, it boasted ten gorgeous stained-glass windows, three of which were modeled on the windows of the abbey, bright colors intersecting into a five-light arch. As everyone stood waiting for Father Kearney to speak, the church bells tolled twelve times. How did it get to be noon already? The rain began to fall again, and Father Kearney motioned for everyone to follow him inside.

They huddled in the entrance, where flickering candles cast dancing shadows on the stone walls. The lingering scent of incense mingled with the slight smell of damp stone. As they stepped farther inside, Siobhán raised her eyes to the ceiling and resisted the urge to point out the intricate design of leaves and flowers painted onto the original wood beams. The church was renowned for its Victorian-era mosaics, and usually Siobhán delighted in showing them off to visitors, but this time the group had more pressing matters on their minds.

Alice stepped forward and grasped Father Kearney's hands in hers. Then she burst into tears.

"There, there," Father Kearney said, patting her hands. "It's been a trying few days, hasn't it?"

His soothing baritone voice seemed to calm Alice at once. She nodded and wiped away her tears. She took a deep breath. "I never imagined this would happen. Never," she sobbed.

"Of course you didn't, petal," Father Kearney said.

"We still want to marry, Father. Is that wrong?" Alice suddenly sounded like a little girl. Paul squeezed her hand as they awaited the answer.

"Love is never wrong, petal," Father Kearney said.

Alice let out a strangled sob.

"Thank you, Father," Paul said. "That's just what we wanted to hear."

"They were hoping to marry here at Saint Mary's," Siobhán said, while Alice tried to get herself under control. "And, weather permitting, hold the reception at the abbey." Siobhán threw a look to Colm before uttering her next words. "And it won't cost you a thing."

If she wasn't mistaken, Colm Cahill visibly flinched. Her words had definitely hit their mark, and when he recovered, he treated her to a searing look. She'd just reprimanded him in public, and he was furious. His eyes flicked to Father Kearney, then back at her, as if weighing his options. What if he was the murderer? It wasn't very smart to rile him up. She would have to be more careful.

"Won't cost a thing?" Susan Cahill said, as if she was on a five-second time delay. From her tone, it was clear that she did not approve of anything that did not cost a substantial amount of money. "Father Kearney." Susan grabbed Colm's arm and then shoved him in front of the priest. The action bordered on violence, with Susan being the aggressor. Maybe *she* was the true bully of the family.

"Her father and I don't approve," Susan announced when Colm fell back without a word.

"You don't approve of the marriage?" Father Kearney asked, glancing at the young couple. His surprise was obvious.

"Not under such a pall," Susan stammered. "Surely you agree."

"The Good Lord is watching over all of us. In good times and in bad," Father Kearney nodded to the couple. "We can also arrange a Mass for Kevin Gallagher, if you'd like."

"Thank you Father," Paul said. "We'd like that very much."

"Thank you," Alice said. "Everyone has been so kind."

"That's the beauty of a small village, my dear. Folks are always willing to lend a hand." He took Alice's hand, patted it, then let it go. "I believe I can adjust my schedule. You can marry here Saturday at noon, followed by a reception in the abbey. Or at Naomi's Bistro, if the weather remains this foul."

"Thank you, thank you," Alice cried. The rest of the guests began to speak with each other in whispers, and some wandered inside the church to kneel and pray or light a candle for Kevin.

"We're so grateful," Paul said. The church door opened with a squeak, and Detective Sergeant O'Brien entered. He stopped to shake himself off. He was a short and stocky man in his sixties with thinning copper hair. He took off his cap and ran a hand over his head, and then gently stomped his feet. He nodded to Father Kearney. "May I have a word with the group?"

"Certainly," Father Kearney said.

"Is it about our belongings?" Susan Cahill asked before he could speak.

Sergeant O'Brien nodded to Siobhán. "Let's speak outside."

"It's lashing rain," Susan said.

You won't melt, Siobhán's da would have said. She kept it to herself.

"The overhang will keep us dry," Sergeant O'Brien said. He placed his cap back on, opened the door, and herded the group beneath the overhang near the church steps.

The wind howled through the driving rain, forcing O'Brien to raise his normally soft voice. "If she's willing, Ms. O'Sullivan will collect everyone's things from the castle." Siobhán was trying to figure out who Ms. Sullivan was when it dawned on her that he meant her.

"I'd be happy to," she said, hoping she didn't sound too eager. "Not a bother."

"Why Siobhán?" Macdara asked. He didn't seem pleased with the development.

O'Brien flicked him a look. "She arrived at the castle after the victim had been murdered. Her siblings have verified that she was at Naomi's Bistro before she headed off for the castle. So she's the only one of you lot who isn't an official suspect."

"Not a bother," Siobhán said again. "Anything you need."

O'Brien nodded. "You'll be accompanied by the castle security guard."

Val. He was hardly protection. Siobhán nodded anyway. "Yes sir."

"I'll go with her," Macdara said.

Sergeant O'Brien shook his head. "With all due respect, Garda Flannery, you're not in the clear." He literally tipped his cap to Macdara.

"Siobhán can't possibly handle everyone's things on her own." Macdara sounded truly outraged. Was he jealous she got to go to the castle and he didn't? Or was he truly worried for her safety?

"Of course I can handle everything," Siobhán said. He was going to mess this up for her. She tried to send him a look. He refused to meet her eyes. Being the protector, as usual. Infuriating. And sweet.

"There are plenty of guards at the castle. They've been instructed to lend a hand," O'Brien said.

"Is she going to carry them on her scooter?" Macdara persisted. "In the rain?"

Paul stepped forward. "She can use our driver and limo."

"Perfect," Siobhán said. "Problem solved."

"Can we talk?" Macdara reached for her hand.

"After I'm back," Siobhán said, avoiding his touch. "Right now I need to make a list!" She reached in her handbag and pulled out her biro and a notebook.

"A list," Macdara said. He narrowed his eyes.

"Of everything everyone needs from the castle," Siobhán said. *And jot down a few notes about each suspect.*

"Of course." Macdara's voice was dripping with sarcasm. He was being a bad sport. Was it her fault that she'd just been handed the keys to the castle? It wasn't until she was in the limo rummaging through her handbag that Siobhán encountered the envelope of alibis. It was still tucked inside, signed and sealed, but not delivered. She had completely forgotten to hand it over to O'Brien. She stopped short of smacking herself on the forehead.

She told herself the slip of the mind had nothing to do with the fact that she was entertaining the idea of having a peek before turning them in.

Chapter 11

When the limo pulled up to the castle walls, Siobhán had fifteen minutes before she was due to meet Val at the front entrance. Perfect. She knew just what to do with the extra time. The rain had ceased once more, but in the distance, thunder cracked and dark clouds hovered, suggesting another round was imminent. If she hurried, she might be able to make it up to the hill before it came lashing down again. There was just enough time to go to the crime scene and have a look at a tree.

Situated at the top of the hill where Kevin was found was one particular large ash tree. Not only was it good for climbing, but from the first branch you had the most magnificent view of the Irish countryside. She and James used to sneak into the woods when they were younger and climb it. It dawned on Siobhán that the murderer could have climbed the tree and been waiting for the victim. Kevin was tall. He was struck on the back of the head. She still wondered if a short person would have had enough strength, not to mention good enough aim, to kill him from behind with one blow. If not, the suspects would be limited to the tall members of the wedding party. But then it dawned on Siobhán that a short person could have climbed the tree and struck Kevin from above. She wanted to suss out her theory before presenting it to O'Brien.

Guards were situated around the castle grounds, and at the closest entrance to the woods. This time Siobhán would enter from the other direction. If she ran into a guard, she would make up an excuse for why she was sneaking into the crime scene. Perhaps some kind of a message from Macdara. He would be furious with her, but she wanted to check on this right away. She cut through the castle grounds from the back until she came to the alternate entrance. This one was hidden from view from the castle windows, making it a perfect place to hide from prying eyes. If Siobhán had been the killer, this would have been the entrance she'd have used. The path was less worn, and the brambles were thick on either side. The guards should have immediately checked everyone's tracksuit for brambles and thorns. Did the guests have extra tracksuits? Had anyone asked Carol or George for an extra tracksuit? She'd have to ask the Huntsmans.

Soon she neared the top of the hill, where a tent had been erected over the body. Crime-scene tape marked the perimeter around it.

Darn it. The tree was outside of the tent, but just inside the taped area. She gazed up at its branches. It was just as she remembered. Sturdy limbs, with the first being low to the ground. One could have easily climbed it, perched on a branch, and poor Kevin could have been standing at the peak, completely unaware that a person was directly above him, waiting to strike.

But could you climb the tree with a large rock in your hands? She would have to find one similar to the murder weapon and try it herself.

There were three guards standing around the scene, just outside of the tape. They all had booties covering their feet and gloves on their hands. She glanced around and saw a cardboard table set up on the other side of the tent. Atop it were two boxes. Booties and gloves. Still crouched down, she scuttled up to the table and grabbed a pair out of each box. Then she hurried back to her hiding spot, just before the peak of the hill. She quickly donned the protection. Now for a rock.

She should come back when there was nobody here. But that would be too late. She could ask permission. *Do ye mind if I climb the tree and see if I can lob a large rock at the back of one of your heads?*

Maybe this hadn't been such a brilliant idea. Here Sergeant O'Brien had literally given her a free pass to the castle, and she was going to muck it up by climbing a tree within the crime scene tape.

And even if she could climb the tree with a large rock, Siobhán still hadn't figured out how the killer knew that Kevin would be at the top of the hill that morning. Several people seemed to have morning walking routines, but Kevin was not one of them. He definitely seemed more like the type you'd find sleeping in a lassie's bed instead.

Just then a few of the guards started talking about a break. After discussing what type of toastie each wanted, two finally broke off and headed down the hill in the opposite direction. The third guard took out a cigarette and sat in a folding chair just outside the crime-scene tape. This was her chance. She couldn't find another large rock, so she'd just have to imagine she was holding one.

Siobhán was able to reach the first branch of the tree without stepping inside the crime tape. She grabbed the branch with both hands and for a second was suspended above the crime scene, her toes grazing the forbidden ground. She stretched one leg over a nearby branch. How long had it been since she'd climbed a tree? She assumed it was like riding a bike, but as she threw her second leg over the branch, her body hanging like a sagging bridge, she amended the thought. Nothing like riding a bike. She was having a hard enough time climbing it with her handbag hanging off her; no way could she have climbed the tree with a big rock in her hand. But maybe a smaller, nimbler person could have pulled it off. Or maybe they were able to place the rock in a bag and climb up. Still, it wouldn't have been easy, and in Siobhán's mind, this just wasn't the way it went down.

The branch her legs were dangling from bowed slightly, and she heard a crack. The guard's head lifted, but he looked straight ahead instead of behind. Siobhán continued to dangle. She didn't trust that the lower branch would carry her weight, and she would have to jump off and try again in order to position herself on the higher branch.

Siobhán was calculating the quietest way to drop from the tree when one of the guards returned. Siobhán froze as he looked past her. Surely he saw her? He plopped down in the empty chair next to the other guard, and the two of them sat with their backs to her as she dangled. Apparently some time-tested observations were true, such as nobody ever looks up, for the guards kept their heads level or down at all times. She hung on to see if she could catch a bit of their conversation.

"The state pathologist will be here within the hour," the one who just sat down said.

"Thanks be to God. Not that we need her. Not many crime scenes where the murder weapon is left right next to the body."

"Aye. No mystery there. One blow to the back of his skull. Poor fella never saw it coming."

"But why wouldn't the killer move the rock? Toss it downhill even?"

Good question. Her hands scraped against the branches. She really wanted to get down, and it was time to meet Val. But she didn't know how to drop without being heard.

"I doubt the lab will be able to lift prints off a rock that's been sitting in the woods. Anyone had access to it. No point in hiding it."

That was a good point as well, like.

"Still. Mighty bold of them."

The killer is someone bold. Hardly narrowed the field. Except... Brian wasn't bold. Martin wasn't bold. Faye wasn't bold. Of course, they could all be acting the fool.

"Aye. Mighty bold of the victim to be clutching a stolen garda cap."

"Surprised Macdara didn't notice it was gone."

"He's been a bit preoccupied lately with that lassie."

Siobhán's face flushed, and her hands began to sweat. They slipped on the branch she was trying to cling to. She held on tighter.

"I wouldn't mind giving her a go m'self," the shorter one said.

"He'd kill ye," the other replied.

For the love of Jayus, talk about something else.

"Something still doesn't add up. You're having a walk in the woods, see a large rock, and pick it up. And then there just happens to be a man standing with his back to ye, and so you lob it at him?"

No. That didn't make sense at all. The killing was planned. The killer was lying in wait with the rock. The real question was—how did they lure Kevin to the top of the hill?

Siobhán couldn't dangle any longer. She untangled her legs, and before she could prepare for a soft landing, her hands slipped from the branch. She let out a cry and crashed to the ground. The guards leapt out their chairs, toppling them over as they sprung up. Their hands went for their batons. From her prone position, Siobhán thrust her hands up where they could see them. "Just me," she said.

"Siobhán O'Sullivan?" From the one who had spoken so crassly of her.

"Right you are." Siobhán was dying to get up; the ground was slick with rain and mud, yet she didn't want to startle them further.

"What are ye doing?" They inched closer as she stared at the sky through the canopy of branches.

She was definitely going to have a sore head and a wet backside. "The detective sergeant sent me."

The guard's eyebrow shot up. "O'Brien sent you to climb a tree in the middle of the crime scene?"

Siobhán waved her hands and stuck a foot in the air. "I have booties and gloves." The gloves were ripped now, but they didn't need all the trivial details.

"Step out of the crime scene."

"Of course." Siobhán slowly got to her feet and tried to step over the crime-scene tape. It was too giant of a step, and she tripped over the tape, landing on her face. She was quickly hauled up by both guards.

"For feck's sakes."

"Sorry." She pointed at the tree. "I was up there." The guards looked at the tree as if it was another suspect.

"I thought the killer could have been hiding up there with the rock." As they stood staring at her, mouths agape, Siobhán explained Macdara's theory of the killer hiding the rock the day before. "So it could have been premed-itated. And if the killer was hiding up in the tree, it could have been a short person as well, like." The guards looked at each other, then back at Siobhán, then up at the tree. "But now I'm not so sure. It wasn't easy to climb, and I didn't even have a rock in my hands."

"O'Brien sent *you* to fetch the things from the castle?" He looked incredulous.

"Why wouldn't he?" Siobhán snapped.

"You're a bit clumsy," the other one said without a trace of sarcasm.

"What was the exact time of death?" Siobhán asked, ignoring the comment. The answer came in the form of a double stare. "The proprietors will probably be wanting Kevin's key back." More staring.

"Was it in his pocket?" Her eyes flicked to the tent.

"You best be getting to the castle now," the tall one said. "Pack up their things."

"Of course." Siobhán began to remove the booties and gloves.

"And thank you for adding a suspect to our list," the short guard chimed in.

She stopped, her head shot up. "Pardon?"

A slow grin came over his face. "Seems we could be looking for a monkey."

The other guard laughed. "Or an orangutan."

The first guard frowned. "What's the difference?"

"I dunno. Different color fur?"

"Do they have fur or hair?"

"I dunno. Are orangutans orange, like?"

"Why wouldn't they just call them orange-a-tangs?"

Jaysus. No wonder Macdara was so complimentary of her detecting skills. It no longer felt like such a grand compliment. *Seems we could be looking for a monkey.* What cheek! Hers was a good theory, and even if it didn't pan out to be true, at least it got her closer to the truth. And that's what this was all about. Edging closer and closer to the killer. The killer was either bold and tall, or short and acrobatic.

They could laugh all they wanted, but she had just made large strides toward the solution. As they continued to bicker about the difference in primates, Siobhán hurried away. No doubt her shenanigans were going to get back to O'Brien, and by extension Macdara. Her ideas were spot-on, even if her actual maneuvers had been a bit on the awkward side. As she hurried down the hill to the castle, Siobhán found herself thinking what a great detective she would be if only she could slink around sight unseen.

Chapter 12

Val was waiting for Siobhán by the castle door with a key in one hand and a lantern in the other. "Electricity is out," he said, hoisting up the lantern and plunging half of his face into shadow. He looked as if he'd aged ten years since she saw him last. He was taller than she remembered too. She suddenly wished Macdara had accompanied her, after all. Lightning flashed, illuminating the stained-glass window in the turret. Thunder cracked against the dark sky, and soon it was raining buckets down upon the stone castle. "Not a day for the faint of heart," Val said, his voice dropping an octave. Siobhán was forced to edge in uncomfortably close as the wind moaned around them.

A strip of crime-scene tape rattled by, sending a shiver through Siobhán. Val flicked his eyes over her. "We meet again."

Siobhán nodded. "Under much darker circumstances."

Val relaxed slightly. "I've never known anything like it in my life." He watched the rain for a second before turning the key in the lock. The enormous door opened with a massive groan of protest. They quickly stepped into the horseshoe-shaped foyer and wiped their feet on the mat that covered the stone tiles.

"Did the crime scene reveal any clues?" Siobhán asked as they removed their raincoats and hung them on an ancient coatrack.

Val arched his eyebrow. "How would I know?"

"Ah," Siobhán said. "You weren't curious then."

He appeared to wrestle with whether or not to answer as they removed their wellies. "Of course I was curious." Val began to put on a pair of loafers he'd stashed underneath the coatrack. Siobhán had been in such a hurry she'd forgotten to bring an extra pair of shoes.

"Your hearing is off then." She would have to be careful not to slip in her stockings. The tiles beneath her feet felt like ice.

"Beg pardon?"

"Surely if you were curious and your hearing is sharp you would have caught a few snippets of the guards talking."

"I might have heard a word or two," Val said.

"Well, give me a word or two then."

Val lowered his voice and leaned in as if someone might be lurking and listening. "The Huntsmans have been cleared."

"Oh?"

"They had cameras in their room for reasons I won't even try to guess—and one aimed on the reception desk."

This was certainly news. "They had cameras set up in all the rooms?"

"No. Just the reception desk. And their bedroom."

"Oh." She certainly didn't want to go down that road with Val.

"I agree; let's not dwell on it." They stepped into a circular entryway. Spanish tiles made up the floor, and a large chandelier hung above them. Siobhán could have sworn it was swaying. Or perhaps she was hypnotized by the lantern in Val's hand. Rooms spun off to the left and right, while a narrower hallway led straight ahead. The room to the left was closed with a pair of pocket doors. To the right was a parlor room. Val turned toward it.

If memory served, the reception desk was through the parlor doors to the left. So the Huntsmans had a video to prove their alibi. She still wanted to question them. She turned to Val. "Where are the Huntsmans now?"

"Left for Manchester. Said they're terrified to be around a killer."

Terrified to be around a killer, or terrified to be around *the* killer? Was it possible one of them knew who the murderer was, and that's why they'd fled? Otherwise— why flee so soon? Had they abandoned the castle for good? She had an illogical thought that the guards should have cleared this with her first. "Anything else?"

"That's all you're getting," Val said. He reached over and flipped a switch. The lights flickered, then came on. "Now there's a bit of good luck," he said turning off the lantern. He set it down. Even with the lights back on, it was still extremely dim, and there was a weighted stillness to the space, as if the entire castle had been holding its breath. Siobhán could only imagine the century of secrets the stone walls could tell if only they could talk. Val stepped into the parlor room and gazed across the room to yet another pair of pocket doors. Just beyond them lay a double staircase leading to the upper floors. Val lifted his eyes to the balcony on the second floor. "Each room has a garment bag and a box. That should be enough to gather their things."

Siobhán took a moment to study the parlor room. A baby grand anchored the back left corner, and a series of antique flowered sofas adorned the middle. The walls were filled with oil paintings and tapestries of rich landscapes and stoic portraits. It was so like a museum that Siobhán half expected a red velvet rope to surround the perimeter. She had only been to the castle once, when she was a child and it was owned by an Irish couple. It was Christmas Day, and a blanket of snow had canceled the O'Sullivans' plans to visit a relative in Dublin. Then their cooker had broken down on top of that, and their poor mam was beside herself. All the shops were closed. "To the castle!" her father had exclaimed.

Oh, what a magical day. They had a feast of turkey and ham, and potatoes, and rolls slathered with butter. Homemade pie with ice cream for dessert. Afterward, they were allowed to play on the castle grounds. It was the first time Siobhán could remember seeing snow. It looked like a blanket of dust, the kind she purposefully used to let accumulate on her night table just so she could draw in it. But this dust was cold, and her father said you could pile it up and make balls out of it to throw at each other. James was the first to make one, and he threw it squarely at Siobhán's chest. It bounced right off her winter coat. She laughed and made one to throw back, although hers seemed to explode before reaching him. Then James tackled her, and they rolled around in it until their mother threatened them with early bed. Oh, what a day! It was like the heavens had rained magic down on the ground. Her father told her angels made the snow. When they returned to the village, Siobhán joyfully exclaimed to anyone who would listen, "We got angel dust for Christmas!"

Their neighbor and friend Mike Granger had quipped: "Of course you did. That explains a lot."

Every time she thought of it now, she nearly brought herself to tears of laughter. But not this time. This time there was no joy. Siobhán turned her attention back to the room.

A knight in shining armor stood next to the gold and marble fireplace, a floor-to-ceiling bookcase dominated the wall in back of the piano, and another glittering chandelier hovered above the large Persian rug laid out on the stone floor. Siobhán couldn't help but feel sorry for anyone who lived in this castle. She much preferred her cozy, comfortable bistro. Home should be like a soft cushion to fall upon at the end of a hard day.

"We'd better not dally." Val crossed through to the pocket doors. The transom above them held a stained-glass window that appeared to be a family crest. Every new detail of the castle filled Siobhán with wonder. Oh, she could only imagine the fascinating owners the castle had housed over the years, the least of which, in her opinion, were the Huntsmans. She couldn't believe they had just abandoned the castle. There were too many questions they needed to answer. Val was already ascending the right-hand staircase. Siobhán had an urge to take the left and beat him to the top. One person could be going up one staircase while another was coming down the other, and if it was timed just right, they might not even be aware of one another. *Just like Kevin might not have been aware of someone coming up the hill.*

When he reached the top of the stairs, Val flicked on another set of lights. Faded rose-colored wallpaper and sconces lined the hallways. Siobhán hurried up the stairs, not wanting to fall behind. As she did, she tried to imagine Kevin walking down these steps the last morning of his life. What was he thinking about? Who was he going to meet? When they reached the first landing, Siobhán stopped and looked left and right. "Should we start with Kevin's room?"

"The victim?" Val sounded thoroughly shocked. "His room isn't to be touched."

Siobhán thought as much, but she kept trying. "I assumed they'd want his things packed up as well."

"No." Val's eyes flicked to the closed door as if he was half afraid of it.

"I wonder why they won't turn over the hotel key." Siobhán kept her voice light and casual.

"What key?"

"There must have been a room key found in one of Kevin's pockets."

A know-it-all grin broke out on Val's chubby face. "Why, his pockets were completely empty, Ms. Detective."

"He'd been robbed?" Siobhán slipped and didn't disguise the surprise in her voice.

Val clamped his lips shut, then realized he'd been tricked into letting that tidbit slip and glared at her. "And you said there wasn't a robber in the village."

"Do you smoke?"

If the abrupt change in conversation startled Val, he didn't let on. He stood taller. "Never touched me lips."

"Good on ye. Do you know anyone around the castle who smokes Newtons?"

"Funny you should say that. The old guy does."

"Which one?"

"The one that was having a walkabout the morning they found the body."

Martin Donnelly. "How do you know?"

Val sighed. "He said he was down to his last two. Asked if I knew where he could buy a new packet."

"When was this?" If it was the morning of the murder, that could be a definite clue. It meant Martin had been in the woods, not heading for Kilbane as he had said.

"The very first day they arrived," Val said.

So the packet may have been dropped Tuesday and not Wednesday. And as offensive as Siobhán found it to mar the beauty of the woods with trash, the difference between litterer and murderer encompassed more than just a few letters. Still. Just because she couldn't prove what day Martin dropped it didn't mean she couldn't confront him about it. If he had dropped it the morning of the murder, perhaps she'd be able to suss it out from his reaction.

Val was growing impatient. He crossed to the door directly across from Kevin's. "The maid of honor," he announced as he opened the door to Brenna's room.

It was of modest size, with faded rose wallpaper, decorative crown molding, and a four-poster bed. It was stripped of all sheets. A garment bag and suitcase lay on the bed. The nightstand drawers were empty and open. But that's where the tidiness ended. Brenna's clothes were strewn everywhere. Thrown over chairs, heaped on the bed, dangling every which way from hangers in the closet. If she hadn't have already met Brenna, she might have wondered if the room had been ransacked.

Val began taking clothes out of the closet and throwing them into the suitcase.

"Stop," Siobhán said. "I'm supposed to do that."

"Then why aren't ye?" He was trying to hurry her along.

"She's not going to be happy if she finds out your paws have been all over her delicates," Siobhán said.

His pale Irish skin flushed scarlet, and he stepped back to the door. "From what I hear, she might not mind." He mumbled it, but Siobhán caught it clear as day. So he had been keeping his ear to the ground. And it sounded as if the guards knew that Kevin had spent the night in here. At least they were making progress. What had Kevin stolen from Brenna? Looking around, it was hard to imagine he'd want anything from her room. Siobhán slid her hand into every piece of clothing of Brenna's that had a pocket. She found nothing.

"Where are her personal effects?" Siobhán asked when all the clothes had been folded or hung.

"Like what?"

"Makeup, toiletries, letters."

"Letters?"

It had occurred to Siobhán that the red ribbon could have been tied around a letter. Was it a love letter? "Books? Notes? What did she have on the nightstand or in the drawers?" Siobhán pointed to the empty drawers.

"The guards have taken some possessions out of each guest's rooms. They'll get them back when the investigation has concluded."

Shoot. So this was just going to be a regular errand. She wanted to look under the bed and lift the throw rug, but the lad was staring at her. Besides, it appeared as if the guards had been quite thorough.

Val came forward and picked up the luggage bag. "We're to place each suitcase, box, and garment bag outside the door to each guest room. The guards will load them into the limo." Siobhán nodded, but she really had her mind on the mattress. If anyone seemed like the type who would hide things under the mattress, it was Brenna. The minute Val was outside the door with the luggage, Siobhán lifted the mattress and began to feel around underneath. Once more, she found nothing. Then she dropped to the floor and peered under the bed. She had to wait for her eyes to adjust. When they did, she was disappointed. Barely more than a few flecks of dust.

Suddenly she felt a firm grip her arm. Val seized her and hauled her up. She was so startled, and his grip so tight, that for a moment she forgot to breathe.

"Just what do you think you're doing?" He'd gone from harmless to hateful in a matter of seconds, and his previously jovial voice was now laced with a murderous rage. Maybe the suspects weren't just limited to the wedding guests. Maybe someone had better take a second look at the baby-faced security guard.

Chapter 13

The minute Siobhán was upright, and glaring, Val dropped her arm and stepped back. "Why are you looking at me like that?"

"You had no right to manhandle me." She rubbed her arm where he had grabbed her.

He cocked his head and studied her for moment, then looked away. "Let's move on." So much for an apology. Siobhán hugged her handbag to her side. If he touched her like that again, she was going to text Macdara. Was she alone in a deserted castle with a killer? He was already walking ahead; for him the incident was entirely forgotten. It enraged her even more.

He came to a halt in front of a door. "Faye and Martin Donnelly." He opened it and gestured for her to go in first. She didn't like turning her back to him. She felt around for the light switch and flipped it on as fast as possible. As if he wouldn't have the guts to kill her when the lights were on.

Like in Brenna's room, the sheets had been stripped, and the bedside drawers were empty and open. Why had the guards been specifically looking through the drawers? She had a sneaking suspicion they'd been searching for the contents of Kevin's pockets. Find his things, you find his murderer. Siobhán could hardly imagine the killer being dense enough to hide Kevin's belongings in his or her room, but she understood the guards had to at least give it a go. Surely if they had found anything, they would have arrested someone by now.

Compared with Brenna, the Donnellys had a lot less clothing even between two of them, and everything was perfectly hung or folded. It took no time at all to get them into the suitcase and garment bags. But this time, dipping her hand into one of Martin Donnelly's pockets revealed a folded piece of paper. Siobhán's stomach fluttered in anticipation. There was nothing more intoxicating than an unread note. There was no time to examine it or Val would catch on. She shoved it in her handbag, then turned to look at the jacks. The bathroom was completely bare. Not even a toothbrush lay on the counter.

"All the bathrooms have been stripped of belongings?"

Val nodded. "They can buy new toiletries in town."

"But what did the guards want with everyone's tooth-brush?" DNA? She wanted to talk to them so bad.

Val cocked his head and studied her. "You think you're clever, don't you?" His voice was laced with disdain. Perhaps all those years of working for the Huntsmans had soured his view of the residents of Kilbane. The dislike was mutual.

"We all have the capacity to be clever," Siobhán said. "Some of us just choose to use it." They fell into a silent rhythm as they went from room to room. Ronan had the fewest clothes, and what he did own was black. His bathroom door was closed. She went to open it.

"Don't," Val yelled, but it was too late; she'd already flung it open and flipped on the lights.

"I said don't!" Val came up from behind. "I clearly said, 'Don't.'"

Photographs of Alice covered every inch of the bathroom walls. A close-up of her lips. Alice walking across the field. Alice holding a flower. Alice brushing a strand of hair away from her mouth. Alice kneeling down by the garden. Alice laughing. Alice with a wounded look on her face. That was the only photo that included another person. In it the back of a man could be seen in a distance, and Alice was watching him. Colm Cahill, Siobhán was sure of it. Siobhán stepped closer. Alice appeared to be standing near the gardens in the back of the castle, and Ronan had obviously caught her in a painful moment. Colm glared at her in the background, and Alice wore the wounded expression of a child abandoned in a crowd. Had they just gotten in a row?

"Heavens," Siobhán said. This certainly put Ronan in a suspicious light. Had Alice inadvertently hired her stalker? Was it possible that Kevin had discovered Ronan's obsession with Alice? Had he confronted him? Threatened to tell Colm or Paul? Perhaps Kevin had even tried to extort him. After all, Ronan had been given five thousand euros for the smashed camera. Imagine Kevin doing the damage and then having the nerve to ask for the money that was supposed to replace it. That could certainly push a man to murder. Especially a man as intense and odd as the likes of Ronan. But she was just speculating, spinning her wheels. There was no proof Kevin tried to steal Ronan's money after smashing his camera. Macdara was right; Siobhán had to be very careful about jumping to conclusions. Still, the pictures spoke for themselves. Ronan was obsessed with Alice Cahill.

"I told you not to open it." Val's voice was hard and threatening.

Siobhán continued to stare at the pictures. "She doesn't look like she's aware that he's following her every move."

"You can't say anything to her."

"Why not? He's clearly obsessed. She should know."

"The guards are watching him. Do not interfere."

"You mean they're using Alice as bait?" Siobhán cried.

"No one is going to harm a hair on her head," Val said. "We're watching her."

If Ronan was so enamored of Alice, you would have thought he would have wanted to kill Paul. Not that Ronan stood a romantic chance with Alice, but who knew what was going on in his unhinged mind? Jealousy could have driven him to murder. But he didn't go after Paul. Unless…

Everyone looked alike in those tracksuits. She'd heard several people make the same comment. What if Kevin wasn't the intended victim? Both Colm Cahill and Paul Donnelly were the same height as Kevin. Not to mention Macdara. From behind, in the darkness of the woods—smashing someone in the back of the head—

Had the killer struck his intended victim, or was it a case of mistaken identity? If the wrong man had been killed, was the killer waiting to strike again? Was Ronan the murderer? A madman in love with Alice? Could Paul's life be in danger? Or even more terrifying—Macdara's?

"I need to speak with the guards," Siobhán said.

"No. You need to clear the rooms." Val opened the next room. The minute Siobhán saw a suit with a pocket square, she knew they were in Brian's room. His was the neatest by far, with all of his garments organized by color. His room was the quickest to pack, and she didn't find anything of significance. It was hard to get a read on that Brian. It could be said that people who had everything under control were hiding something. What effort it must take to be so perfect all the time. Siobhán always found imperfect things to be the most attractive. Like Macdara's lopsided grin.

She sighed. "Who's next?" She was eager to get this over with and speak with Macdara about everything she'd learned. If Kevin wasn't the intended victim, that changed everything.

"Colm and Susan Cahill." He opened the door and immediately cried out. "My God!"

When she finally edged her way in, Siobhán saw a tornado of clothing on the floor. The drawers weren't just empty, they were completely out of the nightstand and turned upside down. The mattress was overturned. This wasn't the work of the guards. She was so stunned, she barely had time to register another odd site. The room had two separate beds. Had the Cahills requested that? Was their marriage troubled? Or had married life simply drained all the passion out of the pair?

Siobhán grabbed Val's arm this time. "Who had access to the room?"

"No one," Val said. "Just the guards."

And you. "And the Huntsmans." *Except they hightailed it out of town.* Or had they? If anyone could have snuck back into the castle, it was them. There were probably loads of secret passageways.

"You have a key," Siobhán said.

Val looked genuinely offended. "Me?"

"I'm just saying."

"Out. Out. I have to call the detective sergeant." He began backing her out of the room.

"Susan and Colm Cahill will demand their things."

"We're not touching anything. I'm calling the guards." He maneuvered her out into the hall and then shut and locked their door. He removed his mobile from his back pocket and was about to dial when Siobhán stepped in.

"We should check Alice and Paul's room first." He glanced at her, then looked at his phone, undecided. "They'll want to know if anyone else's room has been ransacked. Do you want to tell them we didn't bother to check?"

He shook his head, then looked left and right. "Their rooms are one floor above, and they're at opposite ends of the floor."

"Give me the key to Alice's room while you check Paul's," she said. "Come on. There's no time to waste."

He hesitated, then slipped a key off the ring. "Don't pack or touch anything. Just see if it's been tossed."

She headed toward the stairwell on the left, while Val hurried down the hall to the opposite end. Siobhán jogged up the long stairway. She had only four more steps to go when the lights flickered and then extinguished, plummeting Siobhán into the pitch dark. She grabbed the railing and felt for the stair with her foot. Instead she came into contact with something solid, yet not hard. Like a human leg. She made the connection just as she heard a loud grunt. A figure towered over her in the dark. Hands clamped down on her shoulders, and she screamed. Her handbag was ripped away, and a hand pressed hard against her chest and pushed.

Siobhán's stocking feet slipped on the stair treads, and her body hurtled backward despite her mind screaming for it to stop. She was airborne, free-falling for several terrifying seconds. She landed with a thud on the hard steps, first the back of her skull, then her back, and bottom. She slid down the last several stairs before coming to a stop on the cold stone tiles at the base. She hadn't so much as screamed; all the wind had literally been knocked out of her. For a few seconds, she lay at the bottom of the stairwell as her heart pounded in her chest, terrified to move and find out that she was paralyzed or had broken bones. Tears pooled in her eyes.

Stupid, stupid, stupid lass. Who goes around a castle in stocking feet? Then again, who viciously pushes another human being down a dark stairwell? A killer, that's who.

She took a shallow breath and would have been ashamed if anyone ever found out that, in this moment, every part of her cried out for her mam. All she wanted was to be pulled in by her soft arms and wrapped in a hug. She should have gone clothes shopping with her brood. She didn't need this. Waves of pain rippled through her as she tried to take deep breaths and calm her nerves. Her handbag. She pawed around in the dark even though she knew. The person at the top of the stairs had ripped it from her arms. Her handbag was gone.

Slowly, slowy, slowy, she sat up. Then came to her feet. The lights flickered back on with a hiss and a pop. Someone had deliberately cut the power just as she was coming up the stairs. Anger surged through her, giving her the jolt of bravery she needed to move. Siobhán stared up to the landing to see if she could make out a figure on the floor above. But she saw no one. She gripped the bannister. She should turn around, call the guards, or yell for Val. What if the person who shoved her was just waiting to do it again? Or what if they decided to come down for her, finish what they'd started? Fear buzzed around her like an army of wasps, and she nearly turned and ran. Then fury set in, and before it vanished, she used the anger to surge back up the stairs. They weren't going to get away with this. With each step, her heart hammered louder in her chest. When she reached the top this time, she was stunned to see her handbag sitting on the landing.

She stared at it for a moment as if it might be ticking. She bent closer. No sound. No smell. She nudged it with her toe. Nothing jumped out. She grabbed it, slung it over her shoulder, then made a beeline for Alice's door. Hands shaking, heart still thundering, she unlocked it and stepped in. She wanted nothing more than to flee the castle, but she could hardly leave without the bride's wedding dress. Despite her determination, her heart was still Irish dancing in her chest. She could have been killed. Who had pushed her, and why? If they were after her handbag, why didn't they just take it? Was someone toying with her? Val?

Val said the electricity had gone off due to the storm. But it was no accident that the lights went out when they did. Was there a control switch at the top of this stairwell? She could have asked the Huntsmans if they had bothered to stick around. How could the guards be so incompetent as to let them go?

Siobhán forced her attention back to Alice's room. Unlike her parents' ransacked room, it was all in order, filled with photos of her and Paul, congratulatory cards, and a bouquet of fresh flowers. Siobhán approached the closet and slid it open. There she was greeted by a gorgeous designer wedding gown. It was so silky Siobhán longed to touch it. A slim, long gown with a V neckline trimmed in delicate Irish lace and pearls. Sleeveless and clinging, no doubt to show off Alice's stunning figure. When you looked like Alice Cahill, the dress was the understudy, because she was the star. Hanging next to the dress was an elegant veil trailing to the floor. Siobhán was reminded what this weekend had meant to Alice. Her wedding day. Was it possible to still have the fairy tale?

She was about to slip the wedding dress into the garment bag when a rubbish bin underneath the writing desk caught her eye. It was filled with crumpled pieces of pink stationery. Either the guards hadn't noticed it, or they had looked through it and deemed it wasn't important. Siobhán hesitated. She wasn't supposed to touch anything other than articles of clothing. The receipt from Martin's room had been easy enough to slip into her handbag, but she couldn't hide an entire rubbish bin of paper. It looked as if Alice had been writing someone a letter and having a difficult time with it. They wouldn't miss one or two, would they? Siobhán hurried over and snatched the lucky number three out of the garbage. She heard footsteps coming down the hall and dropped three crumpled balls into her handbag.

"Hello?" The door swung open, and Val stared accusingly at her. "What are you doing?"

"A girl can admire a wedding dress, can't she?" Siobhán barked. Val blushed. What if he had been the one to mess with the lights and push her down the stairs? Siobhán tried to wave him away. "Why don't I pack Alice's room while you pack Paul's?"

"Already done," he said. Would he have had time to pack Paul's room and shove her down the stairs? He didn't appear to be sweating or out of breath.

"Maybe you should wait for the guards by the Cahills' room," Siobhán said. She wasn't going to mention what had happened. She didn't know why exactly, other than the fact that whoever shoved her would be expecting her to tell. She wasn't going to give them the satisfaction.

It would be their little secret. Had she been shoved by the killer or someone else? If she told the guards, they would tell Macdara, and he wouldn't let her out of his sight. She didn't want to stop investigating. She was more determined than ever to find the killer.

"Hurry it up," Val said.

Resisting the urge to kick him in the shin, Siobhán set to placing the dress into the garment bag while Val stood and watched. She would have to look at the crumpled notes later, and she hoped it wouldn't cause any fuss that she'd removed them. Helping with an investigation was one thing; interfering with it was quite another.

Chapter 14

The limo pulled up to the Kilbane Inn with everyone's belongings apart from Susan and Colm's. The guards had been just as surprised as Siobhán and Val at the state of the Cahills' room and ordered it sealed until they could go through it piece by piece. Siobhán hadn't been allowed to remove a single stitch of clothing. Susan Cahill was going to explode when she found out. Siobhán expected it might very well be the last straw, and she wouldn't be surprised if Susan declared all-out war. Her heart ached for Alice and Paul. Maybe they should just elope. Margaret O'Shea, the owner of the Kilbane Inn, was already waving at Siobhán through the window. At least Siobhán had been able to throw a little business her way. A frail woman in her early seventies, Margaret had a handicapped leg and got around with the help of a walker. Siobhán could hear it clacking as Margaret made her way to the footpath. At least there was a break in the rain, and the sun was even peeking out.

Val began unloading the boxes and garment bags.

"I've been meaning to speak with ye," Margaret said as Siobhán picked up Alice's wedding dress.

"No need to thank me," Siobhán said. "Let's start with the bride's room." Margaret clacked over to the door to Alice's room and waited for Siobhán to catch up.

"Thank ye? Thank ye? I'm furious with ye." Margaret slammed down her walker.

"What on earth is the matter?"

"You've brought a killer to me inn!"

"Now, Margaret."

"Don't 'Now, Margaret' me. It's one of them that's done it, isn't it?" Her lips curled.

Siobhán sighed. She didn't want to lie. "It looks so."

"I'm not going to get a wink of sleep. I've got me knitting needles under me pillow."

"I'll sleep here myself if that will make you feel better. You can take my room above the bistro." Siobhán felt free to make the offer; Margaret would never leave the inn, just as she would never admit she was thrilled to have the business. She'd have let a room to Jack the Ripper as long as he paid up front.

"'Tis a shame, a woman my age watching over her shoulder."

"I'll ask Macdara to have a guard keep watch."

Margaret's eyes narrowed into tiny slits. "Why haven't you cracked the case yet?"

"Me?" Siobhán said. "I'm not a guard."

"Drop the act, O'Sullivan. We all know you figured out that other mess."

"That's not going to happen this time."

"Bringing danger right to me door, you are."

Siobhán stopped. "Would you rather I send them off to Charleville?"

Margaret waved her hand in dismissal and opened the door. It was a plain room with a small bed. The walls were the color of cream, and except for a wooden cross hanging on the far wall and a mirror above the dresser, there wasn't a stitch of decorations. Maybe Siobhán would whittle a pair of doves for Alice. Siobhán had learned to whittle from her grandfather, who thought the activity would help calm down the young hothead. He was right. She'd taken to the hobby straightaway and was quite good at it. She'd stopped whittling after her parents' death but picked it up again a few months ago. She liked to sit by the fire with a cappuccino and whittle away. The room could definitely use some cheering up.

"I've sprinkled every room with holy water," Margaret said, "seeing as how Father Kearney ignored me request to come and bless the rooms. Still. Perhaps they could do with a few more crosses?"

"I'd say you're all good now," Siobhán said with a forced smile. Margaret watched as Siobhán hung up the wedding dress and placed Alice's box of belongings next to the bed. She made a mental note to bring her some fresh flowers.

"If there's a murder at my inn, I'll be closed down for sure," Margaret said, shaking her head.

"There will not be a murder at your inn."

"How can you be so sure?"

"Everyone is watching now." Siobhán crossed herself. "Besides, it's highly unlikely that we're dealing with a serial killer."

"Serial killer?" Margaret screeched.

"I said highly unlikely."

"How reassuring."

"And the body was found in the woods."

"So?" Margaret shuddered. "That's why I abhor nature!" Margaret spent most of her time at the desk watching soap operas on an old black-and-white telly.

"It suggests the killer wanted their victim in a remote spot. Your inn is far from remote."

"Oh, Jaysus, Mary, and Joseph. I'll never forgive ye." Margaret crossed herself, then removed a small vial from her pocket and sprinkled herself with what Siobhán could only assume was holy water. Heavens. You'd think she'd brought werewolves and vampires to her door.

Siobhán sighed. "Should I ask them to leave?" she suggested once again.

Margaret made a tsk-tsk sound. "That would blacken me name."

"Tell you what. Keep your eyes and ears open, and if you see or hear anything suspicious, I'll have me mobile on twenty-four-seven."

Margaret looked around, then lowered her voice to a whisper. "If I had to guess, I'd say it's the tall man with the loud voice."

"Colm Cahill?"

"That's the one. Yelling at his poor wife and daughter. The bride ran from the room in tears. And they'd only just settled in for a lie-down."

"Where is everyone now?"

"Where does everyone go? Out to the pubs." She made another tsk-tsk sound. "I don't like that young man with the camera either."

"Ronan." The images of the photos he took of Alice swam through her mind. "Apparently he's an up-and-coming artist," Siobhán said.

"Well, I wish he was an out-and-going artist. He's been taking pictures of me. No doubt to have a laugh at my expense." Margaret slammed her walker down.

"Now, Margaret. Perhaps he views you as a worthy subject."

"I'll give him a picture." Margaret made a fist and shook it.

"Where is his room related to the bride's?" He shouldn't be staying here at all. What were the guards thinking?

Margaret cocked her head to the side and looked at Siobhán out of one eye. "That's a peculiar question. Why?"

"I think the bride is tired of having her picture taken too."

Margaret snorted. "She gets her picture taken for a living."

"Exactly," Siobhán said. "Who wants to feel like they're at work all day?"

Margaret's brow furled in confusion.

Siobhán had to get her hands on that camera. If Ronan wasn't the murderer, there was a high likelihood that he had photographed everyone who went into the woods that morning around the same time as Kevin. That would go a long way to helping them nail down the killer. Then again, Siobhán knew she had zero chance of getting the temperamental artist to part with his work. After reassuring Margaret another dozen times that nobody would be murdered at her inn, Siobhán finally slipped away.

All Siobhán wanted to do was fall into her chair near the fireplace, prop her feet up, and have a cup of tea. She was still smarting from the shove down the stairs. Alas, when she opened the door to the bistro and saw that the wedding guests were not in the pub, as Margaret had suggested, but rather lounging in Naomi's as if it was their own living room, Siobhán knew she was never going to get that chance. The place was jammers, and not only with the wedding guests; townsfolk had swarmed the place as well. Technically, they were supposed to be closed down to cater to the wedding guests, but James must have sensed an opportunity to make a little off the lookie-loos. Her brood was running about serving tea and sandwiches, evoking Siobhán's never-dormant guilt reflex. They needed a break too, although from the looks on their faces, they were all too happy to have the colorful and wealthy guests back in the bistro. Siobhán was relieved that Susan and Colm Cahill did not seem to be in the crowd; she wasn't quite prepared to tell them that she hadn't been able to bring back their things.

Alice and Paul were draped in chairs near the fireplace, and Eoin, Ciarán, Ann, and Gráinne were hanging onto them as though the gorgeous couple had volunteered to be life rafts and they were adrift at sea. Siobhán headed for her cappuccino maker as she kept one ear to her brood, curious to see what they were chatting about.

Ciarán was holding up a giant book. "Here it is," he said, thrusting it at Alice. "My *Big Book of Poisons.*" Her eyes widened.

Siobhán dropped her espresso cup with a clatter and was on him in no time. "Your what?"

"From Gorden's," Ciarán said with an ear-to-ear grin. "It lists every poison in the world."

"Why do you need a big book of poisons?" Martin asked. He was hovering near the fireplace with a cup of tea. "Seems a wee one would do the trick." He winked. Ciarán frowned.

Poor Alice was holding the book like it was a dead rodent. Siobhán quickly took it out of her hands. Jaysus, it was heavy. It had a black leather cover with a boiling cauldron on the front.

Siobhán felt like a failure. She had no clue Ciarán had a big book of poison. What else were they keeping from her? Siobhán turned just as James was coming in from the back dining room, his arms filled with plates. She hoisted up the book.

"Gorden's," James said, flashing a grin.

Siobhán sighed. She was always the last to know.

"I'd love to see it," Brenna said, sauntering over from her perch near the window.

"Oh." Ciarán's nose twitched. He only wanted Alice to have it.

Brenna grabbed it out of Siobhán's hands. "T'anks."

"Did you know there are poisonous plants all over Ireland?" Ciarán said, kneeling in front of Alice.

"Well then, petal, it's a good thing I don't have a green thumb." She patted him on the head and laughed, and Ciarán laughed, although Siobhán knew for a fact that he didn't understand the joke.

"I loved everything gory when I was a lad too," Paul said, catching the concern on Siobhán's face. "It's either that or he'll be playing with toy guns and swords."

"But looking at a thing like that at a time like this?" Siobhán turned to see who had just spoken. Nancy Flannery was planted directly behind her, lips pursed in disapproval. Her tone was reprimanding as well, and it was clear that Siobhán was the target.

Brenna chewed on her bottom lip, nodded, and handed the book back to Ciarán.

Siobhán swept up the book. "Why don't we put this away for now?"

"For now?" Nancy Flannery said. "I'd throw it in the trash."

Nancy's comment made Siobhán want to keep the book even more. "Nothing wrong with learning what to avoid in the world," Siobhán said, stopping short of what she really wanted to say: *People can be just as poisonous as plants.*

Ciarán swallowed. "I didn't mean to frighten ye," he said to Alice. "It's just a book."

Alice took Ciarán's hand. "You didn't frighten me, luv."

"You should be studying your school subjects, young man," Nancy said. "Not filling your mind with such nonsense."

"School doesn't start until Monday," Ciarán said. "And it makes complete sense to me!"

"You should be getting a head start," Nancy said. "Mathematics would do you good."

Siobhán wanted to smack her. Then again, she was the old-fashioned sort, and probably lonely. Not to mention she was Macdara's mother. It would do Siobhán good to be patient and understanding.

"Poor lad, running around an orphan," Nancy started to say. The words were like a slap in the face.

"Mrs. Flannery!" Siobhán said. "He's not running around, as you can see; he's perfectly still. More to the point—he's certainly not an orphan."

"What's an orphan?" Ciarán asked, wide-eyed.

"Why don't you put this book back in your room, and we'll talk about it later," Siobhán said.

"His vocabulary could use some work too," Nancy said.

"As could your manners," Siobhán snapped.

Nancy gasped. Siobhán had done it now. And the woman deserved it. But she would never forget the comment and probably never forgive it.

"It's all about plants," Ciarán said, gazing down at the book. "Just regular old plants."

"It was either that or *Zombies of the Peat Bogs*," James said swooping into the group. "I thought this would bore him. Give him less nightmares."

"We need to look for these plants. Dig them all up so no one gets poisoned." Ciarán turned to Nancy Flannery to see if that would satisfy her. Her pinched face looked as if she'd already been chewing on poisons.

Ciarán thrust the book at Siobhán. "I don't want it."

Siobhán took the book and kissed Ciarán on the top of the head. "It's alright, luv."

"Come on," James said. "Let's take the ball out and play."

"Good idea," Siobhán said. She glanced at Gráinne and Ann, who were sitting next to the fireplace just staring at Alice.

"You two go out and play too."

"Play?" Gráinne said rolling her eyes.

"Get some fresh air," Siobhán said. That reminded her. "How did clothes shopping go?"

"What do you care?" Ann said.

"I care very much. I want to see everything you bought."

Ann rolled her eyes, and Gráinne punched Ann's arm. "We'll show ye later."

"Thank you," Siobhán said. It was odd to have Gráinne coming to her defense for once. She was going to have to make a point to spend some alone time with Ann.

"Do you need anything for the wedding?" Gráinne asked Alice. Siobhán frowned. She tried for the life of her to remember the last time Gráinne had asked if she needed anything. She was pretty sure the answer was *never*.

"Aren't you a dear."

"Something borrowed, something blue?" Gráinne's eyes sparkled.

Alice clasped her hands together. "That would be grand, luv. Surprise me."

Gráinne shot to her feet.

"I'm coming too," Ann said, scrambling up.

"I need money." Gráinne held her hand out to Siobhán.

"You don't need money if it's borrowed," Siobhán said. Maybe all of their vocabulary needed a little work.

"Oh," Gráinne said. "Right."

"But you can get your allowance from the register and a little extra. You've earned it." Gráinne and Ann flounced off for the register.

"Sure you can handle this crowd on your own?" James asked.

"No easier than handling you lot," she joked back.

"I'll stay," Eoin said.

"Will ye now?" Paul teased. He could tell that Eoin was in love with Alice. Everyone was in love with Alice. At first, Siobhán had been jealous. Now she couldn't imagine being her. Never getting a bit of peace. At least Ronan wasn't anywhere around, for once.

"Is there anything I can get ye?" Siobhán asked the happy couple.

"We're thrilled just to hide out here," Paul said. "If that's alright?"

"Of course."

"We're going to head to the abbey in an hour," Alice said. "I can't wait to see it."

"Perfect," Siobhán said. "Make yourselves at home. You deserve a rest."

"Did you fetch our things?" Alice looked so hopeful.

"Your things are in your rooms back at the inn," Siobhán said. "There's a bit of news, but I'll fill you in later." She had no intention of breaking any more bad news. Not until she had had a bit of a rest herself.

"Lovely," Alice said. "Thank you very much."

"Not a bother." Siobhán left the couple to themselves—and Eoin—and finished clearing off tables. The bistro was now closing, and Siobhán gently herded the remaining townsfolk out the door and turned over the CLOSED sign. Then she tucked the book of poisons behind the register. She wished Chris Gorden had opened a different kind of shop. Something a little more cheerful. Would her mam and dad have squashed the poison book straightaway, or would they have thought it was a normal part of being a lad? She went into the kitchen. Chef Antoine was standing at the cooker with Brian. They appeared to be in a heated argument.

"And now this," Chef Antoine was saying. "Too many changes!"

"Just do it," Brian said. He whirled around and brushed right past Siobhán and went out the swinging doors. Siobhán just looked at Antoine.

He sighed, took his hat off, and wiped his brow.

Siobhán offered a sympathetic smile. "What changes did Brian ask you to make?"

Chef Antoine raised a bushy eyebrow. "Just wedding details." He shook his head as if perplexed by the whole business.

Siobhán wanted to push for more details, but she could tell Chef Antoine would stubbornly refuse to answer. Besides, she still needed to have a look at the items in her bag that she'd taken from Martin and Alice's room, as well as the envelope of alibis. She liked Chef Antoine. She just couldn't see him as the killer. Not that killers couldn't be likable. But he was so obsessed with being a chef that she just didn't picture him being distracted by anything else. Now, if Kevin had threatened his livelihood somehow—maybe. But that certainly hadn't been the case. Siobhán threw one more thing at him before heading out the door. "Would ye at least help me weed out the herb garden when we get a free moment?" She smiled and blinked her eyes.

"That I will do," he said, sounding genuinely thrilled. "We can hang herbs from the ceiling, no?"

Tears came to Siobhán's eyes. "My mam used to do that."

"Well, then," Chef Antoine said with a smile, "we must do it too."

Chapter 15

Siobhán hurried down the street to the field in front of the abbey, crossed over the timber bridge atop the Kilbane River, and stopped to gaze into the water. It was swollen from the recent lashing, and the grass was slick and shiny. She felt a moment's peace, and who knew how long that would last? She dug into her handbag, diving past the crumpled balls of paper from Alice's rubbish bin, and felt the slip of paper from Martin's blazer. Where were the alibis? She checked once, twice, three times. Why did she carry such a big bag? But it wasn't that big. The envelope with the alibis was gone.

So that was why she had been shoved down the stairs, and why they hadn't bothered taking her handbag. They wanted the alibis. Why hadn't she checked right away? She had been in shock, and in such a hurry. And then she'd completely forgotten, just assumed it was still there. Had the killer done this or someone else? The person could have killed her if he or she had wanted to. Siobhán hated to admit it, even to herself, but she had been extremely vulnerable. It would have been easy to follow her down the stairs and finish her off. But the person simply took the envelope out of her handbag and disappeared. What would they find in the alibis? Maybe nothing. Maybe a lie that would end up catching a killer? She'd had her chance to suss them out, and she'd completely blown it.

What was she going to tell Macdara and O'Brien now? She'd be forced to come clean or lie. But it wouldn't be a little white lie this time. Not the kind of lie she could justify. From now on, she would examine any piece of evidence right away. Starting now, starting with Martin's receipt. It was from Mike's Market. Martin had purchased a newspaper, a breakfast biscuit, and juice. It was from the morning of Kevin's murder. This was proof that Martin was in town checking out the walls, like he said he was. Why hadn't he produced the receipt as an alibi? Perhaps he'd forgotten he had it? But it was the back of the receipt that interested Siobhán. In scratchy handwriting it read:

> *Limerick Pub. Half nine. Friday morning.*
> <u>*Don't be late.*</u>

Don't be late was heavily underlined. If the appointment had anything to do with the wedding, Brian would know. She thought back to his secret conversation with Susan under the passageway, and just recently with Antoine. *Shipment. Permission.* Was the receipt related? Siobhán would have to question Brian as soon as she could.

Next she dug out the three crumpled pieces of paper from Alice's rubbish bin. She opened the first one.

> *Dear Paul,*
>   *I'm so sorry*

> *Dear Father,*
>   *How could you?*

> *Dear Paul,*
>   *Please forgive me. I cannot*

Siobhán's heart squeezed. So much for having the perfect life. *How could you?* What exactly had Colm done? *Forgive me.* Siobhán felt a pinch of shame for reading Alice's private words. There was little difference between these notes and a diary. Maybe she was just writing down her fears and they didn't mean anything.

Or maybe she had done something that needed forgiving.

This was the part she hated. Accusing everyone. Siobhán imagined that the rest of the crumpled letters in the bin were along the same lines. Letters Alice couldn't finish and most likely never intended to send.

Even so. There had to be something to them. Were her father's attempts to stop the wedding starting to work? Had Alice been writing a breakup letter to Paul? Was she having second thoughts about marrying Paul?

Siobhán shoved the notes back into her handbag and headed down the dirt path leading to the entrance of the monastery. The remains of the building and grounds were always a striking vision, the bell tower a welcome sight. The sun was starting to set, sending shards of sunlight beaming through the gaps in what remained of the monastery walls. Every time Siobhán was here, she could picture the monks going about their day, cooking, tending the grounds, brewing beer. If only she could go back in time. Then again, as a woman she would never have gained access to the comings and goings.

The monastery was made up of two stories. The ground floor held the church, the refectory, the kitchen, and the Tomb of the White Knight. The upper floor made up the monk's dormitories, and a final set of stairs led to the bell tower. Although just the bones of the structure remained, there were still carved heads hidden in walls, gorgeous arches, recessed niches, and of course the remains of the five-light window, said to be the most gorgeous in Ireland. She entered a hallway leading to the sections of the ground floor and could hear angry voices rising from the centre. Uh-oh, sounded like there was a row afoot.

She wound her way through until she reached the centre, which housed the Tomb of the White Knight. The friary was founded in 1291 by an ancestor of the White Knights, and the tomb was dedicated: *To Edmund FitzJohn Fitzgibbon, the second to last of the White Knights*. The slab of his tomb was broken in two, and dripping water had carved a small hollow in the gap. The imperfection of the tomb was said to be a sign of God's displeasure at Edmund's treatment of Catholics—he had been loyal to Queen Elizabeth I, daughter of Henry VIII. And of course it was Henry VIII who had ordered the dissolution of all monasteries in 1541. Ah, trouble and turbulent times, as then as it was now.

Susan and Colm Cahill were standing at opposite ends of the space, each with their arms crossed. Paul was sitting in a folding chair near the tomb where Alice was pacing back and forth. "It's my wedding. Not yours. Mine." She whirled on her mother.

"You're paying for it, are you?" Susan said.

"No," Alice said. "But neither are you. Daddy is."

"How dare you? It's *our* money."

"That's enough," Colm said. "Bickering in this run-down eyesore like a couple of commoners."

Run-down eyesore? Siobhán felt her temper flare. She suddenly wished they were all gone, the lot of 'em. She wanted to go back to life in the bistro and get started researching online universities. She should walk away from them right now. Walk away from the wedding, and the drama. And the killer.

Alice's eyes flew to Siobhán, and she cried out. "Don't listen to him. This is a very special place. We're thrilled to have our wedding here." Tears came into her eyes, and she was so tense Siobhán could almost see her vibrating. She threw her arms up. "I'm so happy," she bawled. Paul looked as if he wanted to go and comfort her, then sank his head into his hands instead.

Siobhán glanced around. She was afraid if she didn't choose her next words carefully, she'd send Alice plummeting off a cliff. "I'm glad you like it."

Brian ran in, his sharp appearance for once somewhat askew. His tie was loosened, and his hair not as slick. "Some bird is dive-bombing the reception table."

"I hardly think that's reason to bother us," Susan said. No sooner had the words come out of her mouth when a blur of black came whizzing down from the sky, headed directly for her head. She screamed and dropped to the ground as it did a flyby. Alice and Paul hurried to help Susan up. Colm watched from afar.

"It must have a nest of baby birds somewhere," Siobhán said.

Colm began to pace, shaking his fist at the sky. "Find it and get rid of it!"

Siobhán clenched her jaw. Now, on top of everything else, she was expected to be some sort of bird wrangler. How entitled this man felt. Everyone was beneath him; everyone was put on earth to do *his* bidding.

"You don't mean," Brian said, "kill the baby birds?" He whispered the last bit.

"Of course not," Siobhán said.

"Poison them," Colm said.

"No!" Brian and Siobhán yelled simultaneously.

The bird swooped again, this time straight through the middle of the crowd, treating them to a warning cry. They parted and ducked.

"Let's move out of the crypt for now," Siobhán said. "Until we can get someone to find the nest and gently move it to a safer location."

Everyone began to look up, scanning for a nest. "There are so many little crevices," Brian said. "Hello, haystack. Got a needle?"

"Deal with it," Alice said. "Just deal with it."

Brian looked as if she had slapped him across the face. "Yes. Certainly," he said, and then hurried away as the rest of the group moved out of the crypt and into the larger open space, where hopefully they would be safe from momma bird. The ever-changing Irish sky was now the color of a dusty pearl, the emerald grass was slick from the recent lashing, and the nearby river was having a chat with fishes and birds, answering their plops and caws with murmurs and gurgles. It would have been a lovely close to the matinee of the day if not for the company she was keeping.

Susan popped up in front of Siobhán, her face stretched like a violin string. "Are our things in our room?"

Siobhán couldn't stall any longer. She took a step back. "I have some bad news."

"Don't tell us they found another body!" Colm shouted, sending his voice bouncing across the field.

"No, no. Of course not."

"Did you get my ring?" Alice held out her hand and wiggled her fingers as if she expected Siobhán to place said ring on her finger.

"Your ring?" Siobhán felt the first vestiges of worry crawling up the back of her neck. *What ring?*

"My diamond ring. In mam and da's room." Alice fixed her eyes on Siobhán, who stared back. Alice stepped closer. "Right on the dresser." Alice turned to her mother. "Isn't that where you kept it?"

"Of course it is," Susan said. "Surely you have the ring." She fixed Siobhán with a laser stare.

"I'm sorry." Siobhán's palms grew slick, and her heart thudded with guilt as if she had been the one to raid the Cahills' room. She suddenly understood why innocent people confessed to crimes. "I wasn't able to pack up Susan and Colm's room."

"What?" Susan said. "You mean you didn't bring our things?"

"This is outrageous," Colm said. "Who's your superior?"

Alice held up her hands. "Mam and Dad, would you let Siobhán speak?" Alice nodded as Siobhán. "Go on."

"Someone ransacked your mam and da's room."

"What?" Susan shrieked.

"Everything was turned upside down. We had to tell the guards."

"Of course you did," Alice said. "Why didn't you tell me earlier?"

Siobhán lowered her head. She should have told her earlier. "I'm sorry. I wasn't looking forward to sharing more bad news."

"I see," Alice said. "I understand." But her tone said otherwise. She definitely wouldn't appreciate Siobhán going through her rubbish and reading her personal correspondences.

"After we discovered the room had been turned inside out, the guards wouldn't let us touch anything. So I don't know what was there and what wasn't."

"If someone broke into our room, of course they stole the ring," Colm said.

"How could you let this happen?" Susan said.

"Me?" Siobhán said. "I wasn't even at the castle when it happened."

"That security guard," Colm said. "He must be questioned and then fired."

Alice lifted her head to the muted sky. "I'm cursed. My wedding is cursed." A bird cawed in the distance.

"Don't say that, darling," Paul said, taking Alice by the hand. "We don't need the ring to get married."

"I need to talk to your mother," Alice cried, pulling away from her groom-to-be. "I need to turn my luck around."

The distinctive warning cry from the bird rang out, and it swooped again, sending everyone running farther out into the field. They stopped when they reached the river. The banks were starting to swell, as if mirroring the anger of the group. "See?" Alice shrieked. "Cursed!" She turned on her father. "Are you happy now? Is this what you wanted?"

"You think I stole the ring? Perhaps bribed the bird to wreck havoc?" Colm said.

"I wouldn't put it past you," Alice said.

"My own mother's ring?" Colm threw Paul a pointed look. Paul visibly winced.

"There you go again," Alice said. "Putting down the man I love. In front of everyone. In front of me."

Paul must have noticed confusion stamped on Siobhán's face for he turned to her with an explanation. "I

153

wanted to buy Alice an engagement ring. But she wanted her grandmother's ring."

"Because it's so beautiful, and reminds me of her," Alice said caressing her engagement finger.

"Because she knew Paul couldn't afford one," Colm said.

"Daddy," Alice said, "when did you get to be this person?"

"Why don't you just come out and say it?" Paul said. "I'm not good enough for your daughter."

"You're not good enough for our daughter," Colm said.

"Daddy, please," Alice begged.

Out of the corner of her eye, Siobhán caught sight of Macdara strolling across the field. Angry voices disrupted the private smile she shared with him. She had actually tuned Colm and Paul out for a second, but they were still hollering at each other. Paul set his jaw and curled his fists. Alice flung herself at her groom-to-be as if her touch could diffuse his anger. Macdara immediately assessed the tension and physically stepped between the posturing men. When they each took a step back, he turned to Siobhán. "What's the story?"

Siobhán swallowed and turned to face the Cahills. "Susan and Colm's room has been ransacked."

Alice cried out. "Someone stole my diamond ring."

"There's a bird dive-bombing the abbey," Brian cried. Apparently, everyone was ready to unburden themselves.

"This godforsaken village!" Colm said, clenching his fist and raising it to the sky.

Siobhán couldn't have felt worse. "We don't know for sure if the ring has been stolen."

"Of course they were after the ring," Susan said. "What else?"

"I'll call the guards at once," Macdara said. "See what I can find out." He stared at Siobhán. "Anything else?"

Ronan is obsessed with Alice. Alice may have second thoughts about marrying Paul. Martin is sneaking out to meet someone in Limerick at half nine in the morning on Friday. The killer could have climbed a tree, but probably didn't. Somebody shoved me down a flight of stairs and stole the alibis. Ciarán is an orphan obsessed with poison, and I hate your mam. "No," Siobhán said. "Nothing else."

He studied her for another second before stepping a few feet away to place the call. She was such a terrible liar! And he was such a good detector.

"Brenna was right about the robberies," Alice said. Her hands flew over her mouth. "We never should have come here. This is all my fault." She grabbed Paul. "We should postpone the wedding."

"Finally," Colm said. "Finally my only daughter is showing a bit of sense." He shook his fist again, this time triumphantly, as if he had just won a boxing match.

"We're not postponing the wedding," Paul said. He turned and took Alice's hands. "The more the universe conspires to stop me from marrying you, the more determined I am."

"You don't think we're cursed?"

"No. We're blessed. And I'll fight anyone and anything that tries to come between us." His voice rang with passion and pain. Had Kevin tried to come between them? Colm certainly had. And if Siobhán's theory was correct and Kevin hadn't been the intended victim...

Heavens. What if Paul had done it thinking he was taking out Colm Cahill, the man who stood between him and the woman he loved? Macdara would be furious with her for even thinking it. But if she said nothing, and it was true, it meant that Alice was marrying a murderer. Siobhán couldn't drop him as a suspect just because he was well loved.

"Blessed me arse," Colm said. "There's nothing but doom and death around this marriage."

"Shut it, Daddy," Alice snapped.

The group was coming unglued before her, and without pints of the black stuff, Siobhán didn't have the first clue how to put them back together. She stepped gingerly toward Alice. "Who knew you were keeping the ring in your parents' room?"

Alice thought about it. "Me. Ma. And Dad." She pointed at her parents as she called them out.

Siobhán glanced at Colm and Susan. They glared at her in response. "Did you happen to mention it to anyone? Or talk about it openly?"

"I didn't know a thing about the bloody ring," Colm said. "Except that Paul didn't have to pay for it."

"That's quite enough," Alice said.

"Don't bother," Paul said. "He'll never change his mind about me. And I don't care. Do you hear me, old man? I don't care."

Colm stuck his chest out. "Just who are you calling old man?"

"You," Paul said. "I'm calling you old man."

"If Alice marries you, she's cut out of the will."

"Daddy," Alice said. "Not this again."

"I mean it. You think I don't mean it?" Colm's voice shook with rage.

"Just do it then. Stop holding it over my head." Alice turned her back on her father.

Siobhán couldn't believe how much drama was erupting because of a stolen ring. She approached Susan. "Did you mention the ring to anyone? Anyone at all?"

"Of course not. Although." Susan put her index finger up to her pursed lips. "Never mind."

"What?" Alice said. "You must say it."

Susan sighed. "I asked the Huntsmans if there was a safe in the room."

"Thank God," Alice said.

"There wasn't," Susan said.

Alice visually crumpled. "It's cursed! My wedding is cursed!"

"Darling, please stop saying that," Paul said. His left eye began to twitch.

"Was anyone else around when you asked them?" Siobhán pressed.

Susan blinked rapidly. "Come to think of it, the French chef was there."

"Are you sure?"

"I said so, didn't I? I was surprised to see him standing behind the reception desk. I didn't realize he was allowed to leave the kitchen."

Antoine. Had he stolen the ring? He'd also been the one to discover the body. Was there some kind of connection? But she liked Antoine. He was in her bistro, cooking up a storm. In her bistro, around her brood. Was she a fool for trusting him?

Another thought hit Siobhán. She turned to Alice. "If it's an engagement ring, why weren't you wearing it?"

Tears came into Alice's eyes. "I was. Until Mrs. Huntsman warned me about the robberies. She gently suggested that only a nutter would wear the ring around Kilbane."

"That's when she gave it to me for safekeeping," Susan said.

A silence fell on the group. Siobhán ached for her little village. There weren't any robbers in Kilbane. But the possibility was getting harder and harder to ignore. What if there were? What if there were a robber loose in Kilbane—one who had quickly graduated to murderer?

Chapter 16

After the wedding guests departed for pubs, and the inn, and a bite to eat, Siobhán found Brian back in the abbey, in the Tomb of the White Knight, wrestling with a large ladder. He had it leaned up against one of the walls, and he was sweating profusely. His normally kempt appearance was melting, and even the peak made by his hair was starting to droop. He caught Siobhán's eyes. "I'm afraid of heights." *Afraid of heights.* The sweat dappled on his brow supported his statement. He was short, and therefore if he was the killer he had climbed the tree. If one was afraid of heights, it seemed highly unlikely they would climb to the peak of a hill and then climb a tree.

"Did you even find the nest?" Siobhán asked. Brian pointed, and she followed his gaze all the way to the top of the wall. Tucked into the stone she could see bits of straw poking out and hear the faint chirps of baby birds.

"Oh, dear," Siobhán said. "The ladder will never reach that high anyway."

"Thank God," Brian said. "We'll have the reception at your bistro then, so?"

Siobhán continued to study the wall. Truthfully, she knew a few rascals about town who could probably climb up to the bell tower and then crawl along the top of the wall until they reached the nest. She just wasn't sure she trusted any of those same lads to handle the nest carefully.

Not to mention the fact that momma bird could swoop in and peck an eye out at any moment. She hated to disappoint Alice but was starting to think the bride-to-be might have a point about the wedding being cursed. Surely she didn't want the reception so badly she was willing to kill a nest full of baby birds. "I'll give the volunteer fire department a bell," Siobhán said. "It's not a kitten up a tree, but it has to come in a close second."

"I'm sure they'd do it for Alice," Brian said.

Did Siobhán detect a whiff of jealousy? Where beauty goes, envy follows. The blessing and the curse. "It is hard to resist a bride in distress."

"Let's get out of here before that beast dive-bombs me again," Brian said, racewalking toward the field.

Siobhán hurried to keep up. "I need a word with ye."

"As long as we can walk at the same time."

They gravitated to the medieval wall and began to walk along it as twilight tripped across the sky.

"Did you get Susan's shipment all sorted?" Siobhán asked casually, as if she'd been privy to the conversation from the beginning.

Brian blinked rapidly. "She told you?"

"She thinks of me as the help," Siobhán said. That part was true.

"She thinks of everyone as the help."

"It's sorted then?"

"You tell me. You're the one with the in with the guards."

Permission to go to Limerick. So it was connected with the note on Martin's receipt. But how? "I'm sure it will get sorted," Siobhán said. "I just don't see why it has to stop in Limerick."

"It's ridiculous, if you ask me. The original cases are still being shipped to the castle."

"I wondered," Siobhán said. Cases of what?

"The Huntsmans will probably be thrilled."

"Wouldn't you be?" Siobhán asked.

"I don't have a taste for it personally," Brian said.

"The Huntsmans have gone to Manchester," Siobhán said, still fishing in a mystery pond.

"What?" Brian came to a screeching halt, and Siobhán nearly ran into him. She was still sore from the tumble down the stairs and thankfully managed to avoid a collision. She'd have bruises up and down her body by the morning. So much for the sleeveless dress she wanted to wear to the wedding.

"They were cleared of the murder and then ran off to Manchester," Siobhán said, letting her disdain show.

"Cleared how?"

Siobhán flushed, thinking of the camera in their room. "I'm afraid that's official police business."

"They left? They just left?"

Siobhán nodded. "Abandoned the castle."

"I knew it couldn't be them." Brian seemed to get lost in something in the distance. "But it doesn't seem fair that they just get to leave."

"How did you know it couldn't be them?"

"Bad for business killing off your guests."

"True."

"Is that security lad still there?"

"Yes."

"He'll probably get all the bottles to himself."

Bottles. Shipment. Martin owned a transportation company. What bottles would be delivered for a wedding? The mystery pond was starting to clear up. "Why don't we just have double the champagne at the wedding?" Siobhán said with a laugh. "At least they won't have to drink mead."

"Mi na meala," Brian said with a smile. *The month of honey.*

Siobhán nodded and smiled. Another Irish tradition. The newlyweds would celebrate by drinking mead, which was made from meala, or fermented honey. Served in unique goblets, the brew would be shared by the couple for one full moon after their wedding. Thus the term honeymoon. It was believed that this potent brew would bring auspicious beginnings to the couple, as well as aid in fertility. And that it probably did; it was hardly a surprise that hearty drinking was responsible for many conceptions. Siobhán loved knowing the colorful histories behind words and phrases. The Irish language was full of surprises and phrases that were widely used to this day. It was sad that so many didn't even know the origins of sayings they passed off. She appreciated that Brian was in the know.

However, now Brian was giving her a look that suggested she should go straight to an alcohol rehabilitation facility. She'd nailed it. Martin Donnelly had convinced Susan Cahill to use his lorry to transport a new shipment of champagne. But why? Especially since they couldn't stop the old supply from arriving. What was so important about the new champagne supplier?

"The cases that were sent to the castle are from France, correct?" Siobhán asked.

"Of course."

"What about the new shipment?"

"I had nothing to do with that."

"I just wondered if you knew why she had to change suppliers?"

"It's just an excuse to use his transport company." His tone suggested that he was silently calling her an eejit for asking.

"That makes sense," Siobhán said.

"I can't imagine what he said or did to convince her," Brian said. "Imagine the gall? If we didn't already have a shipment of champagne, that would be one thing. But to force her to buy from another supplier just to hire his trucks? Outlandish."

Siobhán was thinking the exact same thing. And why on earth were they meeting the lorry in Limerick instead of having it drive the extra distance to Kilbane? She made a mental note to speak with Macdara. She would try to speak with him privately after this evening's impromptu wake at O'Rourke's.

Siobhán started to walk away from Brian when she remembered something she'd been dying to ask him. "The tracksuits from the castle?" she asked.

"What about them?"

"Did every room have just one set for each guest?"

He wrinkled his brow. "I only had one. Thank God they didn't force me to wear it."

"I wondered if the castle had extras. Any idea where the Huntsmans might have kept them?"

"Oh," Brian said, as if he finally understood where she was going with her questions. "The tracksuits were only for the wedding guests."

"Excuse me?" Siobhán felt those little pricks up and down her spine.

"They were a special gift."

"I don't understand."

163

Brian rolled his eyes as if Siobhán were the biggest eejit on the planet. "They were a gift from the Huntmans to wish Alice and Paul a happy wedding."

"I see," Siobhán said. She couldn't believe this. Why hadn't she followed up on this earlier? The Huntmans wanted the wedding guests to have identical tracksuits. Did that mean anything?

"Why are you asking so many questions about the tracksuits?"

"I'm just following up on everything I can," Siobhán said. She didn't want Brian to start snooping around or gossiping about her theories.

"Ridiculous gift, if you ask me," Brian said. "Although I do have to give them credit for including all of us, and getting all of our sizes correct to boot. Now, that's class."

"Yes," Siobhán said, feeling slightly nauseous. "It certainly suggests a deadly attention to detail."

Chapter 17

Although Siobhán did not normally look forward to wakes, she was hoping that this evening's rendezvous would be a good opportunity to study the suspects. Nothing like the combination of grief and Guinness to get a few heads talking. And of course, it wasn't a real wake; there would be no body—thank heavens—and it wasn't to take place in Kevin's home with his family watching over him, but the spirit of the event was aligned just the same. To say a few kind words and prayers for Kevin Gallagher. He was owed that much. He also deserved justice. Siobhán knew the tidbit about the tracksuits could be a breakthrough. If only she could suss out the anonymous donor. She was definitely going to have to find a contact number for the Huntsmans.

Walking into O'Rourke's felt like walking into a second home. In the window, Declan had his Laurel and Hardy memorabilia displayed proudly. Inside, John Wayne posters adorned the walls, along with obscure European opera posters. Declan could wax poetic on anything from the latest hurling match or who placed what in the horse race, and when you were least expecting it, he might quote a line or two from *Don Quixote*. The pub was normally packed with locals, but Declan had a sign on the door: RESERVED FOR WAKE. The pub would be theirs alone for an hour before the regulars filtered back in to drink pints, swap stories, and listen to traditional Irish music.

Declan O'Rourke was behind the bar, wiping down the counter and treating the wedding guests to the smile he reserved for tourists, which was not nearly as broad as his usual, yet not as phony as the grin he reserved for Americans. He was a large man, both tall and wide, with an infectious, gap-toothed grin. He was equally feared and loved by the lads in town. He was never afraid to toss anyone out on his ear for being too cheeky, but was equally likely to give ossified lads a ride home when needed. In short, Declan O'Rourke was an institution. When all the wedding guests were seated at the bar, he began lining up the pints of the black stuff, along with shot glasses for the Jameson, including a pint and a shot for himself. It was a nice change to see the guests in their own clothing, and most of them were appropriately wearing black. It occurred to her that Ronan, who only wore black, was always ready to mourn. He was pacing the bar with his camera on the ready. Declan hoisted his pint into the air.

"Who would like to say a few nice words about yer man—Kevin, is it?" He glanced at Siobhán.

She nodded. "Kevin Gallagher." She lifted her pint.

"To Kevin," Paul said.

"Let's get this over with," Colm said. "He was your best man—you have a word." Colm nodded to Paul.

Paul cleared his throat and shifted. "I've known Kevin Gallagher all me life. He was always up for a good time. In fact, that was his favorite saying: 'Not here for a long time; just here for a good time.'" Paul laughed, then turned a bit stricken as he realized how fortuitous it had been. "He liked to get a rise out of other lads. Any lad would do.

Got a rise out of you, didn't he, Dara? Swiping off your garda cap." Paul chuckled. Macdara nodded and smiled, but Siobhán could tell it was forced. No doubt he was thinking of where the cap ended up. Siobhán couldn't help but think it was rude of Paul to bring it up again. But now was not the time to air such grievances. "Kevin loved betting on the horses. Betting on anything, really. He was always scheming about how to get rich. And he could never turn down a pretty girl. He was a bit of a dark horse alright. But he didn't deserve to be done like that. God bless him. Rest in peace, my friend. Rest in peace." Paul choked up, then hoisted his pint. Everyone followed suit, and there was a moment of silence as they drank.

"He was very sweet to me," Alice said next.

"You mean sweet *on* you," Brenna said.

"Who wouldn't be?" Ronan said. He was the only one standing, leaning against the counter with his camera stuck to his chest, gawking at Alice. She visibly reddened. Siobhán felt her anger flare. It wasn't right that the guards hadn't hauled in the stalker and warned Alice of his secret trove of photos.

"Who else would like to say something?" Declan asked, hoping to move this along. "How about you?" He nodded to Susan.

She looked startled, but Declan could get his way with that stare of his. She lifted her glass. "He was a lover of women," Susan Cahill said. "Did I mention he accosted me on the stairs?"

A joint "Yes" rose from the group. Susan sighed and adjusted Colm's blazer underneath her bottom. She'd refused to sit directly on the stool. Colm and Susan had sent their driver into Charleville to buy them a few new outfits. Susan was in a black dress, surprisingly fitting for a wake. The blazer she was sitting on was from Colm's suit. Siobhán thought Susan would be thrilled to be wearing decent clothing again, but this was the most nervous Siobhán had ever seen her. She was barely able to sit still.

Unless.

The blazer was positioned so that she was sitting on the breast pocket. Maybe she was wiggling around like that because there was something in the pocket. Siobhán had to be careful because now she was staring at the woman's arse. If there was something in the pocket, it had to be just a wee thing. Why, nothing more than a large pebble would fit in—

Or a ring...

Was Alice's diamond ring in that pocket? Colm had said the ring belonged to his mother. She could see him taking it just to stir up trouble, throw out another roadblock to wedded bliss.

"Mrs. Cahill, would you please stand up?" Siobhán heard herself say.

"What are ye doing?" Macdara whispered in her ear.

Susan dismissed her with a flash of her hand. "I've nothing more to say about the lad."

"I think something has been spilled on your stool."

Susan shrieked and flew off it faster than a fool could lose his fortune. Colm shot out of his stool and reached for the blazer.

"Look," Siobhán shouted and pointed to the front door. Everyone turned. Siobhán lunged for the blazer and had her hand deep in the pocket before Colm had turned back.

"What in the devil are are you doing?" His bark was almost as bad as Declan's. But she wasn't going to be stopped, not when Alice possibly thought of her as a thief. Sure enough, she could feel something that felt like a ring.

"This!" she pulled it out. It was a ring alright, but not a woman's. Instead, Siobhán found herself holding up a man's claddagh wedding band embedded with emeralds. Siobhán's eyes flew to Colm's hand. His ring finger was barren. Siobhán's mind flashed back to the double beds in the Cahills' room. Another sure sign that there was trouble in paradise.

Colm towered over Siobhán. "How dare you?"

"Calm down," Macdara said, cutting in front of Colm. "I'm sure there's a reasonable explanation." He threw Siobhán a look. *There'd better be.*

Brenna hoisted her pint. "It's not enough that you stole Alice's ring. Now you're going for Mr. Cahill's right under his nose, like!"

Siobhán spoke up. "I noticed Mrs. Cahill couldn't get comfortable, and I thought she might be sitting on something in the pocket is all."

Susan's face had gone quite pale, and instead of biting at Siobhán, she was glancing at the exit as if she wanted to flee.

"Hand it over," Colm said. "I should have you arrested."

"Daddy," Alice said. "Why aren't you wearing your wedding ring? You always wear your ring." Tears pooled in her eyes.

Siobhán waited for him to make the excuses she often heard married men use: I was doing such and such manly activity and I didn't want to lose it, it was starting to make me finger sore, I've lost a few stone and I'm afraid of it falling off. Instead, he didn't offer a word. He simply picked up his pint and started to drink.

"Let's not get into a row," Susan said. Interesting. She didn't seem to mind in the least that he wasn't wearing his wedding ring. Nor did she seem surprised.

Brenna got in Siobhán's face. Her hair was pulled back in a loose bun, and her cleavage was spilling over her tight black dress. But unlike the first morning Siobhán met her, Brenna's face was heavily made up, and her eyes were bright and flashing. Siobhán could smell the beer on her. "Where's Alice's ring?"

"Siobhán didn't steal my ring," Alice interrupted. "I couldn't say the same about you." Although Siobhán felt bad that Brenna was being thrown under the bus, she was relieved to hear that Alice didn't think she was a thief.

"Me?" Brenna said. "You think I stole your bloody ring?"

"We're here to remember Kevin," Paul said. Behind them a camera snapped away. Siobhán glared at Ronan. Instead of looking appropriately shamed, Ronan slid up behind Alice and whispered something in her ear. Alice's face drained of color, and she turned on Brenna, screaming above the din.

"You took a thousand euros from my father?"

Ronan cocked his head, stared at Alice, and then began to photograph the meltdown.

Brenna dropped her jaw. No words spilled forth.

"What's this?" Paul stepped forward.

"This is a wake for Kevin Gallagher. What else can we say about the lad?" Colm said, desperately looking around for help.

"Paid her a thousand euros for what?" Paul said.

"To seduce you," Alice said. "On Wednesday evening. Brenna was supposed to seduce you, Ronan was supposed

170

to take a photo of it, and I was supposed to call off the wedding."

All heads turned to Colm, especially Declan, who was leaning on the counter as if he was watching a riveting football match. Colm slid his empty pint to Declan and downed his whiskey. Declan began to refill the pint without taking his eyes off the drama.

"So that's why you were so over the top," Paul said to Brenna. "I thought it was the drink."

Alice whirled on her father. "How could you?"

How could you? The same thing Alice said in her note. That she was reacting like this was a surprise, so the note must have referred to something else. No doubt Colm Cahill had been working behind the scenes, doing whatever he could to stop this wedding. Earlier, when he'd threatened to cut her out of his will, Alice had responded as if she'd heard him threaten that before. Could that be what *How could you?* had meant in her crumpled note?

"She's lying," Colm finally said. "I didn't pay her a pound."

Brenna pointed at Colm. "You gave me a thousand euros tied up in red ribbon!"

"Yep," Ronan said. "Same as."

Red ribbon.

Alice threw up her arms. "That's Daddy's calling card whenever he wants to bribe someone. A stack of money tied up with red ribbon."

That's what Kevin took from her room. Brenna hadn't been upset over the ribbon—she had been stewing over the stolen money. Kevin had slept with her, then upon waking, he had stolen a thousand euros from her. Was that motive for murder? Could make a woman go mental, alright. Especially one who is tipped to the mental side already. But if Brenna had killed Kevin, why give Siobhán the red ribbon? There would be no need for her to try and find her money if she had killed him to get it back.

"How could you?" Alice cried out again. "You're supposed to be my maid of honor. I thought we were friends."

"You only asked me to be your maid of honor when Sheila Fehey turned you down," Brenna said.

"She didn't turn me down; she broke her ankle."

"I wasn't your first choice."

"You weren't my second or third either. But it was too short notice to ask a real friend. I would have been better without one at all." The curtain of wealth and class was starting to drop. Alice and Brenna now sounded a bit like Maria and Aisling, squabbling over a lad or where to go on a Saturday evening. Siobhán felt an ache, missing her girlfriends, even when they were at their worst.

"I'm sorry," Brenna said. "Don't be mad. I knew Paul wasn't going to fall for my seduction. It was easy money. That's all."

"That's all?" Alice sputtered. "That's all?"

Brenna cried out in frustration. "You're rich. A thousand euros is nothing to you. It's certainly nothing to your father. But it's a lot of money to me, alright? And I don't even have it anymore."

Bingo.

"What does any of this have to do with Kevin's murder?" Paul said. He turned to Colm. "Did you pay Kevin too?"

"He paid him to knock over my camera," Ronan said, startling all of them by speaking. Once again Siobhán was reminded how easy it was to forget Ronan was there at all.

The perfect cover for a murderer trying to hide in plain sight.

Alice put her hands on her head. "Is Kevin's murder all my fault?"

"Of course not," Paul said. "Why would you say that?"

"Daddy stirred all of this up to stop the wedding. Kevin would still be alive if you and I had never met."

"You can't start going down that path," Paul said. "It's not our fault."

"I'm only looking out for you," Colm said. "You're out of his league."

Paul pointed to Colm. "Kevin said the exact same thing to me on Wednesday evening. The exact words—out of her league. You *did* pay Kevin to rattle me."

"What does any of this matter now?" Colm said. "It still hasn't worked."

"And it's never going to," Alice said. "Why don't you get that?"

Paul took Alice's hand. "Nobody could ever, ever love this woman as much as I do."

Colm's eyes flashed. "Are you sure it's Alice you love, or my money?"

Alice gasped. Paul shook his head.

"There's not a single man better than my son," Faye said. She downed a shot of whiskey, stood up, and pointed to Colm. "You had best watch your tongue."

Siobhán glanced at Declan, thinking he was going to toss them all out on their ears any minute now. Instead, he was grinning and hanging on every word.

"Now, now," Martin said. "We all just need to calm down." He flicked a nervous glance at Susan. She refused to look back at him. As the guests all started shouting over one another, Siobhán tried to piece together what she had learned.

Wednesday night Colm had paid anyone he could to try and break up the wedding. Brenna to seduce Paul. Kevin to try and discourage Paul. Ronan to take incriminating photos...

Kevin had woken up in Brenna's room, spied the euros on the table, and taken them. Quite risky. He had to know Brenna would figure out he was the thief. Presumably he'd already been paid by Colm as well. Kevin got drunk the night before. His room was directly across from Brenna's. Did he wake up and think they were in his room? Did he mistake the money for his own?

Money aside, why had he gone up to the hill? He certainly didn't have a morning walking routine. And if Brenna was still trying to get her money back, that meant she didn't have it. She just wasn't a good enough actress to pull this off. That meant—someone had the money. Follow the money and you find the murderer?

Unless Kevin was killed by one person and robbed by another. Siobhán sighed and downed her whiskey.

Apparently Ronan had snapped enough photos of the wedding guests shouting accusations at each other, for he soon slipped away and headed to the back of the pub. Siobhán followed him. He ducked out onto the patio, and Siobhán became his shadow.

The outdoor area was decorated with the usual debris of old coffee cans filled with cigarette butts, a rickety picnic table and benches, and an old Guinness sign. Ronan went straight to the corner and hunched over his phone, texting away with one hand while removing a cigarette from his shirt pocket and lighting it with the other. It was as if she had finally earned her cloak of invisibility. It was satisfying to be the one sneaking up on him for a change.

That lasted as long as the thought, for just then his head shot up, and his eyes blazed as he stared at her. She wondered if he was on drugs. He exhaled, and cigarette smoke hovered between them, heavy and stale. Siobhán coughed.

"You shouldn't sneak up on people like that." He had a smoker's rasp. His black hair seemed extra spikey, his nose ring extra shiny.

"You're one to talk." She glanced at his camera. "I went into your bathroom in your room at the castle."

His eyes grew wide, and he swallowed. "So?"

"The guards saw your wall of pictures."

"So?" Defiance lit his eyes.

Siobhán didn't know what to expect, but this surly attitude was not it. He didn't appear to feel guilty in the least. "You must have a portable printer." It was the only thing she could think to say. After all, how did he print all those pictures?

He held his arms out. "Guilty. Cuff me." He stared at her. "Rough me up." He winked, and then his mouth seemed to curl in on itself.

"The pictures don't seem very wedding-like."

He spread his arms open like he was about to take flight. "I was hired to snap away all weekend."

"I'd like to see all the photos you took before Kevin was killed."

"As you said yourself, they're on the wall."

"Those are only of Alice. Every single one of them. One might say you are a little obsessed with her."

A smile crept over Ronan's face. "An artist should be obsessed with his subjects. That's what makes it art." He took a step closer. "I'd like to take a whole lot more of you."

Siobhán crossed her arms, hating the way he was sizing her up. "You must have digital copies of all the photos you've taken."

A scowl came over his face. "Not from the first few days, thanks to Kevin knocking the camera out of me hands."

"You were pretty angry about that, weren't you?" He still was. His face was easy to read.

"Not angry enough to kill him." He held steady eye contact. It was unnerving.

"What about the camera card?"

Ronan glanced toward the door. His bangs fell into his face, and he blew on them. "Someone took it."

"Who?"

Ronan scowled. "If I knew that, I'd have it back by now."

"When?"

"Must have been when the camera fell. I was busy trying to pick up pieces of the lens. But now we've just learned that the whole thing had been a ruse. So why are you questioning me instead of trying to figure out who took the camera card?"

"A ruse?"

"Colm just admitted he paid Kevin."

"He paid Kevin to plant seeds of doubt in Paul's mind."

"Don't be an eejit. He paid Kevin to knock into me so he could steal the camera card."

"Why on earth would Colm Cahill want your camera card?"

Ronan just stared at her.

"Come on. If what you say is true… There must be something incriminating in one of the photos you took."

"Must be."

He was infuriatingly calm. "Have you looked for the card?" Siobhán pressed.

Ronan stepped up yet again, closing the gap between them. "Why would I do that?"

Siobhán was taken aback. There was something exciting about him, although she loathed to admit it. She knew plenty of young women who fell for his type. The bad boy. The rebel. She would much rather have a true man like Macdara, but now, with him standing so close, his eyes trying to penetrate her, trying to rattle her by getting as close as possible, his swagger and confidence— well, she had to admit, even with his beanpole figure she could see how other lasses might lose their heads near this one. "Why wouldn't you look for it?" She stammered.

"Because if we're right, then Kevin was killed over that card. Do you think I want him coming after me next?" Ronan stepped back, crushed out the nub of his cigarette in a coffee can, then lifted a new pack out of his camera bag. Newtons. He stared at her as he lit one.

"Or her," Siobhán said, eyeing the pack. Val told her the old man smoked Newtons. They weren't a ubiquitous brand. Had Val lied to her on purpose? Or were his powers of observation inept? There was no way of proving when the pack had been dropped, but Ronan just moved up a notch on her suspect list. Maybe the simplest solution was that he killed Kevin to get his camera card back. Then again, Ronan had just put his cigarette out in a nearby coffee can instead of tossing it to the ground like most of the lads did. Perhaps it was just because Siobhán was here.

"What?" Ronan tilted his head back and exhaled. Smoke curled up into the night sky.

"Or *her*," Ronan repeated as if it had just registered what Siobhán meant. "The killer could be a woman." He winked at her. "Was that a confession?"

"Excuse me?"

"You said the killer could be a woman." His eyes raked over her body. "You're definitely a woman." He held out the pack of cigarettes, offering her one. She shook her head.

Siobhán tried to steer the questions back to the case. "If the killer was after the camera card, wouldn't he or she have come after you already?"

Ronan shrugged and tapped his cigarette, scattering ashes onto the patio. "Too many eyes. They could be waiting for the right moment. Or maybe they've figured out by now that I don't have digital copies."

"I don't believe you."

"You don't believe what?" Ronan cocked his head and studied her, genuinely curious.

"I think you do have copies."

Ronan shrugged. "Suit yourself."

"If you let me see those photos, I swear I won't breathe a word to anyone, and I'll help keep an eye on you."

"Everything alright here?" Macdara strode onto the patio. Ronan dumped his cigarette into one of the old coffee cans once more and slipped past Siobhán without another word. Macdara's eyes followed Ronan until he was completely gone before turning back to Siobhán.

"Did you know?" Siobhán asked.

Macdara eyed her. "Know what?"

"What the guards found in the jacks of Ronan's room?" Macdara sighed and looked away. He did know.

He knew all about the wall of pictures. "You were supposed to tell me everything."

"Not everything. Just anything I can."

"I thought you were officially a suspect."

Macdara grinned. "What can I say? Is it a good t'ing or a bad if your colleagues can't see you as a killer?"

"Alice deserves to know that she has a stalker."

"We made some calls to Dublin. Talked to several galleries. When Ronan is fascinated with a subject, this is what he does. He explores them through photography. He has no criminal record."

"That's of very little comfort."

"There's more."

"Go on."

"Ronan is not just taking photographs for the wedding. He was also hired by the *Irish Enquirer*. The more photos he produces of Alice, the more he gets paid."

"Disgusting. I'm surprised the Cahills didn't anticipate that and make him sign a contract."

Macdara raised an eyebrow. "Maybe Alice thought it wasn't necessary, given his celebrity status. Either way. It makes him greedy, but not a dangerous stalker."

Siobhán sighed. "Every lead is turning out to be a dead end."

"Well then, maybe this will interest you." Macdara grinned.

"Don't draw it out."

"Chef Antoine and Brian have been approved to do wedding errands. A delivery is coming into Limerick tomorrow—"

"The Limerick Pub? Half nine? Cases of champagne?" Siobhán couldn't help but jump in.

Macdara's mouth dropped open. "Jaysus," he said. "Now who's holding out on whom?"

They began to talk over each other. "Can we go? Can we spy—"

"The guards have approved a little spy operation—"

Macdara stopped. "Dammit, Siobhán. You aren't letting me surprise you."

"Sorry. Go ahead."

Macdara sighed. "If we know everything, then why are we going?"

"We don't know why the lorry is stopping in Limerick instead of coming into Kilbane."

"Why did Susan switch to Martin's transport company?"

"Exactly. She's not exactly the type to throw favors anyone's way."

"Martin might have something on her."

"Something incriminating."

"So you're still up for it?"

"Are ye joking me?" Siobhán grinned.

Macdara approached Siobhán and placed a hand on her waist. He was wearing that cologne that drove her insane. "Can we listen to some music and have a proper date the rest of the night?"

"Of course." Siobhán felt a shiver of attraction run through her as he gently kissed her on the lips. She had best keep her head about her and remember that they were at a wake. They headed for the door. Macdara stopped just before crossing back inside.

"O'Brien wants the packet of alibis."

"Oh," Siobhán said. "Of course." Her stomach twisted.

His eyes bore into hers. "Tell me you didn't open them."

Siobhán did her best to keep her face neutral. "I swear I didn't open them."

Macdara sighed with relief. "I'm sorry. I didn't mean to accuse you."

"It's okay. I was tempted."

"Do you have them in your handbag?"

"Not at the moment."

Macdara looked around. "Probably a good thing. You wouldn't want anyone to lift it."

"I definitely wouldn't." *Wouldn't want anyone shoving me down a flight of stairs either.*

"Make sure you get them to O'Brien first thing in the morning."

"First thing." She hated lying and wasn't even sure why she was doing it. Other than the fact that nothing ruined date night more than confessing to losing a packet of alibis.

Chapter 18

Upon her return from the wake, Siobhán entered Naomi's Bistro and sank with relief into the chair near the fireplace. James had been tending to the fire, and it was crackling away. What an exhausting couple of days. She'd missed being around her family. To her surprise, they were all awake and waiting for her.

The back windows were open, and the sound of crickets filtered in, along with the faint hoot of an owl. Ann brought her a cup of tea, and Ciarán sat on the floor next to her and put his head in her lap. Her breath caught as she ran her hands through his hair. He needed a trim. Her mam would have never let it get this long. Tears came to her eyes. Often she was ambushed with a combination of grief and fierce love at the same time. Her thoughts were starting to change from missing her mam and da (which of course she did) to feeling bad about what *they* were missing. Ciarán seemed to have grown an inch overnight. James was sober and staying that way, Eoin was possibly turning into a ladies' man, and Ann and Gráinne were blooming like spring flowers. Well, they would have still had their hands full there.

Eoin's lanky body was draped over the counter, his head buried in a comic book, Gráinne and Ann were splayed out at a table, and James stood with his arms crossed, staring at Siobhán.

"Well?" Gráinne said when there had been a few minutes of silence.

"I swear I don't know anything new," Siobhán said. "I'm letting the guards handle it."

Ciarán lifted his head. "We should make the list," he said. He scrambled to his feet.

"No list," Siobhán said. "I don't want to think about it anymore this evening."

"Tell us everything you've learned about Alice." Ann placed her hands underneath her chin and leaned forward eagerly.

"Like what?" Siobhán said, feeling a twinge of jealousy.

"What is her dress like?" Gráinne added.

"And what is she like?" Ann repeated.

"She's a little stressed out," Siobhán said. "But she's lovely, really. And so is the dress."

"Who's the designer?" Gráinne asked. She was becoming more and more label conscious. On one hand, Siobhán didn't like it; on the other hand, maybe she would become a famous fashion designer.

"It's a gorgeous dress, with lace and satin and pearls— slim line—and it looks very dear," Siobhán said. "That's all I know."

Gráinne rolled her eyes. "Useless."

"Can we go to the wedding?" Ann said. "I would die to go to the wedding."

"As I said, it's all a bit stressful right now, luv," Siobhán said.

"Who wouldn't be stressed out?" Gráinne said. "The wedding is supposed to be all about the bride. All anyone is talking about is the murder. I can't believe they're going through with it."

"They have to go through with it," Ann said. "So love can win."

Love would only win if the murderer was brought to justice. Every second counted. "How are you getting on with Chef Antoine?" Siobhán couldn't help but ask. So much for not talking about it. It seemed there was no avoiding it.

"He didn't do it," James said.

"Ah," Siobhán said. "You like him."

James shook his head. "Not necessarily. But the man doesn't think about anything other than his culinary talents. Unless Kevin had stolen one of his precious recipes or chef knives, I don't think he'd have time to be bothered by such business."

"He won't let me touch them," Ciarán said. "They're sharp."

"Good advice," Siobhán said.

"Doesn't seem to stop him from leaving them all over the place," James said. He held up his hand before Siobhán could react. "Don't worry. I'm keeping my eyes peeled."

Ann thrust up her finger. "Chef would definitely kill you if you tried to take a bite of crepe before it's on the plate."

"We should start making crepes," Gráinne said.

"This is an Irish bistro," Siobhán said.

"I love his accent," Gráinne said. "And he made us croissants this morning. To die for!"

"Yum!" Ann said.

"I like the crepes better," Ciarán piped up. "Did ye know you can eat them with chocolate?"

"Is Chef Antoine making the wedding cake as well?" Siobhán asked. She would never tell anyone, but champagne and wedding cake were close to her two favorite things in the world. She would probably spend more time picking out the cake than she did her dress.

"Bridie is making the cake," Ann said. "But it's a surprise."

Siobhán's mouth watered. If Bridie was making the cake, it would probably be traditional. Fruitcake made with honey, soaked in Irish whiskey and frosted with a sweet white glaze. Green icing as trim, and perhaps a shamrock on top for good luck. Siobhán couldn't wait.

"It has seven tiers," Gráinne said.

Ciarán's head popped up. "Why would a cake be crying?"

Gráinne and Ann howled with laughter, then filled a frowning Ciarán in on the difference between tears and tiers.

"She's been giving us samples," Eoin said. "It's the best I've ever had in me life."

Bridie was a woman of many talents. Why hadn't she given Siobhán any samples? She hoped Ciarán wasn't eating too much sugar. It made him mad hyper. It should be added to his *Big Book of Poisons*.

"No wonder you haven't missed me," Siobhán said. "You've had crepes and cake."

"And Trigger," Ciarán pointed out, scooping up the dog, who wriggled in his arms.

"Eejits," Eoin said, shaking his head. "She's searching for compliments, do you not know?"

Siobhán laughed. Maybe he would be a hit with the ladies. She ambushed him in a hug. He pulled away as fast as he could, but she still held onto his hand. "You missed me?"

"You've barely been gone." Eoin dashed back to his comic. "But I don't trust the Frenchy."

"Eoin's just jealous," Gráinne said.

"Am not," Eoin said.

"Are too," Ann said. "Because Alice told Antoine she wanted him to be her forever chef."

Eoin shook his head, disgusted. "I can cook," he mumbled. "I could cook for her forever."

Trigger broke free and began racing around the bistro, chased by Ciarán. "His paws are muddy!" Siobhán exclaimed. She reached for the mutt as he scooted by, and he growled. The rest of the lot howled with laughter.

"He does hate you," Gráinne said. "Have you been mistreating him when we weren't looking?"

"Of course not," Siobhán said.

"Maybe he doesn't like the way you smell," Ann said. "They've very sophisticated noses."

"There's nothing wrong with my smell," Siobhán said. "He just wants to be alpha dog, and I'm not going to let him get away with it."

Trigger trotted over to James, who picked up the pup. He licked James's neck.

"Now we've mud all over the dining room. I'm tellin' ye, he cannot be inside. This is a bistro. We could be shut down, like."

"Settle," James said. "We'll get it clean by brekkie." Siobhán sighed, flopped back into the chair, and closed her eyes. "You still haven't cracked those college catalogs," James called over his shoulder.

The stack of catalogs on her bedside table swam through her mind. She'd planned on studying history. But at the moment, she was so thoroughly immersed in the present that the appeal had lessened. But James was right. If she didn't start studying something, she'd spend the rest of her life just running the bistro. It had to be done, but it wasn't her dream. Macdara had said she was the best investigator on the case. And she wasn't even a guard. She'd had trouble getting that out of her mind. She'd even imagined herself in the garda uniform, gold shield glittering on her cap. Garda Siobhán. Garda O'Sullivan. Garda Siobhán O'Sullivan.

Suddenly she became aware of Ciarán hovering over her, his freckles inches from her face, his breath warm and salty. "He might like you if you give him treats."

"I have to blackmail him to like me, do I?" Siobhán said.

"Works for me," Ciarán said. She ruffled his hair.

"He still won't like her as much as Ann like ze French chef," Eoin said.

"Shut your gob!" Ann screamed. "You're the one drooling over Alice."

"Can't blame him for that," James said, sauntering back into the dining room.

Siobhán was starting to feel even more relaxed. There was nowhere else she'd rather be than at Naomi's Bistro on Sarsfield Street with her cheeky siblings having a go at each other. It struck her that the chaos of family was much more comforting than the calmness of strangers.

Chapter 19

Early Friday morning, Siobhán stood outside Detective Sergeant O'Brien's makeshift office at the gardai station. He normally worked out of Cork City, but he had been given a temporary room in Kilbane. It had one window, one chair, and a desk. O'Brien was sitting in front of a stack of papers, but his attention was elsewhere. The desk was wobbling, and he kept dipping underneath trying to secure it, then popping back up to test it out. She had to come clean about the envelope of alibis and getting shoved down the stairs at the castle. Especially before heading off to Limerick with Macdara. O'Brien was at his desk, culling through papers. "Come in."

Siobhán approached, still trying to practice the best way to go about this. He looked up and waited.

"I should have shared this with you when it happened," Siobhán began. He gestured for her to sit. She let it all out as fast as she could, from the electricity getting shut off to getting shoved down the stairs. By the end of her tale, her voice was warbling.

The crease in O'Brien's forehead deepened. He slammed his hand down on the table, making it rock. "You withheld evidence and failed to report a crime." His eyes briefly flickered to the legs of the table.

Siobhán reached into her handbag, balled up a tissue, and stuck it under the desk. "I didn't realize the envelope of alibis had been stolen until much later."

O'Brien jiggled the table. It remained still. He smiled at it, but when he looked up at Siobhán, he was glaring again. "You're interfering with my investigation."

"I have no idea who it was. None at all."

"I'll try and verify where all the wedding guests were when this happened," he said. "How did Macdara take the news?" He immediately registered the look on Siobhán's face. "Ah," he said. "You kept it from him." The implication was clear: she was a liar.

"He worries about me." She hadn't come here to discuss her personal life, and it made her extremely uncomfortable.

"He should. I was wrong to send ye to the castle on your own."

"No. I can handle this."

"Not anymore. You're to take three steps back now."

She wanted to protest, tell him what a good investigator she was, but that would only backfire. "Yes sir."

She waited for him to mention the outing to Limerick. "Anything else?" She shook her head. It didn't seem like the right time to ask about the garda application process as well as a dozen other questions she had. "Ms. O'Sullivan?"

"Pardon?"

"Anything else?" He wanted her out.

Can I have a look at the police reports? "No, nothing at all, Detective Sergeant." She turned to go.

"If anything else happens—anything at all—and I don't get wind of it directly from you? I'll have you arrested."

"Yes sir."

"That's all." Siobhán went to the door, then stopped. O'Brien shook his head. "For the love of God, what?"

"I was just wondering. Would you like to hear my theories so far?" She was prepared to tell him that he should contact the Huntsmans. That she didn't think Kevin was the intended victim. That someone could have used the tracksuits to his or her advantage. That her mind kept circling back around to Colm's missing fax.

"Theories like the killer could have climbed a tree but probably didn't?" O'Brien said with a straight face. Of course the guards had squealed on her. They all thought she was a right joke. If she decided to become a guard, maybe this is what it would feel like all the time.

Siobhán flushed. "And a few more."

"I appreciate it, Ms. O'Sullivan. But keep your theories to yourself. I only want the facts."

So much for asking for the Huntsmans' telephone number. "Yes sir." She made her escape before he could remember to cancel her trip to Limerick.

–

Siobhán and Macdara stood in Limerick City, on Crescent Street, named for the half-moon shape made by the terraced buildings on either side. They had situated themselves at the base of the Daniel O'Connell monument, perfect for ducking behind if they needed quick cover. The air was crisp, but the skies were clear. Across the street from where they were staked out, Antoine and Brian were planted in front of the Limerick Pub. Brian was buried in his iPad; Antoine was smoking and pacing. They had no idea they were being watched, and Siobhán felt slightly ashamed.

Macdara checked his phone. "I have another bit of news, but you have to keep it between us."

"Go on."

"Kevin's pockets were empty."

"He was robbed—"

"He was robbed—" Macdara caught up to what she was saying. Stopped. Shook his head.

He had wanted to be the first to break the news. "But you confirmed it, so t'ank you."

Macdara nodded. "They didn't find so much as a hotel key. And Paul said that Kevin always wore a gold watch and chain. Belonged to his grandfather. But they didn't find either on him."

"Staging it to look like a robbery," Siobhán said.

"Or it was a robbery," Macdara countered.

"Kill a man over a gold watch and a chain?"

Macdara shrugged. "It happens."

"He was killed from behind."

"So?"

"So? The killer wouldn't have been able to even see the watch and gold chain."

Macdara sighed. "They could have spotted it on him earlier."

"I don't buy it."

"I'm not selling it. I'm just going over the options."

"I can't believe you've been discussing this with Paul." The anger in her voice was unmistakable. She'd meant to keep it in, but really, what was he thinking? Whether Macdara liked it or not, old friend from university or not, Paul Donnelly was a suspect. It was downright irresponsible to leak evidence to him.

Macdara stared at her. "You're jealous because Paul knows something about the investigation that you don't?"

"Makes me sound petty when you put it like that."
Macdara glanced away.

"He's a suspect."

"So am I," he snapped.

He was way too close to this case. She could only imagine how he was going to react when he found out about her being shoved down the stairs and having the alibis snatched. Or getting reprimanded by O'Brien. "Where did everyone go when I was at the castle getting their things?"

"Most of them went back to the inn to rest," Macdara said. "I believe a few went to the pubs."

"What about Alice and Paul?"

"To the inn. Why?" He was on high alert.

"No reason."

"Don't give me that."

"I'm just making conversation." Macdara relaxed. She felt guilty that he bought her little white lie. "Has anyone else reported any robberies?"

"Nothing out of the ordinary. Peter Hennessy is convinced that someone keeps taking his ladder. But every time I go into his hardware shop, I find it leaning up against a different shelf. He's getting forgetful."

"So that doesn't count."

"A few reports have been filed on the travelers. But that's also nothing new."

Travelers was the polite name for itinerants. *Tinkers*, *gypsies*, and *bleeding thieves* were other names she often heard them called. They set up their caravans on the outskirts of Kilbane, and there was no love lost between their camps and the locals. They illegally hooked up to the town's electricity lines, their horses and dogs were so skinny you could see ribs, their children didn't go to school, and quite often you couldn't understand a word they were saying. Siobhán didn't feel comfortable around them, but she also didn't like the names they were called. There were definitely a few heads in town who would love to pin a murder on one of them.

Siobhán sighed and held up the binoculars. Antoine and Brian were conversing now. Siobhán wished they could hear what they were saying, but it was obvious to anyone looking on that they were in a great state of agitation.

"Stakeouts aren't nearly as exciting in person as they are on telly," Siobhán remarked, biting into a chocolate.

"Christ, I know. We've only been here ten minutes, and I'm itching to move," Macdara said.

"Jaysus. Has it been that long?"

Macdara laughed, wrapped his hand around her waist, and pulled her in for a kiss. Siobhán shoved him away. "We're on duty."

"And your mouth is too busy with the chocolate to bother with the likes of me."

She was startled how well he knew her.

From down the street came the rumblings of a lorry with a rattling muffler. It troddled into view, black smoke belching from the exhaust pipe. It lurched up to the pub with a screech. Passersby backed up; some pointed and laughed. This beat-up piece of tin couldn't be carrying the shipment, could it? She peered through the binoculars again. MARTIN'S TRANSPORT was stamped across the side. "We were right."

"Martin's Transport," Macdara said. Siobhán handed Macdara the binoculars. "I can see it with me own eyes. It's only across the street, like."

Siobhán grabbed the binoculars back. "Suit yourself." Antoine and Brian were now unloading boxes from the back of Martin's wreck and into the boot of the lorry they'd rented. Thick black exhaust continued to belch into the air. "Pretty clear why Susan didn't want that mess pulling into Kilbane," Siobhán said. Another letdown.

"Hardly a mystery," Macdara agreed. "The real question is why? Or, more to the point, how? How did Martin Donnelly convince Susan Cahill to switch to his transport company? What does he have on her?"

"What if it isn't Martin who has something on her?" Siobhán probed. Macdara waited. "Could it have been Faye? Or Paul?" Her voice cracked.

"Could be," Macdara said. A clipped and guarded answer. He didn't want to appear to be biased.

"Faye trying to help out her husband, or Paul trying to help out his father."

"I get it," Macdara said.

"And Paul was angry with Kevin. So angry he fired him as his best man."

"And that makes him a killer?"

"We have to consider everyone," she said softly.

"I'll find out who the original suppliers were—"

Siobhán held up her hand. "All France for the champagne, Farm to Table in Dublin for the produce, the meat from a butcher in Cork, the cake from—"

Macdara grabbed her hand. "I get it. You're three steps ahead of me." He was definitely browned off.

It was more likely six steps ahead of him, but once again nobody liked a braggart. Siobhán held up her notebook. "Helps to have one of these."

"And be a Nosy Nellie."

"That too. Now shall we go to the chipper before heading back?"

"Curried chips?" Macdara asked, his voice brightening. Siobhán nodded. Nothing sorted sore feelings like a basket of curried chips. Macdara took her hand and squeezed. "You're my soul mate."

By the time they reached Macdara's car, hands full with their curried chips, twenty minutes had passed. Macdara came to a sudden stop, and Siobhán almost coated his back with the delectable sauce. She looked around him to see what had arrested his attention. It was the windshield of his car. Written in bright red lettering, three words were scrawled on the windshield:

STOP OR DIE

Chapter 20

Cars wooshed by, birds circled and cried overhead, and the Shannon River gently flowed while Siobhán and Macdara stared at the threat on the windshield.

"You have to appreciate the brevity," Macdara said after a long pause.

Siobhán edged forward and examined it. "Why, it looks like lipstick," she said.

"Are you sure?" Macdara asked.

"No. That's why I said, 'It looks like lipstick.'" She glanced in the direction of the Limerick Pub. "Brian or Antoine?"

Macdara shook his head. "Now, why would Brian or Antoine be carrying around red lipstick?"

"That's what I would do if I was a man and a murderer," Siobhán said. "Throw us off the scent. Besides, you never know what one does in private, now do ye?"

Macdara grimaced. "Don't put thoughts like that in me head."

"Don't be so judgmental. Besides, a man can walk into a shop and buy lipstick as a gift for a woman, can he not?"

"Alright, alright," Macdara said, throwing up his hands. "But if Brian or Antoine saw us, then they know we know they're here."

"So?"

"Why would they risk it when it would be super easy for us to figure out it was one of them?"

"And yet we still don't know," Siobhán said. She edged closer. She wanted to touch the substance and see what it was, but of course she wasn't going to tamper with evidence. It definitely wasn't blood, but the color was a warning, along with the words. Siobhán glanced down the street, trying to ascertain which stores had cameras that might have caught anyone approaching the car. "We can get them to pull the CCTV footage."

"Cork will have to call into Limerick for them. It's not going to be quick. Until then I'm going to have to drive with this on the windshield."

"Maybe you should call some of your colleagues now. They might want us to leave the car here."

Macdara sighed. Then nodded. He took out his mobile and walked a few feet away. Siobhán stared at the message. They would have to suss out what everyone else had been doing while they were here. Was the killer nearby? Watching them right now?

The killer was getting worried, which had to mean they were getting close. It was broad daylight; someone had to have seen something. So the killer was also getting careless. Was it only a matter of time before they fatally slipped up? They should canvass every single establishment right now. The car was parked on a side street, not directly across from any buildings, but it wouldn't hurt to ask.

When Macdara returned, his face was scrunched with anger. She was about to ask him what on earth was the matter when it dawned on her. O'Brien had told him everything.

Macdara pinned his beautiful blue eyes on her. "Shoved down the stairs?"

"I had on stocking feet."

He took a protective step forward, although his jaw was clenched in anger. "Are you hurt?"

Siobhán shook her head. "Just a bit sore."

"I'm a bit sore as well. You aren't supposed to be here. Did ye know that?"

"I did not specifically know that."

"O'Brien didn't tell ye to back off?"

"He might have done. But he did not specifically cancel this prearranged stakeout."

Macdara jabbed his finger at her. "You lied to me."

"I didn't lie. I omitted."

"Omitted a lot, didn't ye?"

Siobhán's mind raced. What else? "The tree?"

Macdara frowned. "The alibis," he said. "What tree?"

"Right. The alibis and the shove." *And the tree. And Val manhandling her.* "I'm sorry."

"We're getting a taxi home, I'm dropping you back off to the bistro, and you'll be done with this whole mess."

"I'm still invited to the wedding."

Macdara's eyes flashed. "You were never invited to the wedding."

Siobhán thrust her chin up. "Alice invited me."

"Did she now?"

"Indeed she did."

"O'Brien just went ballistic. I had to talk him out of arresting you."

"Me?"

"You're withholding evidence and interfering with this investigation."

"You're the one who said I was one of the best investigators they have."

"I was wrong. You're not trained for this. This is all my fault." A taxi pulled up to the curb. He had called it as soon as he'd finished his call with O'Brien. Macdara opened the back door and gestured for her to get in.

"I thought we should talk to a few shop owners—"

"In." Siobhán got in the car. Macdara got in after her and slammed the door shut. "It's your car," she said. "I think the message was meant for you." Macdara gave her a sideways glance. She didn't want to joke about either of them dying, but it worked. A tiny smile broke out on his face. "You have to stop," he said. "I'm not joking."

She smiled and nodded, suddenly feeling very drained. Maybe he was right. She wasn't a trained investigator. She had a bistro to run, young ones to mind. University catalogs to peruse.

STOP OR DIE

She couldn't shake the feeling that Macdara might be in danger. And she really couldn't shake the feeling that one of Macdara's oldest and dearest friends might just be the killer. Colm was bearing down on him, trying to break up this wedding. It was working too. Alice was having doubts. There was no other way to explain those letters in her rubbish bin. What if Paul had read them? Wouldn't he kill to keep the woman he loved? She didn't want the killer to be Paul, but that was exactly why she had to clear him. If he was innocent, she would prove it. And if he wasn't? Well, no one else was going to go there. From what she could see, O'Brien was spending more time fixing wobbling tables than investigating this case. Macdara was barred from investigating, and he was way too close. Paul might have even planted Macdara's cap at the scene to throw suspicion on him. Again, she didn't want it to be true, but it was a distinct possibility. Either Kevin was wearing that cap, or someone wanted to set Macdara up for murder. She wasn't the one who should stop investigating. She was making headway. She was rattling the killer. She was going to keep asking questions. She would do her best to keep under the radar. And she knew just where her next line of inquiry should begin.

—

Siobhán found Martin Donnelly in Butler's Undertaker, Lounge, and Pub, which was her very last shot since asking around and hearing from several sources that it wouldn't have been unusual for him to have snuck out for a nip. A wave of sadness hit Siobhán as she entered the establishment; she hated the pall, and the dim lights, and the sad boxes of tissues on nearly every surface. Her parents had been taken care of here, as was everyone else in town, and if she had her way she'd never walk in here again. Martin Donnelly was alone at the bar, hunched over at the very last stool. John Butler, the undertaker and bartender, peeked out from behind a pair of red curtains upon her entrance. He was a middle-aged man with a rather formal and theatrical appearance. His eyebrows were penciled in. He had a gaunt face and a slim build. He always wore a buttoned-up suit and often carried a cane. Today he looked like a man who didn't want to see or be seen. He raised his eyebrow as if to ask her if she was here for a drink, and when she shook her head no, he disappeared again without another word.

"Martin?"

His head jerked up in surprise, and when he met her eyes, for a second she saw a flash of what felt like rage. Just as quickly, he recovered and even offered a smile, which Siobhán found way creepier.

"You found me," he said.

"Small village."

"I'm beginning to notice."

"You're blackmailing Susan Cahill." Some people you had to warm up, but Siobhán got the feeling that Martin would say more if he was knocked off-kilter.

"She's lying!" He shot up from his stool and knocked over his pint. Siobhán grabbed a box of tissues and began mopping it up, a reflex from working in the bistro.

Siobhán decided to play along with his suspicions. "I figured as much. I wonder why would she lie?"

Martin's left eyebrow began to twitch. "What exactly did she say?"

"What do you think she said?" Siobhán tried to say it with as much attitude as possible.

"It was a gesture, that's all. We're family now." He sounded as if he was trying to talk himself into it. He also sounded as if he hadn't been the mastermind.

"I think it's admirable that Paul is looking out for you," Siobhán said. It was a shot in the dark.

The twitch grew more pronounced. "I don't know what you mean." But he did know what Siobhán meant. Had Paul insisted that Susan use Martin's transport company?

Siobhán sat down next to him. "You must be very conflicted about this marriage."

"I never said any such thing!"

"I can only imagine how I'd feel if Colm and Susan were about to become part of my family."

"I have no feelings," Martin said. He lifted his pint. "This helps." He guzzled the remainder of his pint. "Publican!" John Butler did not appear.

"You argued with Kevin the night he died?" Since almost everyone seemed to have had a run-in with Kevin, this wasn't exactly a shot in the dark. More like a shot in the dim.

"Wrecked chicken," Martin muttered.

"Pardon?"

"You've heard it. I know you've heard it."

"Wrecked chicken?"

"Go ahead. Have a laugh."

Siobhán kept perched on her stool even though she'd rather run from the place as if she were on fire. "I don't know what you're on about."

"Are ye messing?"

"No. Haven't heard a word."

Martin harrumphed. "You already know I have me own transport company."

"I do, yeah."

"Had an awful mess about six months back. Had a little accident. I was transporting chickens. Loads of 'em. Hit a bump in the road, and me truck veered off into a ditch. Rolled onto its side. Poor fellas. Most of them didn't make it."

"I'm sorry."

"Ah, well. They weren't going to make it much longer anyway, you know."

This was not the conversation Siobhán planned on having, and she really didn't know how to respond, so she just nodded and made a comforting tsk-tsk sound.

"But Kevin thought it was mighty hilarious. All night long he says to me, 'What's for dinner tonight, Martin. Wrecked chicken?'"

Martin looked outraged, and Siobhán did her best to copy his expression. "But do you think I would kill him over that?" He shook his head. "Pah."

Siobhán believed him. Sitting before her was a shrunken man. She couldn't imagine him bashing anyone with a rock. She couldn't even imagine him expending the energy to lift a rock unless he thought there was a pint buried underneath. "What about your wife?"

"You leave her out of this." Suddenly Martin was in Siobhán's face, his finger pointing directly at her, his jaw clenched with rage. "She was right about one thing. This bloody wedding was a huge mistake!"

He stood, and turned. "It was one of the Cahills who killed Kevin. You mark my words. That insufferable couple would do anything to get their way. Anything!"

With that, he stormed past her and slammed out the door. John Butler appeared through the curtains and stared at her. "Oh my," he said and disappeared as quickly as he came. Siobhán hurried out of the depressing lounge. So either Faye or Paul had convinced Susan to use Martin's company to deliver a new shipment of champagne. One of them had something on her. Which one, and what exactly were they holding over her head?

–

Charleville, County Cork, was situated in the Golden Vale, on a tributary of the River Maigue. The area was renowned for its lush, rolling pastures. It was bordered to the west by the Galtee Mountains and backed up by the picturesque Glen of Aherlow, a delightful valley that drew many an eye, tourists and locals alike. The third largest city in Cork, Charleville was the closest city to Kilbane, and Siobhán loved not only the change of scenery but the plethora of shops. It was the most logical place to come for the bits and bobs needed for the wedding, starting with flowers.

Alice, Brenna, Susan, and Siobhán had no sooner stepped into the flower shop when an argument ensued between mother and daughter.

"White lilies," Susan said, gravitating toward a bouquet.

"No," Alice said. "Lilies make me think of death." She shuddered. "We've had enough of that."

"Marriage is a form of death, dear," Susan said. "Besides. They're traditional."

"Bells of Ireland are traditional too," Siobhán suggested. "Or wildflowers."

"I'm not paying for wildflowers," Susan said.

"You don't pay for wildflowers, Mother, you pick them." Alice rolled her eyes and glanced at Siobhán. "I loved the flower arrangement Siobhán had on her table. White roses with two red in the middle. That's what I'd like."

"We need flowers for all the tables," Susan said.

"The beauty of a small wedding, Mother, is that we only have one table."

"Everyone is going to sit at the bridal table?" Susan sounded horrified.

"I'll get one bouquet to take down the aisle, and you can get whatever else you want for the table at the abbey. Except white lilies. Anything except lilies."

"The abbey," Susan said with a shiver. "I still can't believe you want to have the wedding there."

"I think it's lovely."

"At least Antoine and Brian were able to meet the champagne shipment in Limerick today," Siobhán said casually, watching Susan carefully for a reaction. Oh, that Botoxed face. It was impossible to see any change of expression on the woman at all.

"Champagne shipment to Limerick?" Alice said. "I thought the champagne had already been delivered to the castle?"

"We don't know where the Huntsmans were storing it," Susan said. "So we had to scramble at the last minute to get a new shipment in."

She was quick on her feet, Siohban had to give her that. "It was mighty nice of you to use Martin's transport company," Siobhán continued.

This time Siobhán could read Susan's expression: pure rage.

"You did?" Alice said. She'd clearly been left in the dark.

"He's family now, isn't it?" Susan said.

Alice threw herself into her mother's arms and hugged her. When she released her, Susan stumbled back, her expression even more horrified than before. Like hugging a cactus, Siobhán supposed. She felt another grip of grief as she immediately felt one of her mother's warm hugs wrap around her.

As Alice and Susan were ordering the flowers, Brenna clutched Siobhán's arm, then dragged her out the door and onto the footpath.

"You're hurting me," Siobhán said. Charleville was much busier than Sarsfield Street would have been, with

205

numerous folks going in and out of shops and restaurants. It was the warmest day they'd had so far, and Siobhán had a sudden urge to go for a run. Or have a basket of curried chips. Yes, she'd much rather have the chips.

Brenna waved her hand in front of Siobhán's face until she looked at her. "Have the guards said anything to you or yer man about me?"

"Like what?"

Brenna's expression belied her impatience. "About me and Kevin in the same bed that night."

"No." Everyone assumed Siobhán was tapped into the vein of the gardai. Little did they know how ostracized she was.

"Do you think I'm still a suspect?"

"Everyone is a suspect."

"Even your precious Macdara?"

Siobhán frowned. *Was Brenna threatening her?* Had she killed Kevin and planted Macdara's cap at the crime scene? If Kevin had the cap and Brenna slept with Kevin, she would have had access to it. "What do you care what I think?"

Brenna clutched Siobhán's arms. "They have to cancel the wedding. You have to make them."

Fear tickled the back of Siobhán's neck. "What aren't you telling me?"

Brenna looked away and lowered her voice. "Colm Cahill does not approve."

"He's made that clear."

Brenna's eyes were wide with fear. "He's never going to let the wedding go on."

"Stop talking in riddles. If you want my help, then out with it."

Brenna paused as a mother walked by, pushing a stroller. "I hear you've been asking around about Ronan's pictures from that night."

"How did you hear that?"

"Ronan thinks I'm a worthy model."

Siobhán rolled her eyes. That man would take a picture of a tree stump and call it art.

"I can probably get him to invite me into his room," Brenna continued.

"I won't even ask how."

"Seduce him, like."

"Got it."

"He backs all his photos up to his laptop."

This was news. "How do you know?"

"You're not the only one who keeps her eyes open."

"Let's say you do get hold of his laptop. Then what?"

"I can transfer them all to a USB while he's sleeping."

"The guards have Ronan's laptop."

Brenna laughed. "You're so naïve. He has another laptop. I've seen it with me own eyes."

Siobhán should tell her not to do it. It was too dangerous. Leave it to the guards. "What's in it for you?"

"You'll get your garda friend to protect me." There it was again, pure panic in Brenna's voice. Siobhán wished she were a lemon she could squeeze to get the juicy bits.

"Protection from whom?"

"Colm Cahill."

"Again. What aren't you telling me?"

Brenna's expression finally broke. "I know why Kevin went to the top of the hill that mornin'."

"Why?"

"There was a note."

Siobhán tingled. "A note."

"It was a total misunderstanding. It wasn't meant for him."

The bell jangled, and Alice and Susan emerged from the flower shop. "There you are," Alice said. "What are you two whispering about?"

"Lilies," Brenna said. "We're whispering about lilies."

Chapter 21

Siobhán practically had to drag Macdara into Chris Gorden's comic shop. He didn't like the Yank, mostly because Chris made no effort to hide his crush on her, but Paul insisted on the clandestine meeting spot. Chris Gorden was at the counter, laughing with a pair of teen-aged girls. He had American movie star looks, although she much preferred Macdara's tousled charm.

Siobhán and Macdara tried to sneak past the counter. "Hey Siobhán," Chris called out. They stopped, and it wasn't lost on Siobhán how the teenaged girls smiled at Chris. They weren't from Kilbane. Colleens were trav-eling from Charleville to come to the shop and flirt with the foreign owner. It was highly unlikely that these lassies had come to check into the comics.

"How ya?" Siobhán called out politely. She could practically feel Macdara simmering behind her.

Chris's grin widened. "How's Ciarán liking his *Big Book of Poisons*?" Siobhán didn't want to untangle that knot in this moment, so she smiled and gave Chris a thumbs-up. Chris winked at her. "I have volume two, if he's interested."

"The lad is starting school," Macdara said. "He shouldn't be wasting his time with gore."

"You're not a fan then?" Chris said, gesturing around the store.

Macdara shook his head. "I'm not."

Chris folded his arms. "So why are you here?"

"None of your business."

"Now, lads," Siobhán said. They ignored her.

Chris folded his arms across his chest. "Graphic novels are a form of art, you know."

"Looks to me like you're promoting nothing but violence," Macdara said.

Chris glared. "Mankind has always been dark. Always been violent. You should know that."

"I should?" Macdara shifted.

"Of course. You're a guard. And you live in a walled town. You think the walls were built for decoration?"

The girls laughed, and Macdara tensed. "I know me own history. A year ago you probably couldn't even find Ireland on the map."

"Indulging in story is a healthy outlet for violence. Maybe if the killer had read a few comics, he wouldn't have taken such drastic measures."

Macdara shook his head, Siobhán tugged on his sleeve, and they hurried to the back of the store.

"Good to see you, Siobhán!" Chris called after them. "Drop in anytime. By yourself!"

"Wanker," Macdara said.

Paul was standing in the very back corner of the shop, lurking near a poster dripping with fangs and blood. He almost looked as if he belonged in the pages himself: his hair was uncombed, his face full of stubble, his eyes bloodshot. When he lifted his hand to scratch his chin, it trembled.

"You look like you've lost the plot," Macdara said. "What's the story?"

Paul started to pace the two-foot section. "I wanted to talk where no one else could overhear."

As Macdara waited, Siobhán glanced around at the few lads in the shop, all so buried in comics they wouldn't notice an actual zombie apocalypse outside the door. "This should do it," she said.

"Do the guards have anything on the killer? Anything at all?" Paul sounded absolutely desperate. Macdara hesitated. Siobhán prayed he wasn't going to feed Paul any information. "All this business is pushing me over the edge." Paul's voice was hoarse.

"I can imagine," Siobhán said.

Paul stepped up to them and threw open his arms. "For the love of God, help me."

Siobhán felt a pair of eyes on them and looked up to see Chris Gorden a few feet away, pretending to stack books. Macdara steered them to the next aisle and lowered his voice. "Talk to us."

Paul's face lost all color. "Alice is going to kill me."

Macdara's eyes widened. "Literally?"

"No, not literally. Well, maybe literally. I certainly wouldn't blame her."

"What did you do?" Siobhán asked.

Paul looked left and right, then lowered his head. When he spoke, his voice was barely audible. "I don't think we should go on with the wedding."

Siobhán gasped, and Macdara took a step back. "The past few days you've been pushing for it."

"I know. I know. I don't want to hurt Alice." His voice rose. Macdara placed a finger to his lips. Paul nodded.

"You don't want to go on with the wedding this weekend, or you don't want to go on with the wedding at all?" Macdara whispered.

Anger welled in Paul's eyes. "That man."

"Colm," Siobhán said.

Paul pulled out a handkerchief and mopped his brow. "He just offered me a bribe!"

"You're joking me," Macdara said.

"Name my price, he said. A hundred thousand euros? Two hundred? A million? What was it going to take to get me to walk?"

"A million?" This time it was Macdara who needed to be shushed. "Surely you're not considering it?"

"How could you even ask me that?"

"You said Alice was going to kill you."

"Only because now I'm keeping yet another secret from her." Paul's eyes flicked to Siobhán.

"You can trust her," Macdara said.

Yes, Siobhán thought. *But can we trust him?*

Paul clenched his fists. "What if that was Colm's plan all along? Create secrets between us? Wait until the last minute to tell her everything I haven't told her." Paul was starting to babble. Chris Gorden came into the aisle. This time he wasn't holding a stack of books to shelve. He began adjusting books already on the shelf. The trio moved toward the front of the store.

"You're not saying you think Colm killed Kevin?" Siobhán blurted out.

Paul ran his fingers through his hair. "The night before Kevin was killed, he and Colm were speaking in whispers on the back patio."

Macdara's expression told Siobhán that he didn't like that he was hearing about this now. He didn't like that his friends were just as capable of lying to guards as everyone else. She would have to make an effort not to say she told him so. "What were they saying?"

"I missed the beginning. But it was clear that Colm was furious. I think he threatened Kevin."

"You think?" Siobhán said.

"I was just stumbling back to relieve myself, if you must know. I didn't realize Colm and Kevin were back there until I almost fell into them."

Macdara leaned in. "This isn't news. We already know Colm was throwing money around to anyone willing to stop the wedding." Macdara stopped suddenly. "Did you say secrets you've been keeping from Alice? More than one?"

Paul visibly reddened. He nodded.

Macdara looked stricken. "Did you sleep with Brenna?"

"That cow? Of course not!"

Siobhán was taken aback. She'd never heard Paul speak of a woman in such derogatory terms. And from the shocked look on Macdara's face, neither had he. How well did Macdara really know Paul Donnelly? Paul must have picked up on their discomfort. "I'm sorry. I'm sorry. I'm just so wound up. I don't know what to do. I don't know who to trust."

"We can't help you if you won't tell us what's really going on." A few of the lads nearby were looking at them now. Macdara picked up a comic and leafed through it. "Vampires and witches, and shite. Jaysus. Whatever happened to good old Westerns? Horses and guns."

Siobhán suppressed a smile. Imagined him as a wee lad, dreaming of being a cowboy. And, she had to admit, she liked that he was a little bit jealous.

"Colm put a private investigator on me a few months back," Paul said, snapping her back to the moment.

Macdara slapped down the comic. "Can't say I'm surprised."

"And when he didn't find anything on me, he turned them loose on me mother and father."

Faye and Martin. "That's out of bounds," Macdara said. "And?"

"You know my father had some bad business."

"I'm aware. Poor chickens." Too late, Macdara made a noise that sounded an awful lot like clucking.

"Almost lost his license."

"Go on."

"Colm was having him tailed day and night, trying to catch him drinking and driving again. One more strike and it would be off to jail."

Either Paul didn't know about the switch to Martin's Transport or Macdara's old friend was a new liar. And a good one at that. Beads of sweat started to form on Paul's forehead. "Out with it, lad," Macdara said.

"The night before Kevin's murder, several of us saw Colm Cahill kissing another woman in the pub."

Siobhán felt a tingling sensation crawl up her spine. This was big somehow. She would need time to think on it. She turned to Macdara. "Does that ring any bells?"

Macdara shook his head. "I spent most of the evening talking to my mam. I don't recall seeing Colm with another woman, but it's not out of the realm of possibility."

"Messy business," Siobhán said. Was that why Colm wasn't wearing his wedding ring? "Who was the woman?"

Paul shook his head. "A local. That's all I know."

Macdara sighed. "Is there more to the story?"

"They disappeared shortly after. But not before Ronan snapped a picture."

Siobhán stepped forward and made a concentrated effort to keep the excitement out of her voice. "What did this local woman look like?"

"Middle-aged. Chestnut hair. Bubbly and chesty. I only saw her from afar."

Annmarie?

"Did Colm find out there was a picture?" Macdara asked.

"I think Ronan tried to sell it to the highest bidder. I never trusted that lout, but Alice can be easily impressed."

Siobhán finally had a few pieces she could put together. "Is that why Colm asked Kevin to knock the camera out of Ronan's hands?"

"Exactly. That's it," Paul said.

And then the camera card mysteriously disappeared in the scuffle. Just like she'd mentioned to Macdara on the hilltop. She gave Macdara a look that she could only pray he'd interpret as: I told ye so.

"Are you going to buy something?" Chris Gorden popped up behind them.

"No," Macdara said. "I'm going to buy a birdcage and use a few of these as lining." He gestured to the comics.

Chris Gorden frowned. "No loitering." He smiled at Siobhán. "Except for you. You can loiter all you want."

"Let's go," Macdara said. "Wanker," he said again under his breath.

Once outside, the three stood silent, as if mulling over their options. Siobhán wanted Paul to keep talking. But taking him for a pint in his agitated condition wasn't the smartest idea. She knew just the place. "Care to walk to the abbey?"

Macdara nodded. "I could use some fresh air," he said.

"I'll follow you." Paul gestured for them to lead the way.

They headed toward the town square and then cut right down a side street until they reached the banks of the river. Once they crossed the bridge and traversed the field, they entered the monastery grounds. Macdara cut directly through until they reached the stairs leading to the bell tower. "Up for a climb?"

"You bet," Siobhán said, hoping her enthusiasm would spread to Paul. He was starting to look guarded, as if he regretted speaking with them.

"I suppose," Paul finally said.

"Good lad." They raced each other to the top, where the view was long and the walls high. They stopped to pant. "Jaysus, we're getting old," Macdara said.

"Speak for yourself," Siobhán said. Macdara pinched the back of her arm, and she yelped.

"I'm lucky I'm settling down," Paul said, winking at the two of them. They hopped up on the wall. "You two ever think about doing the same?"

Siobhán felt the heat rush to her head as Macdara gazed out at Kilbane. Rolling fields of green. The stone wall winding along, Saint Mary's steeple rising in the background. Someone was mowing their lawn, and the scent of freshly cut grass mingled with the heather. "Back to Colm Cahill," Macdara said, ignoring Paul's question. "What aren't you telling us?"

Paul took out a pack of cigarettes. Marlboros.

"You smoke?" Macdara asked.

"If you had to deal with the Cahills, you would start smoking too."

They waited while Paul lit up. He puffed for a few moments, exhaled, and then began. "You know my mother is a solicitor."

"Back to work after a long absence," Siobhán said. "Good on her."

"Her latest client wants a divorce. Only there's an iron-clad prenup."

Was Paul talking about himself?

"Did you sign a prenup?" Macdara asked.

Paul gave a wry laugh. "Of course. Colm insisted I sign one. I don't mind. I'm not after the Cahill money. And it was one of his solicitors who drew up our agreement. My mother has a different client."

Paul was making them pull every word out of him. He paused between sentences, taking his time smoking his cigarette. "Go on," Siobhán urged when she could stand it no longer.

"If this client divorces her husband without cause, she'll get nothing. But if there's any proof of hanky-panky—an affair—the woman will receive half of his fortune." Paul stubbed his cigarette out and waited. In the distance, church bells tolled.

Siobhán leaned forward. "You don't mean?"

"Yep."

"Susan Cahill," Siobhán whispered.

Faye Donnelly's client was Susan Cahill.

Chapter 22

Amongst the older generations, divorce was practically unheard of in Ireland. There were plenty of jokes about the secret to an Irish marriage, mostly involving bottomless pints and couples not speaking to one another for the rest of their miserable lives. Couples who grew apart often lived apart, but even then divorce was never an option. Marriage was a sacred contract that held up even when love fell down.

Macdara kept a brisk pace, heading for the gardai station with Paul. He'd tentatively agreed to give a statement to the guards. Siobhán held back, mulling over everything they'd just learned. If Susan was divorcing Colm, and Ronan had snapped the picture, that would allow her to inherit half of Colm's vast fortune. Either way, trouble was very much at hand. Cahill versus Cahill. Not a pretty sight. What was Ronan playing at?

Another question remained. Who had the picture? Had one of them killed to get their hands on it? They were equally capable, and equally motivated.

Siobhán joined Macdara and Paul outside the station. Paul wanted to smoke another cigarette before he went in.

"It can't be an accident that some local woman happened to hit on Colm in the pub," Macdara said. "Right when there was a camera following Colm."

Paul nodded. "Heck of an accident."

"We need to track down this local woman," Siobhán said. "Get a signed statement that Susan hired her to hit on Colm Cahill." Maybe not as bad as an actual hit on her husband, but diabolical nonetheless.

"My mother is going to be furious with me," Paul said. "Confidentiality means everything to a solicitor."

"Can't worry about that now. Lives are at stake," Macdara said.

Paul's eyes narrowed at he stared at the town square. "I realize."

"Would you recognize this local woman if you saw her again?" Siobhán asked gently. Folks passed through the square with a nod or a wave, and she nodded and waved back.

Paul flicked his cigarette to the ground. "Hard to say. It was dim and crowded."

"Why didn't you say anything earlier?" Macdara asked. "The guards will want to know."

Anguish was stamped on Paul's face. "Alice doesn't know. Our wedding isn't the ideal time to find out about her parents' divorce. She's going to be furious with me too. Everywhere I turn, a woman is going to be furious with me."

Siobhán sighed. He was right, and she wasn't going to console him with a lie, no matter how wretched he looked. The Irish skies were gray, the air slightly damp, and the recent rains had washed the air with a fresh earthy scent. Macdara regarded Paul. "Tell me the truth. Did you take the camera card?"

Siobhán held her breath.

Paul vehemently shook his head. "How could you even ask me that?"

"Desperate men take desperate measures."

"I swear. I've nothing to do with it."

"What's your theory?"

"I believe Kevin swiped the camera card. And that's why he was killed. It's either Ronan, Susan, or Colm."

Ronan, Susan, or Colm, Siobhán repeated silently. *Or you.*

"Wouldn't your mother know if Susan was in possession of the photo?" Frustration rang from Macdara's voice.

Paul shook his head. "Susan is a client. My mother only betrayed her confidence so far."

Siobhán chewed on the possiblities. Whichever way it worked out, Kevin tried to play someone for a fool. Played them against each other, ready to cater to the highest bidder. A fatal mistake.

Macdara nodded to the blue station door. "Once you walk in and start talking, there's no unringing this bell."

Paul mopped his brow again and nodded. "Then what should I do?"

Macdara clamped his hand on Paul's arm. "Besides the guards, don't say a word to anyone."

Paul grimaced. "I don't know what to do with myself."

"Go to Sheila Mahoney's salon and get yourself sorted," Macdara said. "You look like hell."

Paul turned to go inside, then grabbed Macdara's arm. "Tell them." He stopped and looked around. "If anything ever happens to me. Tell them. It's Colm Cahill or Susan Cahill who done it."

—

The minute Siobhán entered the bistro, hands full of wild-flowers, Ciarán launched himself on her like a torpedo.

She staggered back with his arms around her neck and scrawny but strong legs wrapped around her waist.

"Where have you been?"

"Cheeky lad." She bent over, cueing him to jump off; instead he continued to clutch her.

"We have to do the list."

"No."

"Get off, you dolt." Gráinne appeared, and in less than a second, she untangled Ciarán from Siobhán and planted him on the floor.

"T'ank you." Siobhán laid the flowers on the counter.

Ann appeared and swept them up. "I'll get a vase."

"Thank you?" Siobhán wondered what was afoot. One sister being helpful was a pleasant shock; two was downright suspicious.

"There you are," James said, popping his head out from the kitchen. "Let's get on with this."

"Get on with what?"

James held up a manila envelope. It looked awfully like the envelope with the alibis. Siobhán reached for it. James held it above his head.

"Where did ye get that?"

"It was slipped under our door."

"Oh my God." Why? Because whoever had stolen it had either deleted an alibi or changed one. Now they were all ruined. She should take them to O'Brien right away and tell him everything.

"We have to call the detective sergeant," Siobhán said.

"Or," James said, "we have a little peek first."

"Peek," Gráinne and Ann chorused.

"Peek," Ciarán shouted.

"Eejits!" Eoin called from the kitchen.

Siobhán caught James's eye. "There's a bit more to the story."

James narrowed his eyes. "Like what?"

He wouldn't react any better to her encounter on the stairs than Macdara. And if he knew she'd been threatened with arrest if she continued investigating, she'd never get a look inside that envelope. And doctored or not, she so wanted to get a look inside that envelope. "Never mind. We peek, but not the young ones. Then we put everything back exactly the way we found it and then take it to O'Brien."

"Agree." Eoin was in the kitchen, Ann was busy with the vase of flowers, and Gráinne and Ann were in the back garden, playing with Trigger. James nodded for Siobhán to follow. They headed outside.

"They're going to hate me," Siobhán said as they hurried past the window.

"You'll be promising them chips, and telly, and sweets as usual."

Siobhán shrugged. There was no use denying it. It was better than them hating her. They entered Mike Granger's fruit and veg shop at the end of the street. Mike had been a dear friend of their father's and still looked after the O'Sullivans whenever he got the chance. He was at the counter and waved to them as they walked in. A balding man in his late forties, he was wearing his usual baseball cap and drinking a Diet Coke. "How ya?"

"Grand," Siobhán said. "Just here for a few bits and bobs."

He nodded and then turned his attention elsewhere. James grabbed a basket. "We'll pretend that's our shopping list," he said, pointing to the envelope. They hurried down a back aisle, past the other shoppers. The area in front of the vegetables was clear. "Jaysus," James said. "We forgot to steam it open."

"Eoin is right," Siobhán said. "We're eejits."

"We need a knife."

"Or." Siobhán ripped it open. O'Brien already knew the envelope had been snatched. No use preserving the seal.

"Why did you do that?"

"It was left on our doorstep," Siobhán said. "Who's to say he or she didn't rip it open."

"Smart," James said picking up a turnip and throwing it in the basket.

The first alibi Siobhán lifted out of the envelope belonged to Ronan. He wrote in all capital letters.

> SMOKED CIGARETTES
> TOOK PICTURES
> MURDERED KEVIN

"He's some cheek," Siobhán said.

James studied the confession. "The first two items are true. What if the third is as well?"

"He's definitely in the running," Siobhán said. She was dying to tell him of her other Ronan discoveries, but she needed to keep as much as possible close to her chest. Rumors and suppositions were dangerous animals that had to be penned in.

James pulled out the next one. Brian's. He had each day meticulously listed and every second accounted for. Siobhán went to the morning of the murder.

6:00 AM Awoke.
6-6:30 Shower and dress. Gray pinstriped suit with pink pocket square.

6:35   Tea and croissant in the kitchen with Chef
        Antoine.

6:40   Outside to begin erecting tents. Saw Martin
        Donnelly down the street. Saw Val at the gate.

6:45   Witnessed argument between Carol Huntsman
        and Colm Cahill at the front desk.

Siobhán read the last line again. That was the argument about the missing fax.

"It's almost too much information," James said.

"Maybe that's the point. Distract us."

"Seems a stretch."

"I agree. It's also very neat and tidy. Just like him."

"Too messy to kill someone with a rock to the back of the head?"

"Exactly. He seems like he'd go for a tidy method."

"Is there a tidy way to murder someone?"

Siobhán thought about it. "Poison?"

"Not for the recipient." James shuddered. Drink was a form of poison. Siobhán wondered if he was thinking the same thing.

She glanced at Brian's notes again. "There's a witness to everything he's listed. Easy enough to check. I'd say if we can confirm everything here, then we can safely eliminate him as a suspect."

"I'll check on these alibis," James said.

"You?"

"Can't have you diving into this alone."

She hesitated. If she demanded he stay out of it, he'd dive in even deeper. Besides, she couldn't do it all alone, and if anyone could handle himself, it was James. "Be careful."

He flashed a grin. "Who's next?"

The next alibi was written by Brenna. She only included the day of the murder. Either she hadn't been paying attention to Macdara's instructions or she didn't want anyone to know what she'd been up to before the day. Her handwriting was pretty but messy, kind of like herself:

> *Out to the pub Wednesday evening. In bed by half one. Visitor at two in the morning. Rose at 8 am Thursday. Tea and croissant. Out on the grounds with Alice, Faye, and Mrs. Cahill by half eight.*

"Visitor?" James raised an eyebrow.

"Kevin."

"You're joking."

"Nope."

"Do the guards know?"

"Yep."

"So we've learned nothing."

"Throw something else in that basket, will ye? The turnip looks lonely." They moved over, and James tossed in a few apples.

Siobhán slid Brenna's alibi back in the envelope. "We should check these accounts with Val."

"Who's that?"

"He's a security guard at the castle."

"Could he be a suspect too?"

"He's a bit of a dark horse alright."

"Why would he kill your man?"

"He's got a temper. It could have been impulsive. He also seems protective of the Huntsmans."

"A temper?" James said. He stepped forward protectively. "Did something happen?"

"Nothing I can't handle." The door to the shop burst open, startling them. Paul Donnelly stood just inside the doorway, breathing heavily. When he spotted Siobhán and James, he hurried over. Siobhán shoved the envelope behind her back. Not suspicious at all, like.

Despite the heavy breathing, Paul's hair looked as if it had been recently cut, and he had shaved. A groom preparing for a wedding. But his expression was anything but joyful. "I can't find Alice."

"I should think not," Siobhán said. "She and her mam have a huge to-do list."

"Mrs. Cahill is the one who just rang me. She said Alice didn't show up for a fitting."

A bride not show up for a wedding dress fitting? That was alarming. Paul held up his mobile. "I've called everyone. No one has seen her. She's not answering a single text or call. I never should have let her out of my sight."

"When was the last time you spoke to her?"

"She rang me from the flower shop."

"I was with her then," Siobhán said.

"Was everything alright?"

"Besides arguing about lilies, everything was grand." Brenna had never gotten around to telling Siobhán her secret. How she knew why Kevin had gone to the hilltop that morning. Something about a note. After Alice and her mother interrupted them, there had been no chance to follow up.

"I'm going to find Macdara and see if he'll drive me around," Paul said.

"I'll look around the shops in town. She could be running wedding errands."

Paul looked hopeful. "So no reason to alert the guards?"

"Let's not panic yet," Siobhán said. "If we don't get anywhere with everyone searching, we'll definitely call the guards."

"I'll follow up with our messages," James said, taking the envelope of alibis from Siobhán. "Then I'll say hello to O'Brien."

"Thank you." Siobhán should have been the one dropping off the alibis. But finding Alice was more important.

"It could just be cold feet," Siobhán said to Paul as they exited the shop. "That's normal."

"Normal," Paul said with a twinge of sadness. "I'd give anything for a little bit of normal."

Chapter 23

The bell jangled as Siobhán stepped into Courtney's Gift Shop. One of the tiniest shops in town, Courtney's made up for the lack of square footage by being neat and cheerful. They sold accessories for women, many of them handmade by Bridie. Annmarie stood behind the counter, her hands fumbling in the cash drawer. Her head was tilted unnaturally to the side. When Siobhán drew closer, she could see Annmarie was actually on her mobile, cradling the phone without her hands. She rolled her eyes at Siobhán, slammed the register shut, and then used a free hand to pick up her mobile as she continued her phone conversation. "I won't. I won't. I won't. Yeah, yeah, yeah. I won't. Bye-bye. Bye, bye, bye, bye," she sang and hung up with a sigh. "My mam is reeling from the news of another murder in Kilbane. She wants me to move to Spain with her."

Siobhán could only imagine how painful the news was after losing Courtney.

"My sister loved this shop," Annmarie said with a sigh. "If I were to abandon it, I'd feel like I was abandoning her." She sighed. "At least this time the killer is from outside Kilbane."

That hadn't been determined at all, but Siobhán wasn't going to fan the flames of fear. She also wanted to grill Annmarie to find out if she was the local who was seen kissing Colm, but finding the bride was the first priority. "Have you seen Alice Cahill recently?"

Annmarie gazed out the window. "I was hoping she'd be with you. I've been waiting here every day, and no one has so much as popped their head in. I heard you took them shopping in Charleville instead."

"Not instead. We had to order flowers."

"So they'll be coming in here?"

"I hope so. First we have to find the bride." Annmarie was browned off that they hadn't visited; now was definitely not the time to get any information out of her. Siobhán was headed out when Annmarie called for her to stop.

"There's something else. I'm not sure if I should mention it." Annmarie practically flew out from behind the counter.

"Go on."

She played with the pearls around her neck. "Have you heard anything?"

"Anything?" Siobhán said. Maybe this was exactly the right time.

"I don't know. What's the gossip?"

Annmarie definitely looked guilty of something, Siobhán decided to play it cool. "Right now I'm just looking for the bride."

Annmarie's face scrunched with worry. "I saw something." It came out as a hurried whisper.

Siobhán stepped forward. "Go on."

"I mean, I could be wrong."

"Please." Was she going to confess to kissing Colm? Did Susan hire her?

"It's one of the travelers. I saw him pass by me window. He was wearing a gold watch."

Siobhán had to stop and recalculate. "That's what you wanted to tell me?"

Annmarie frowned. "Don't you think it could be important?"

Not as important as you being paid to set up a married man. "Right, right, of course." There was no use getting Annmarie's guard up. She would have to come back at it when she figured out the right approach. Siobhán replayed what Annmarie said. A traveler with a gold watch. That was unusual. First of all, it was rare to see the travelers in town. Secondly, Kevin had a gold chain and a gold watch. What were the chances that it was a coincidence? She would have to look into it as soon as she found the bride.

"Is there anything else you can tell me about the traveler?"

Annmarie frowned. "I think he was wearing a green cap." Siobhán thanked her and hurried out.

—

Siobhán checked the Kilbane Inn next. Margaret was standing out on the footpath with her ear pressed up against one of the doors.

"What are you doing?"

Margaret screeched and jumped back. "Listen!" She grabbed Siobhán, stuck a glass in her hand, and shoved her up against the door. Siobhán hardly had a choice, so she used the glass to listen. Inside, she could hear Colm Cahill and Susan Cahill screaming at each other.

Colm was the first voice she heard. "Just tell me. Is it true?"

"You have no idea." The sounds of something slamming.

Susan screamed something back, but the only word Siobhán could make out was "money."

"I will never let you get away with this," Colm screamed, clear as day. Heavy steps. Getting closer.

Jaysus. Siobhán jumped back, whirled around, and gently started shoving Margaret out of harm's way. As the door burst open and Colm stepped out, Margaret hoisted up the glass and began pretend-drinking out of it as if she and Siobhán were rehearsing a scene out of an amateur stage play.

Colm stopped short when he saw them, his face bright red with rage. "Where's my daughter?" he screamed at Siobhán.

"I was hoping you could tell me," Siobhán said.

"My wife says she ran out of the shop in her wedding dress."

"In her wedding dress?" This was new.

Colm flailed his arms. "Some sort of fitting."

"She ran out *in* her wedding dress?"

Colm clenched his fists. "I just said so, didn't I?"

Susan ran out of the room with a suitcase clutched in her hand.

"Where are you going?" Colm yelled.

"I'm not staying with you for one second longer," Susan yelled back. She stopped in front of Siobhán. "I'll stay with you."

"Me?" Siobhán couldn't have possibly heard right.

"I'd rather stick a fork in my eye. I can't wait to get out of this bloody village. But yes. You."

"There are six of us and only four beds," Siobhán said. Susan started to sob. It was more disconcerting than anything the woman had done or said so far.

"You deserve it," Colm said. He headed back for the room and slammed the door. Susan looked at Siobhán, tears spilling out of her eyes.

"I'm going to tell that photographer to publish his exposé. Every single word."

"Ronan?"

"He's not really here to photograph the wedding. He's here to spy on Alice for that evil gossip rag."

So Susan knew about the deal with the *Irish Enquirer*. Who was her source? "How do you know this?"

"Told me himself. Wanted to see if I would bid higher before he started selling them all his photos. Said he could make a mint off of us unraveling."

And he was probably right.

"The guards have attempted to confiscate all his photos," Siobhán assured her.

"What if he has them all on some little stick?" Susan said.

"A USB?"

"I don't know if it's from the States or not. Who cares at a time like this?"

Siobhán didn't bother to educate her about USB sticks. "I'll have Macdara question him again, but shouldn't you be more worried about the fact that we can't find Alice?"

"Don't be daft. She always does this. She's having a walkabout."

"A walkabout? In her wedding dress?"

Susan sighed. "One minute we were standing there, and I was simply telling her the dress was too tight. The next thing you know, Chef Antoine walks in with her lunch, and she's tearing out of there."

Chef Antoine. Had he said or done something to upset her? "She's always been impulsive and rebellious," Susan continued. "Her trainers are missing from her room. She always has to walk when she's upset."

"Good to know." The morning they met, Alice said she was walking the road outside the castle. People were creatures of habit. Perhaps that's where Siobhán would find her. And if nothing else, it was the perfect excuse to get in a run.

"Where are you going?" Susan called after Siobhán. "You're supposed to take me to your house."

"Ask Margaret if she has another room," Siobhán said. "Unless you want to sleep in the back garden with our new pup, Trigger, we simply don't have the room."

Chapter 24

After changing into her running clothes, Siobhán kept a steady pace and headed down the road toward the castle. Annmarie had given her something new to chew on, but if Siobhán was right about Susan hiring her, she was definitely holding back vital information. And she seemed unusually spooked, although another murder in Kilbane could definitely do that to a gal.

Macdara hadn't answered any of her calls. She left him a message to fill him in on the traveler with the gold watch. She was going to have to pay a visit to the travelers' camp. There no longer seemed to be enough hours in a day, and time flew when she was investigating a crime. She wouldn't dare go as far as to admit that she was enjoying it, but it did challenge her on so many levels. And she welcomed challenges; there was no denying that. Were there any courses in those college catalogs at home that would come close to giving her this kind of rush?

The air was crisp and filled with the smell of wood smoke. Clear skies were above, but it had rained overnight, and Siobhán could feel the vestiges of the damp in her bones as she jogged. Her breathing became labored more quickly than usual. She passed through the entrance gate. She was now outside the walls on the road to the castle. When she was nearly there, she caught a flash of white thrashing around on the ground. Alice, in her wedding dress, was wrestling with someone in the dirt. Siobhán thrust herself forward, running as fast as she could. As she drew closer, she could see that Alice was in a tussle with a man. Siobhán screamed, hoping that might be enough to make him let her go. When she finally reached them, she could see it was Val that Alice was struggling with.

"Let her go!" Siobhán said. But even as the words were out of her mouth, she caught the terrified look on Val's face, and then saw it was Alice who had a firm grip on him. Her nails were dug into his arms.

"She's gone mental!" Val yelled.

"He stole my ring," Alice said. "It's him."

"Let go now," Siobhán said, as she peeled Alice's fingers from Val's arms. Alice's fingernails were caked with dirt, along with her wedding dress and most of her face. Siobhán soon spotted the reason, Alice had been frantic-ally digging in the dirt with her hands.

Val stared up, his face beet red, hands already up in the air. Siobhán knew firsthand that Val was capable of getting rough. Had he manhandled Alice the way he'd grabbed Siobhán in the castle?

"I found her digging," Val said. "Tried to calm her down. She clawed me." He began to walk backward.

"Stay right there," Siobhán said in the sternest voice she could muster. Val backed up a few more feet. "If you take one more step, I'll call the guards and have you arrested."

"But she attacked me!" Val said.

"Who do you think they're going to believe?" Siobhán said. "The pair of us, or you?" It wasn't like her to lie and threaten so, but if there was a valid reason Alice thought Val stole her diamond, she didn't want him out of their sight.

She knelt down on the ground next to the now sobbing Alice.

"He told me he'd buried it somewhere along here," she wailed. "Will you help me dig?"

"I told her no such thing," Val said.

"Not you," Alice said. "Chef Antoine."

"Chef Antoine said he saw Val burying your ring here?"

Alice nodded. "He came to deliver my lunch. And he was nearly crying from keeping this secret from me, but he could see how upset I was about the ring. He said Val steals from the guests and buries the things near his post." She pointed to the entrance gate, which was indeed Val's usual post. Had Val knocked Siobhán down the stairs? He had certainly been there. But why would Val want the alibis? His wasn't amongst them. Unless he was just trying to solve the case ahead of Siobhán?

But the push had been so violent.

Val's eyes flickered, and he looked as if he were about to cry. "He's lying. Miss Cahill, that French barbarian is lying. If anyone's a thief, it's him!"

"Where are the guards?" Police cars were parked everywhere, including the van from Cork University Morgue.

Val pointed to the woods. "They're on the hill with the state pathologist. She's just arrived."

Siobhán took Alice by the hand and hauled her up. "I have to dig," Alice cried.

"No," Siobhán said. "You don't." She pulled her away from the hole, away from Val. "Let's walk."

"He'll just wait until we're gone and dig it up," Alice cried. "I want my diamond ring!"

"I didn't do it," Val said. "She's mental."

"I'm the freaking bride. I'm allowed to be mental!" Alice was screaming now.

"I'll have a guard watch this area," Siobhán said.

"I don't need to be minded," Val said. "I didn't do anything."

"Why are you still here anyway?" Siobhán said.

"What do you mean?"

"The Huntsmans are gone. There are no guests. What are you still doing here?"

"I've been given permission."

"But why?"

"Where would you rather stay? In that sad little inn or in a castle?"

"Seems like it would be lonely."

"I like watching the guards work. I don't plan on being a security guard forever."

He sounded sincere. And the guilt crept back into his voice. That was the secret he was keeping. His ambition. He was embarrassed about his post as a mere security guard. Probably fancied himself a detective superintendent. So if he wasn't stealing trinkets from guests and burying them, why on earth had Chef Antoine said that?

Alice began racewalking toward Kilbane.

Siobhán turned to Val, who was staring after her with a tortured look on his face. "Why would Chef Antoine accuse you of such a thing?"

"I have no idea." Val's face flushed a deep crimson, and he looked away. Siobhán had no time to press him; she had a runaway bride on her hands.

Alice ended up by the river just across the bridge and just short of the abbey. She was staring into the water as if she were thinking about tossing herself in.

"It's peaceful here," Alice said quietly. With her dirt-streaked face and filthy wedding dress, Alice Cahill looked anything but peaceful. Siobhán was grateful Ronan wasn't nearby with his camera. Unfortunately, this would have been the cover photo for the *Irish Enquirer*. People loved it when the rich and beautiful were down and dirty.

"Do you think Val is the killer?" Siobhán asked gently.

Alice whirled around. "What?"

"If he stole your ring, he could have robbed Kevin that morning."

"It's crossed my mind," Alice said. "But…"

"But?"

"Robbing people is one thing. But murder? That seems like too big of a leap."

"I'm inclined to agree. The killing feels very angry to me."

"Meaning someone who knew him."

"Yes."

"Loved him, even." A small sob escaped her lips. Alice slapped her hand over her mouth as if she hadn't expected to say it.

In fact, it was a funny thing to say. Siobhán wanted to keep her talking. "Right."

Tears spilled over onto Alice's cheeks. "Like Paul," she whispered.

Siobhán felt a little zap of electricity. "Like Paul?"

"My father thinks… He thinks…" Alice started sobbing. Great heaves came out of her. Siobhán waited. When the tears finally stopped, she wiped her face with her hands. "It's nonsense! I can't believe I'm even

238

repeating it." She grabbed Siobhán. "Please forget I said that. Daddy's been doing everything he can think of to come between us."

"Your father thinks what?"

"He thinks Paul killed Kevin," Alice cried out again.

"But why on earth would Paul kill Kevin?"

Alice shook her head. "I told you to forget I ever said it."

"It's okay. We're just eliminating him. This is how you do it. You have to walk through every scenario, no matter how outlandish."

Alice took a deep breath and nodded. "Kevin was hinting around that he knew secrets about Paul."

Siobhán stepped forward. "What secrets?"

"He didn't say. That's why I didn't take it seriously; he was just messing."

"What exactly did Kevin say?"

"He said that he could tell me secrets about Paul that would make me not want to marry him."

"Kevin said that to you."

Alice paused. "No. Brenna did. She overheard them that night." Alice's hands flew to her mouth. "Do you think Brenna was lying?"

"Did she say anything else?"

Alice nodded. "She said Paul was furious. Roaring and shouting at Kevin. That's when he told him he'd find a new best man."

"Let's just follow one trail at a time. If Kevin was telling the truth, what type of secret do you think Paul might be keeping?"

Alice's face stilled. "I can't talk to you. You're practically a guard."

"I'm not. I'm just a person."

"You're trying to solve this case."

"Aren't you?"

Alice gazed down at the river, then met Siobhán's eyes. "We're just talking here to clear him. Right?"

"Absolutely."

"Promise me you won't tell anyone."

"I promise." Siobhán crossed her fingers behind her back.

"Paul had dirt underneath his fingernails." Alice covered her mouth again as if she couldn't believe she'd just said it.

Siobhán gently placed her hand on Alice's arm. "When?"

"The morning Kevin was killed. When he came across the lawn and kissed me."

"You're sure?"

"Paul always has impeccable nails. He's tidy to a fault."

"Did you ask him about it?"

"I didn't get the chance. I was about to tease him, ask him if he'd been digging in the dirt with his hands, when Chef Antoine came running out of the woods."

"Why didn't you ask him later?"

"Because he'd cleaned up by then, and of course I didn't think for a minute that my fiancé had picked up a rock and smashed Kevin in the back of the head."

Siobhán edged forward. "And now? What do you think now?"

Alice's blue eyes seemed to pale. Her mouth trembled when she spoke. "What if it wasn't Val at all? What if *Paul's* the one Chef Antoine saw burying something near the wall?"

Siobhán was about to joke that it was impossible to mistake Val for Paul when she thought about it. Val's uniform was the same shade as the tracksuits. They were both tall men. From a distance, spotting someone kneeling down in the dirt, it was possible. Chef Antoine expected to see Val near his post, therefore bolstering his conviction that it was Val.

Alice let out the last of her fears, in a single gush. "What if it was Paul he saw, and what if he was burying Kevin's things? What if my father is right? What if I'm about to marry a murderer?"

Chapter 25

The travelers' camp was overgrown with weeds. It made Siobhán doubly sad. First, for neglecting her father's herb garden, and second, for silently judging them about the state of theirs. She counted six caravans in the field, at least three propped up with cinder blocks and leaning to the side. Toys and debris were flung about the lawn. In the centre of the caravans was a fire pit. Ashes were piled around it. A child sat near the pit, poking at the ashes with a stick. His face and clothes were smeared with dirt. He couldn't have been more than three years of age. She wanted to scoop him up, clean him off, and take him home. Then again, the lads in her family had come home many a time covered in dirt and mud. Alice Cahill herself had just looked like a grown-up replica of the dirty child. Siobhán had deposited her at the inn and called in Gráinne and Ann to tend to her. They were thrilled to do it, and it took some sting out of not letting them read the alibis. Siobhán waved and smiled at the child. He or she (she could not be sure) did not return either gesture.

An old woman came to the door of the caravan closest to the child and yelled something at Siobhán, who couldn't understand a word. The woman came out of the caravan, slamming the door behind her. She picked up the child and disappeared inside. This had been a bad idea. She didn't even know the name of the man she was looking for. She turned to head out when she spotted a green cap near the caravan closest to the exit. Didn't Annmarie say he was wearing a green cap? She went and rapped on the door. After a second, a curtain on the caravan twitched. Siobhán waited. Nothing happened. She knocked again. The curtain opened, and the window popped up. A man stuck his head out. He could have been thirty or fifty, it was hard to tell. Most of his face was concealed by facial hair. But she could see a gold chain around his neck.

"I dinna see a t'ing," he said straightaway.

"Your watch and chain." Siobhán pointed to his neck. "They belong to a dead man."

The traveler cocked his head to one side. "He issna gon ta need it den, is he?" The man was difficult to understand, his word slurring together.

"I need to know exactly where you found them."

"Buried inna dirt. They're mine."

"Near the castle?"

The window slammed shut. The curtain fell back. Siobhán took a step back, thinking that was all she was going to get out of him when the door to the caravan popped open with a squeak. He was so rail thin she wanted to cry out. Clothes hung off him. The watch was taped to his wrist so that it wouldn't fall off. He looked at her and nodded.

Was he answering her question in the affirmative or just greeting her? She decided to go with the former. "Where exactly near the castle?"

"They're mine." He shook his wrist. The tape held. There was a possibility that this was the killer, but he didn't seem to be hiding the fact that he had Kevin's belongings. She was sure he'd discovered the loot after the murder.

"They're evidence." She didn't have a clue as to whether or not he even understood her.

"Git." He threw his arm up like an elephant's trunk, signaling which way she should leave.

"I'm not trying to take them. Just tell me exactly where you found them, that's all." She'd let the guards decide whether or not to come for the items.

"Mine," he said. This was getting her nowhere. She'd have to send the guards back. She felt guilty doing it, but she snapped a photo of him with her phone. He actually smiled, showing his cavernous mouth. Siobhán's stomach turned. Maybe she'd leave a basket of brown bread.

She started to walk away when he called out to her. "I'll give ya da note for a tenner."

—

Siobhán found Brenna in Sheila Mahoney's hair salon. Her head was wrapped in tinfoil, and she was laughing it up with Sheila, who had a cigarette in one hand and a pair of scissors in the other. Siobhán shoved the note under her nose.

More when the deed is done. Meet me at
sunrise. Top of the hill.

"That's it," Brenna said. "Where did you get it?"

"This is the note that Kevin took from your bedroom?"

"I just said so, didn't I?"

"But it wasn't really to him?"

Brenna sighed and rolled her eyes at Sheila, who shook her head in empathy. "Hurry it up," Sheila said. "We have to rinse."

"Who wrote this note?"

"Colm wrote the note. To me. He slipped it under my door Tuesday evening. We met at the top of the hill Wednesday morning. That's when he paid me to seduce Paul."

"Oh, luv," Sheila said, "I would have done that for free." They cackled like a pair of witches and didn't even notice when Siobhán walked out of the salon.

—

Siobhán headed for the gardai station, turning the note over in her mind. So Kevin woke up, most likely with a wicked hangover. He saw the note and the money on Brenna's nightstand. Most likely he thought they were for him. He went to the top of the hill. But whoever was waiting up there hadn't been waiting for Kevin.

Colm Cahill was the intended victim. He was the one who announced he planned on hiking up to the top of the hillside every morning; he was a man of routines, the one the killer expected to find.

And if all that was true, then the job was left unfinished, and Colm Cahill was in grave danger.

There were black smudges all over the note. Something about that tickled a faint memory for Siobhán, but every time she tried to catch it, every time the thought came close, it flittered away again. Black smudge, black smudge, black smudge. The dirt Alice had been digging in by Val's post was brown. So where had she seen a black smudge?

—

Instead of being grateful that she had turned over the note, O'Brien was furious with her.

245

"I told you to take three steps back." Once again they were crammed into his temporary office. Siobhán didn't understand how anyone could solve a crime from behind a desk. No wonder they weren't making any headway.

"That's why I'm giving the note to you and letting you know that the traveler has Kevin's watch and chain. And one more thing—"

"You went and confronted the traveler all on your own. Against strict orders!"

He had her there. Siobhán stood tall. "You said you weren't interested in my theories, so I had to verify it as fact before I brought it to ye." O'Brien's eyes narrowed into little slits, and he motioned for her to leave.

"Kevin Gallagher wasn't the intended victim. I believe Colm Cahill was."

O'Brien rose. He pointed to the door. "Get out."

"I think Colm Cahill is in mortal danger. What if the killer tries to finish what he started?"

"Did you know that the victim had Macdara's garda cap under his hand?"

Siobhán was startled. Why was he asking her that? "Kevin lifted it off Macdara the night before. He was wearing it as a joke."

"The answer is yes. You knew, and you said nothing."

"Surely you're not pointing a finger at Macdara?"

"Right now I'm pointing a finger at me door. Get out."

"This really isn't about me. You need to put a guard on Colm Cahill—"

"I'm going to say it once more. And if you're still standing in front of me, I'm locking you in a cell. Get. Out."

Despite it being an overgrown jungle, Chef Antoine was delighted with the O'Sullivans' herb garden in their little patch of heaven out back. After each new leaf he discovered, he gave a cry of joy, as if he had just discovered a new country. Eoin followed him around with Trigger attached to his heels. Siobhán was pacing around, trying to calm herself down. O'Brien had been so rude. What's worse, she knew she was right. Colm Cahill had a target on his back. Siobhán had texted Macdara that she urgently needed to see him, but he had yet to respond. She knew O'Brien would carry through with his threat of locking her away if she caused any more trouble, but she couldn't possibly keep this development to herself. Not when a man's life was at stake. If no one else listened to her, she would have to warn Colm Cahill in person.

Once in a while she caught Trigger staring at her as if he were plotting her demise. Ciarán was right. She would have to start giving him treats.

"This garden must be tended," Chef Antoine said. "Shame, shame, shame."

Siobhán indeed felt ashamed. She had even resorted to buying jars of herbs at the shop, something her ma and da would have found outrageous.

Chef Antoine began to clear out the weeds, plucking off leaves, smelling them, and either sighing with joy or crinkling his nose. "You need to place little signs," he said. "Mint, rosemary, thyme—" Chef Antoine began rattling off the Latin names.

To Siobhán's surprise, Eoin delighted in them and began to repeat after the chef. Siobhán was thrilled to see him engrossed in something other than comic books or eBay.

"I know this one," Eoin said, brushing a bordering shrub with his foot. "Laurel." He beamed and looked at Chef Antoine for praise.

"Laurus nobilis," Chef Antoine said, coming closer. He bent down and examined the shrub with one eye. Then he shot up. "Non," he said. "Big mistake." He shook his head and wagged his finger at Eoin.

"How so?" Siobhán said. He sounded slightly threatening, and her mother-bear shackles were up.

"This is cherry laurel."

"Lovely," Siobhán said. "I love cherries."

"Will it produce cherries?" Eoin asked. He turned to Siobhán. "We could make a pie."

"Non, non. Unless you want this pie to kill your patrons."

Siobhán stepped back. "Pardon?"

"Cyanide. This foliage has an abundance of cyanide."

"You're joking me," Eoin said.

"Many, many plants have poison," Chef Antoine said. "The world is wild and dangerous, no?"

"What other plants are poisonous?" The thrill was evident in Eoin's voice. Chef Antoine's cool factor had shot up exponentially.

"Socrates, you hear of him?" Chef Antoine twirled the end of his mustache.

Siobhán held her breath. "The philosopher?" Eoin said. Siobhán exhaled. Thanks be to God, he was learning something in school.

"Killed by poison hemlock!" Chef Antoine said. "Ze hell broth."

"Hell broth," Eoin echoed, fascinated. He looked around the garden. "Do we have any here?"

The chef took a moment to cast his gaze around the yard. "No," he said, sounding almost as disappointed as Eoin.

"Wait for me." Eoin stuck his hand up, then ran back into the garden.

"Could this kill animals?" Siobhán asked.

"Animals, they are smart. No eat."

Eoin returned with Ciarán's *Big Book of Poisons.* "What else?" Eoin rubbed his hands together in gleeful anticipation.

"Let's not monopolize all of the chef's time—" Siobhán started to say.

"The leaf of the evergreen yew." Chef Antoine leaned into Eoin and lowered his voice. Eoin began flipping through the book. They were both enjoying this way too much.

"Here it is," Eoin exclaimed, jabbing a page of the book with his finger. "Do we have that?" He sounded extremely hopeful.

"Here? Non. But you will find it in abundance in the churchyard. It is the shrubs that line all along the back."

Siobhán knew the exact shrubs he was talking about. They had always been behind the church. "But they're so pretty," she said.

"Oui, oui," Chef Antoine said nodding his head. "Pretty to look. Not so pretty to eat."

"Deadly," Eoin said.

"Oui," Chef Antoine said, missing Eoin's vernacular use of the word. Siobhán supposed it was better than "awesome," but in these circumstances she'd prefer the latter.

"One more!" Chef Antoine said, seeming as delighted as Eoin. "Tooth of ze wolf."

"A wolf?" Eoin's eyes were huge.

"Grows in the late summer. A flower. Wolf's bane. If you consume this?" Antoine snapped his finger. "Heart attack. Death. Very, very fast."

"Very, very fast," Eoin echoed. He flipped through the book, then showed the page to Chef Antoine, who nodded. Eoin turned the corner of the page down. "Is it still around?"

"Yes. I would say, you can still find for a little while longer. Hidden in amongst herbs and shrubs. Little deadly flower. Little, bad wolf."

"Great lesson, lads," Siobhán said. "How do we get rid of every single poisonous leaf?"

Chef Antoine reached down, grabbed a fistful of cherry laurel, and threw it on the weed pile. "Like this," he said. "Dangerous to eat. Not to touch." Siobhán and Eoin donned gloves and helped pull out the rest of it. Soon they were pulling weeds and piling them up in the corner. After a half an hour, Siobhán was starting to sweat. That was it for her.

"Why don't we go back inside for a nice cup of tea with a sprig of mint?"

"Little bad wolf," Eoin said, mesmerized. "Wait until I tell the lads about this." Just then the back door opened, and Macdara stepped out.

"We have a cyanide back here!" Eoin exclaimed.

"Good for you," Macdara said. "Siobhán? Do you have time for a chat?"

Chapter 26

They went for a walk down Sarsfield Street. It was late afternoon on a Friday, and folks were bustling in and out of the shops, and slipping into the pubs. They found themselves gravitating toward the chipper. Siobhán stopped before going in. "I think Colm Cahill was the intended victim. Not Kevin. And I'm worried the killer is going to try to finish what he started."

"Why are you so sure?"

Siobhán told him about Brenna's note.

"So it was a complete fluke that Kevin was at the top of the hill that morning."

"Exactly," Siobhán said. "But O'Brien didn't want to hear a word of it."

Macdara nodded and lowered his voice. "The story on Ronan checks out. He was hired to do an exposé. Paid a lot of money. Admits the camera card was taken off him—"

"Isn't that motive for murder?" Ronan had been eager to get to the crime scene. Ronan was furious about his camera being smashed up. And Ronan loved stirring up drama and then photographing the aftermath. Had he staged a murder for his sick artistic purposes?

"He had a secret backup of all his photos. I don't think he's our killer."

"You found his backup?"

Macdara nodded. "The guards confiscated a USB."

Siobhán began to pace as she played the scene over in her mind. The prenup. Colm kissing another woman—probably Annmarie. Ronan capturing it on film.

That photo was worth a fortune to Susan Cahill. Or Colm. But if Susan had the photo, and Siobhán was right about Colm being the intended victim, why try to kill him? Why not just kill him in court with the evidence of adultery? She was just speculating. Maybe Annmarie could shed some light on the situation. Siobhán was going to have to pay her another visit. Siobhán sighed and filled Macdara in on Alice's tussle with Val. "Where was she digging?" Macdara looked on high alert.

"Near the wall. Chef Antoine told her he'd seen Val burying something." It reminded her that she'd completely forgotten to ask Chef Antoine why he thought Val was a thief and why he'd waited until just recently to tell Alice. She'd been too preoccupied with her latest run-in with O'Brien. Macdara was frowning. She knew him too well. He was hiding something from her. "What?"

"It's official guard business." Macdara looked away from her.

He was so infuriating sometimes. But this was no time for a fight. "You found Kevin's things buried near the wall, didn't you?"

"Me? No. I didn't."

"Spill it," Siobhán said, pointing her finger at Macdara.

He sighed. "The guards indeed found a small hole had been dug by the wall. Kevin's lighter, ID, and hotel key were found. His watch and gold chain were missing."

"Because the killer buried all the items there, but the traveler dug them up," Siobhán said. "He probably had no idea the items belonged to a murder victim, and of course he only took what was of interest to him."

Macdara nodded. "So Chef Antoine was correct."

"Why didn't Chef Antoine report this to the guards?" Siobhán wondered out loud.

"Maybe he's taking a page from your book," Macdara said.

"What if Chef Antoine only thought it was Val he saw digging? What if he saw someone else?"

"Who else?" Macdara's frown was back.

Siobhán dodged the question. She didn't want to get into another row about Paul. The fact that Macdara couldn't even consider him as a suspect meant he couldn't do this investigation justice. She lobbed a question of her own. "What all did they find buried near the wall?"

"Hotel key. Lighter. Identification." Macdara looked away again. He was holding something back.

"And?"

"I'm not supposed to say."

Siobhán threw up her arms. "I'm not a suspect."

"But you're not a guard either. And O'Brien has made it clear to me too. You are to stay completely out of this."

"Come on!" Siobhán knew she should offer some reasonable explanation as to why Macdara should ignore his superior and listen to her, but there really was none.

Macdara held up his index finger. "Not a word to anyone. And no more investigating."

Siobhán put her hand to her heart. "Not a bother."

"You said that way too quick."

"Not a word to anyone." Siobhán mimed zipping her lips shut.

"And no more investigating."

"Who's investigating? I'm just trying to keep a bride from having a complete breakdown. Did you find the diamond ring?"

"No."

"Are you sure?"

"Of course I'm sure. But we did find a thousand euros and another piece of that red ribbon that you somehow got Brenna to cough up."

"They weren't after the money," Siobhán said, more to herself than Macdara.

"Or they planned on coming back for it," Macdara said.

"Why wouldn't the traveler take the money? Especially when he had the note?"

"We surmised it was a matter of where each item was buried. The euros were found at the bottom of the hole, way underneath the other items, much deeper. My guess is that something—an animal most likely—disturbed the hiding place and the shiny gold watch and chain caught the eye of the traveler. The note must have been toward the top as well. He probably grabbed them as quickly as he could, then saw nothing but the lighter, hotel key, and ID. With so many guards around the castle, I'm sure he grabbed his treasures up as fast as he could. Had he dug a little deeper he would have found the euros."

Siobhán mulled it over. It was a likely theory. She put the traveler aside for a moment. The important bit was the killer. The killer didn't want to be caught with Kevin's possessions and didn't have any other choice but to bury them? Perhaps Chef Antoine had discovered the body sooner than the killer had expected and he or she had panicked.

Paul had dirt underneath his fingernails. Paul would have a motive to kill Colm Cahill. And he was the right height. Easy to lob a rock at the back of his head. Siobhán wanted to discuss all of this with Macdara, but he was liable to blow a gasket.

"Oh, no," Macdara said.

"What?" Siobhán said.

"I can hear the wheels turning in your head."

"With the distraction of a wedding, the killer might let their guard down. We have to make sure we're watching. Carefully watching."

"You're using a wedding to catch a killer?"

"Do you have a better idea?"

Macdara stared at her. "Why can't you just be a normal girl and catch the bouquet?"

"How about I be a normal girl right now and eat curry chips with you?"

"That'll have to do," Macdara said opening the door to the chipper and waving her inside. "That'll have to do."

Chapter 27

Inside Saint Mary's Cathedral, it was beginning to look a lot like a wedding. Bunches of white lilies tied with red ribbon were attached to the ends of the pews. Apparently Susan Cahill had gotten her way. Siobhán wished she could rip the lilies off and replace them with white roses, but, alas, that was not to be. Still, things were looking up. Macdara had spoken with the guards, who had promised to keep an extra eye on Colm Cahill. For once, instead of hurtling accusations at each other, the Cahill/Donnelly wedding guests were putting their attention on something besides murder. There was an almost jovial atmosphere in the air. Brian was humming. Chef Antoine had been in the kitchen since way before sunrise, and Ronan was photographing pre-wedding activities. Even the sun was shining for the big day. The volunteer fireman had safely removed the bird nest from the abbey, ensuring that Alice would get her outdoor wedding after all. Siobhán was actually on her way to help Brian set up for the reception, but as soon as she descended the church steps, Faye Donnelly stepped in front of her.

She was dressed in a warm cream suit with a matching pillbox hat. Her hair was tucked into a bun, and a spot of coral lip balm completed the picture. Siobhán was about to compliment her when Faye put her finger to her lips. Confused, Siobhán looked around.

Faye lowered her head. "I have to talk to you. Alone."

Siobhán looked around once more. There wasn't a soul in sight, just a sparrow flitting about a tree. "We are alone."

Faye swept her eyes over the grounds. "Someone could come out at any moment."

"I'm headed for the abbey. Do you want to walk with me?"

Faye nodded and began to follow Siobhán. "Are you close to figuring out the guilty party?"

"Today I'm just focusing on the wedding. Why?"

"Do you really think that every little bit of information is important?"

Siobhán stopped, turned to Faye. "I do. What is it?"

Faye's eyes were wide with fear. Siobhán's heart sank. Maybe this wasn't going to be the perfect day. Her heart strings tugged. Alice and Paul deserved their day. Faye's eyes clicked nervously up and down the street. "Maybe I should tell the guards instead."

Siobhán knew that if Faye had wanted to tell the guards, she'd be speaking to them right now. "I can promise I'll pass on your information to the guards," Siobhán said, keeping her voice light.

"What about Martin?"

"What about him?"

"He told me you were questioning him. He didn't do it."

Was this all it was about? Faye was worried Siobhán thought Martin was a murderer? "I've been speaking to everyone. Did you know Susan switched to his transport company at the last minute?" Faye's eyes flicked up and to the right. "If the guards have the wrong end of the stick, I'll make sure to straighten them out."

"What end of the stick is that?"

Siobhán began walking again, picking up her speed slightly so Faye would have to run after her. "That you're blackmailing Susan Cahill."

"Blackmail?" Faye said. She sounded indignant. "I simply asked Susan to use Martin's trucks."

Siobhán stopped. "Why?"

"Because business has been slow lately. He was losing confidence. Believe me. You don't want to be around Martin when he's depressed."

"I'm very sorry to hear that. But I meant why did Susan agree to make the switch?"

"I'm not blackmailing her."

"I don't have time for lies."

"How dare you?"

"We all know Susan Cahill doesn't do good deeds. You must have convinced her somehow."

"You know what I do for a living."

Siobhán stopped walking. They were by the Kilbane Museum, nearly to the edge of the field. In the distance was the abbey. "You're handling Susan's divorce. I also know there's an ironclad prenup as well as an incriminating photo that Susan Cahill either has in her possession or would kill to get her hands on."

A slight smile appeared on Faye's soft face. "My, my, my. You are a good investigator."

"Thank you." Siobhán started to cross to the field. Faye was taking her time getting to the point, and Siobhán wasn't going to play games. If she enjoyed pulling teeth, she would have become a dentist.

Faye reached for her. "There's more."

"Go on then."

"I shouldn't have said it." Worry lines appeared in Faye's forehead.

"Said what?"

"During the last meeting I had with Susan, I said something I will regret for the rest of my life." In the distance, the bells from Saint Mary's began to toll. "I said the only way you're going to see any money without that picture is over his dead body."

Despite the sun beating down on them, Siobhán shivered. "Who was the woman in the picture? Describe her."

"Older than you but much younger than me. Brown hair in a bob. Glitzy clothes and makeup and slightly overweight."

Annmarie. Was that why Annmarie had seemed so on edge?

No wonder she was acting so strange, talking about moving to Spain. The store had been struggling ever since Courtney died. Annmarie wasn't normally the sort to do such a thing, but desperate times and all. Siobhán felt a wave of grief for Annmarie. She knew what it was like to never have enough money.

"Susan Cahill doesn't have the photo," Siobhán said. "That's why you're so worried."

Faye looked around again, and then her voice dropped to a whisper. "Everyone looked alike in their tracksuits."

Siobhán suddenly saw what Faye was trying to confess. Without the picture, Susan Cahill would get nothing. "You think Susan Cahill went up to the top of that hill to kill her husband."

Faye's hands flew over her mouth. She could barely manage a nod. When she spoke again, her voice was strangled. "It's my fault. Oh. It's all my fault!"

"Please calm down."

"It was just a silly comment. How was I to know she would take me so seriously?" Faye cried out again. Siobhán was terrified the woman was going to faint dead away.

She grasped her arm. "Don't worry. I'll look into it." Siobhán paused. "You'd be wise not to say a word to anyone until I can check this out."

"You don't have to tell me twice. I can't wait for the day when I can stop looking over me shoulder."

—

The locals came out in droves for the wedding and soon dotted the steps of the church like mismatched figures dropped into an impressionist painting. Sheila Mahoney wore a glittering silver dress that, from the perspective of a hovering drone, might look like a shiny UFO doing a flyby, while her husband Pio stood rigidly by in a baggy tuxedo. On the opposite end of the steps, Peter Hennessy looked well-kept in a dark gray suit with a green bowtie, a marked departure from the denims he used to blend into his hardware store. Mike Granger gave up his cap for a comb-over, and finally there was Annmarie, screaming centre stage in a red, low-cut dress. Heavens. Siobhán was surprised she'd shown up. She prayed she didn't have a crush on Colm Cahill. Alice had been the one to decide that it would be a gesture of good cheer to invite the folks in town, and whether it was out of morbid curiosity or a desire to see love win out, they were happy to oblige.

Siobhán stood on the top steps of the church with Macdara, scanning their surroundings, hoping to spot anything amiss. She had donned an emerald green dress that set her auburn locks aflame and teased the green flecks out of her eyes. She'd caught Macdara sneaking glances at her, which always sent a thrilling shock through her. He was so handsome in his black suit, starched white shirt, and tie. She found herself wanting to touch him, a hand on his arm, an excuse to brush something from his collar, a quick kiss. She resisted the urges, lest he think the wedding was flooding her head with romantic ideals.

Nancy Flannery, to Siobhán's surprise, played the organ, and she was inside warming up. Cheerful melodies floated out on the breeze and buoyed the mood of the crowd. Brian burst onto the scene, sweating in his tuxedo. He wore a lavender tie and pocket square. He pulled a matching handkerchief out of his pocket and dabbed his brow. He was talking out loud, or perhaps to one of them, although he didn't seem to be making eye contact with anyone. Siobhán had to move closer to catch the gist of it. A champagne flute was missing. He'd had all their names engraved as a surprise, but Macdara's flute was nowhere to be seen. Brian finally worked up the nerve to ask Macdara if he'd pinched it. It took multiple repetitions of denial before Brian moved on.

"I don't even want the flute," Macdara confided to Siobhán. "Unless you can drink Guinness out of it."

"I have to side with Brian on this one," Siobhán said. "I go mental when things disappear."

"I'll keep that in mind," Macdara said with a wink.

"It was so nice of your mam to play the organ. She's very good."

"She likes to be helpful."

Siobhán smiled. *Like mother like son.* "I haven't had much time to get to know her."

"She hasn't run for the hills yet; that's a good sign."

"She's been forbidden by the guards to leave Kilbane."

"Well, yes. There's that. But she's still hanging around us, like."

Just then Siobhán spotted Val leaning over to tie his shoe on the church steps. He straightened up, looked at Siobhán, and winked.

"What was that about?" Macdara said.

"He's being cheeky," Siobhán said with a wave of her hand. She didn't want to get Macdara riled up. Had Alice changed her mind about him being a thief and invited him, or was he crashing the wedding?

Bridie hurried by with her hands full of white ribbons. She had on a pretty blue dress with a matching pillbox hat. Her brown curls bounced, and her eyes were bright and shining. "I'm going to help decorate the abbey," she shouted as she flew by.

Next her siblings entered the churchyard. The lads were in suits, and Ann and Gráinne wore dresses. Ann's was pink, which looked gorgeous with her light hair, but Gráinne was wearing a tight black dress that looked more suited to a nightclub than an afternoon wedding. Siobhán kept her gob shut; scolding her wouldn't do any good, and it was too late to ask her to go home and change. Besides, if she asked her to go home and change, then she would have to face the fact that Gráinne would not go home and change. Siobhán's heartstrings pulled at the sight of Ciarán in his suit, and it was grand to see Eoin out of his baseball cap for once. James kissed Siobhán on both cheeks.

"Chef Antoine is still in the kitchen."

"It smells delicious," Ann said.

"Oui," Gráinne said.

"Get a good seat," Siobhán said, gently urging them inside. "I'll be there in a moment." She watched as her brood filed in to the church.

Ronan came out just as they were going in and began scanning the churchyard with his camera. When all this was over, would they stop him from selling his photos?

She'd barely had time to wonder when shouts rang out from the small cemetery in the churchyard. Men's voices, raised in anger. Macdara ran toward the sound, and Siobhán followed. Once they turned the corner, they spotted Paul and Colm standing head-to-head behind a statue of an angel, shouting at each other over the headstones.

"Hurry," Siobhán said. "Quiet them down before Alice dissolves into a puddle." As Macdara headed for the men, someone grabbed Siobhán by the arm. She whirled around to see Brenna standing behind her in a fluffy yellow dress, the kind you might make your maid of honor wear if you loathed the ground she walked on. She looked like a giant baby chick. The dress was so bright Siobhán had to look away for a few seconds. *Jaysus*. Siobhán resisted the urge to cross herself.

Brenna swatted down the layers, only to have them bounce back up. "Alice wants to see you."

"Me?" Siobhán said. "Is she in the dressing room?"

"Yes." Brenna nodded, then flounced away.

—

Siobhán had to get to the dressing room to speak with Alice. They had to postpone this wedding. The killer was going to use the distraction to strike again. Siobhán could feel it in her bones. She was crossing the churchyard to Alice's dressing room in the small building adjacent to the cathedral when her mobile started beeping. She glanced at her screen. The Kilbane Inn. It was Margaret. Siobhán hesitated, then answered.

"I've been checking under the mattresses." Margaret sounded even more frantic than usual.

"What for?"

"Weapons."

"I see. And did ye find any?"

"No. But I did find stolen property."

Siobhán sighed. "Then why didn't ye call the guards?"

"I like you better."

"What did ye find?"

"Not on the phone. Someone could be listening."

"I can't come right now, Margaret. I can come after—"

"After will be too late." The phone went dead. Did Margaret hang up, or had the call been severed? Siobhán glanced at the time on her phone. She had an hour until the ceremony. Asking Alice to postpone the wedding wasn't going to be an easy feat. She wanted to ignore Margaret, but she'd made that mistake once before. Should she visit the bride first or Margaret? Siobhán had once ignored a call for help from Courtney. She'd regretted it the rest of her life. She wasn't going to make the same mistake with Margaret. She caught a flash of yellow coming toward her. "Brenna," she called, "tell Alice I have to zoom back to the bistro. I'll be right back."

Brenna rolled her eyes and continued in the direction of Alice's dressing room. Siobhán would have to take that as a yes.

—

Siobhán's scooter was parked behind the church. She ran for it. This would be the first time riding her scooter in a formal dress, but she had little choice. If there was serious trouble when she arrived at the inn, she would call the guards straightaway. She zoomed down the street, her dress flapping. When she pulled into the Kilbane Inn, Margaret was standing with her walker, waiting, an anxious expression plastered on her face.

Before Siobhán was even off her scooter, Margaret was tapping her walker down the path. She stopped in front of room number ten.

"Isn't that Paul's room?" Siobhán asked.

"You're a sharp one alright," Margaret said.

Siobhán hopped off the scooter and approached. "I don't feel right entering his room."

"I don't feel right with a murderer under me roof."

"Hurry. I don't want anyone to see us." Margaret unlocked the door, and soon the two of them were huddled inside. The bed was made, and the room smelled fresh. His clothes were tossed everywhere—on chairs, on top of the bureau, and on the bed.

"Lucky they can afford a maid," Margaret said.

"What stolen goods are ye on about?"

Margaret waddled to the bed, peeled back the covers, then lifted the mattress. She stuck her hand in and grabbed something. When she turned around, her face had scrunched into a ball of wrinkled anxiety. "He was my favorite," she said, almost sobbing. "To think he's a thief, and maybe a killer."

"Show me."

Margaret uncurled her fingers. Sitting in the middle of her palm was a sparkling diamond engagement ring.

Chapter 28

Siobhán flew back to the church. Paul, Colm, and Macdara were standing outside on the steps. At least everyone was still alive. Paul had stolen Alice's ring and lied about it. Macdara was going to have to face the truth about his friend. Siobhán had insisted Margaret lock it in her safe until the guards were called. And the guards would be called. Soon. But Siobhán wanted more time. Just a little more time. She was close. She could feel it. Macdara saw the look on her face. The three of them came to a halt in front of her. "What's wrong?"

"Nothing."

"I know that look. That's not nothing."

"Excuse me," Paul said. He broke off and jogged up the church steps. Colm stormed off in the opposite direction. *Either the man who is about to give the bride away is a killer, or the man she's about to marry is.* Either way, Alice was doomed. Siobhán was going to have to find a way to stop the wedding.

"You're completely flushed" Macdara said. "What is it?"

"What can I say? Weddings make me all aflutter."

Macdara narrowed his eyes and stared at her. "Liar."

"We'll talk later," Siobhán said. "First I have to see to the bride."

Siobhán entered the dressing room and found Alice standing in front of a mirror. She turned, and Siobhán gasped. Alice was wearing a light blue wedding gown. Her hair was pulled back in a tight braid. A veil of wild flowers adorned her head. In one hand she was clutching a horseshoe and in the other a bell. Unfortunately, she was holding the horseshoe upside down.

"You look gorgeous," Siobhán said, keeping her voice cautious. She stepped up and gently turned the horseshoe in Alice's hand the right way. "So your luck doesn't run out," she said gently. Alice did look gorgeous. The blue was particularly stunning with Alice's eyes. "Where did you get the dress?"

"Bridie helped me," Alice whispered. "She couldn't really get my other one clean."

"Well, you look gorgeous. She even added some Irish lace. Now there's a good bit of luck."

Alice nodded. Or she tried to nod. Her head wobbled instead. All was not well with the bride; that much was obvious. Alice rang the bell. "Faye couldn't find a Child of Prague." Alice picked up a garden gnome from the wedding table. "Do you think it will count if I bury this instead?"

Placing a statue of the Child of Prague in a garden prior to a wedding was supposed to ensure nice weather. Some brides buried it instead. "You should be sorted," Siobhán said, gently taking the gnome out of her hand and putting it down.

"A man has to be the first to congratulate me after I say 'I do,'" Alice said. She put the bell and horseshoe down and picked up a man's shoe from her wedding table.

"And I've asked Macdara to walk in front of me and throw this over my head." Another silly superstition. Only this time, Alice was buying into them. She'd gone completely mental. "I've already stood in the sun, but I didn't see any magpies." She grabbed Siobhán. "I have a confession."

"What is it?"

"I don't even know what a magpie looks like. What do they look like? And why does it have to be three of them? Won't one of them do? Is it because of the Holy Trinity?" Black tears began to run down her face. Siobhán tensed. This had surpassed superstition. Something had happened to rattle the bride. And if Siobhán wasn't mistaken, it had something to do with the mirror.

Siobhán hadn't noticed until now that every time she moved slightly, Alice stepped in front of it. Siobhán made more of a definite move for the mirror.

Alice whirled around, grabbed a robe off the dressing room table, and had it covered before Siobhán could get a look at it.

"What are you doing?" Siobhán said.

"It's bad luck to see the bride," Alice said.

Siobhán cocked her head. "I think that only applies to the groom. And I can still see ye."

"I don't want to chance breaking it," Alice said. "That's at least seven years bad luck. And seven years is when the itch starts. So I'd have seven years of bad luck only to start itching. I can't have that. I won't."

Siobhán had to find a gentle but firm way to break it to Alice that no matter what lucky talismans she drummed up now, this wedding had to be stopped. She took a deep breath. "I have something to tell you." There was only one way to do this. Quick and honest. "I don't think Kevin was the intended victim."

Alice's pretty face clouded over with confusion. "I don't understand."

"From behind in the dark. In the tracksuits. I think the killer thought Kevin was someone else."

"Who?" Alice stared at her with terrified eyes. "And why are you telling me this now? Of all times?" Siobhán blinked. This wasn't going to be easy. Alice was already wound tight. "You think it's my father. Or Paul. They're all about the same height." She began to pace; her heels clicked on the floor, and her dress swooshed along the floorboards.

Siobhán felt awful. But Alice had to know. If Paul was the killer and Siobhán kept silent—well, she couldn't have lived with herself. Siobhán stepped up. "In the dark. From behind," she repeated.

Alice stopped pacing and glared at her. "Are you saying my father tried to murder my fiancé?"

Siobhán swallowed. "Or your fiancé tried to murder your father." It was now or never. "Or your mother tried to murder your father. Or your mother tried to murder your fiancé. Or one of them tried to murder Macdara. I suppose there's a chance that Val is in the mix as well. His uniform is similar to the tracksuits, and he's the right height." There. It was all out. Siobhán thought about how people always said, "Now, that wasn't so bad, was it?" They were dead wrong.

"No. No, no, no, no." Alice began to pace the dressing room.

"I think the killer believed the victim was your father. That makes the most sense."

"Explain."

"He's a man of routines. He'd announced that he was going to walk to the top of the hill every morning."

Alice glanced at the shrouded mirror. "But why? My mother, for example. She's put up with my father for all these years. I won't pretend they had a happy marriage, but murder? Why would she?"

Because she's divorcing him. Siobhán didn't want to be the one to drop that on the bride. "Motives are often complex," she stalled.

"Macdara could have been the intended victim, couldn't he?" Alice repeated, almost sounding hopeful.

"Possible," Siobhán said. "But highly unlikely."

"Macdara could be the killer then," Alice said.

Siobhán felt her anger flare. She took a deep breath and had to remind herself that Alice was in a panic. And in denial. And why wouldn't she be? Of course she'd rather accuse Macdara than someone she loved. Siobhán told herself to stay calm. "Macdara is a guard," she said slowly, trying not to get too defensive. "He's dedicated his life to upholding the law."

"Perfect alibi, isn't it?"

"Macdara doesn't have a motive," Siobhán said.

Alice stared at Siobhán. "You said yourself motives are complex."

"Complex isn't synonymous with nonexistent."

"Macdara has a motive," Alice said.

A pinprick of fear raced up Siobhán's spine. "What are you on about?"

"The night they all went to the pubs, Macdara's mother came right out and asked my father for a loan. He politely turned her down."

"That can't be." Siobhán hadn't heard a word about this. Her mind was spinning, trying to make sense of it.

"Ask anyone," Alice said.

Siobhán took calming breaths. "That still doesn't go to motive."

"It might not, had it ended there. But my father never knows when to stop. The more drinks he had in him that night, the more he began to talk. Macdara overheard him speaking ill of Nancy to half the pub. Calling her a commoner with no manners. That's why Macdara squirreled her out as soon as possible. Paul said you could see steam coming out of his ears."

Paul. Had he made the entire story up? Had he been the one to plant Macdara's cap underneath Kevin's hand? Had he pushed Siobhán down the stairs?

"You have to postpone the wedding," Siobhán said. "I fear that someone is in grave danger."

Tears spilled from Alice's eyes, and the pacing commenced. "Why are you doing this to me? Just let us get married. Then accuse anyone you want."

"We need to call the guards," Siobhán said. "We need to keep everyone safe."

"Do you have proof?" Alice was practically shouting.

"I'm getting close."

Alice threw her arms up. "Close isn't good enough."

"There was the note your father wrote to Brenna—"

Alice put her hands over her ears and turned away. "This was not Paul. Or my mother. Yes, Daddy can be brutal when it comes to business. But my mother wouldn't kill him. There's no reason to kill him!"

Siobhán swallowed. She had to tell her. "Your mother is—"

The door swung open, and Susan Cahill stood on the other side. "What is going on in here?" The mother of the bride was wearing a white suit, bright red lipstick, and a dark glare. Susan turned to Siobhán. "Get out."

Siobhán froze. She didn't want to intrude, but this wedding had to be canceled. She hadn't even had a chance to tell Alice about the ring.

"No, you get out, Mother."

Susan Cahill looked as if she'd been slapped. Then she whirled around and barged out. The door slammed behind her.

Alice placed her hands in prayer position and shook them in front of Siobhán. "Please. Please. Just let me get through this wedding. We'll talk to the guards after."

"There's something else."

"I don't want to hear it! I don't want to hear another word."

"Someone is in danger. We have to cancel the wedding."

Alice snorted. "Did my father pay you as well, like?"

Siobhán felt the words like a slap across her face. She clenched her fists and took a deep breath, and imagined she was sitting by the river whittling a wee flower. That she then used to bash Alice over the head. "This next bit of news is about Paul."

"Get out. It's not Paul. It is not Paul."

"I'm not saying cancel, just postpone."

"I'm not letting you ruin my wedding day. Is everyone out there and ready? Tell them I'm ready now."

"Paul stole your diamond ring."

Alice became preternaturally still. All color drained from her face. She was almost as white as her dress. "You're lying." Her voice was that of a deflated balloon.

"I just came from the inn. Margaret found it under his mattress."

Alice blinked. She set her jaw. "I don't care."

"What?"

272

"Find my father and tell him I am ready right now!"

"Paul stole your ring and lied about it."

"Then he must have an explanation. And after we're married, I'll ask for it."

Siobhán was trying to figure out how to deal with this type of insane thinking when Ann and Gráinne entered the dressing room.

"How ya?" Alice said softly.

Gráinne and Ann approached. Gráinne held out her hand. In it was a blue broach that had belonged to their mam. Siobhán's throat seized up. "Something borrowed," Gráinne said.

"And blue," Ann said. "To match your lovely dress."

Tears spilled down Alice's cheeks as she gathered both Ann and Gráinne in for a hug. Then she pinned the broach to her wedding dress, even though it was hardly more than a piece of costume jewelry. "T'ank you."

Ann and Gráinne were beaming. "Father Kearney wants to talk to ye," Ann said as she and Gráinne headed for the exit. Ann spied a plate of butter cookies on a side table. She swiped one up and stuck the whole thing in her mouth.

"Don't!" Alice cried. Ann's eyes went wide. There was a knock on the door. "Come in," Alice said. She reached for a tissue and handed it to Ann, whose eyes were starting to water. Siobhán didn't have time to figure out why her youngest sister was suddenly tearing up, and why Alice looked so alarmed. The door opened, and Father Kearney strode in. Ann froze, her mouth clamped shut, as Father Kearney began going over the ceremony with Alice. Ann looked like a statue.

"Just a minute, Father," Alice said. She turned to Ann. "It's alright, luv." She thrust another tissue Ann. "I would have made the same mistake. Go on. Spit it out."

"What's going on?" Siobhán asked. Ann spit the cookie onto the tissue.

"Run to the jacks and wash your mouth out."

Ann nodded, tears running down her face.

"What on earth?" Siobhán said.

"Soap," Ann croaked, pointing to the plate of little white circles. She ran for the bathroom. Oh dear. The little soaps did indeed look like cookies.

Gráinne howled with laughter. "She had to wash her own mouth out with soap."

"Poor thing," Alice said. She was being so kind, even after Siobhán had been so cruel. But she had no choice. The closer they came to saying "I do," the more danger they were in.

Father Kearney cleared his throat. Everyone turned back to him. Siobhán slipped away and went after Ann.

She found her at the sink in the restroom, rinsing and spitting. "I'm such an eejit!" she wailed.

"No harm done," Siobhán said.

"You eat one then," Ann said.

"I would if it would make you feel better."

Ann looked up at Siobhán. "Alice is beautiful. You're beautiful. Gráinne is beautiful." Her voice grew in volume and rose in pitch until she was almost wailing. "I'm so ugly. And stupid. I'm such an eejit!"

Siobhán immediately folded her into her arms. Ann was battling a storm of hormones. Siobhán had been the same way. Probably still was. "You are not. You are absolutely gorgeous."

"I am not."

"I swear to ye. You're perfect." Siobhán smoothed down her blond hair. Ann was beautiful too, just lovely. It never mattered what the outside looked like. The most beautiful girl in the world could feel ugly on the inside. It made Siobhán want to weep.

"You have to say that."

Siobhán gathered Ann's hair in her hands. "Lovely blond hair. We'd all kill for it."

Ann sniffed. "Liar. They're always talking about you. Hair like fire."

"Fire burns. Didn't ye hear? Blondes have more fun."

"They do not."

"Cross me heart."

"Don't hope to die."

Siobhán kissed her on the top of the head. "I won't. I don't."

"I don't like all of this," Ann said. "I want things to go back to normal."

"The wedding is almost over. Then they'll be gone, and the trouble will go with them."

"Who do you think did it?"

"I don't like you worrying your pretty head over it. Let's just think happy thoughts for now, pet. Alright?"

Ann nodded. "Would you really eat the soap for me?"

"Only if it would make you feel better." Ann dug in her pocket and brought out another wee soap. She held it out to Siobhán with the faintest of smiles creeping across her face.

Cheeky lass. Siobhán sighed, took the soap, and squeezed her eyes shut as she brought it up to her mouth. *Ah, for feck's sake.* See there? Could probably use a bit of cleaning anyway.

Ann stopped her just as she brought it up to her mouth. She slapped it away. Siobhán smiled. "You do love me." Siobhán swiped at her.

Ann rolled her eyes and disappeared out the door.

T'anks be to God. Siobhán didn't really want to eat the soap.

By the time Siobhán came back out, the dressing room was empty. Siobhán was about to walk out when she stopped. She turned, walked over to the mirror, and ripped off the robe. On the mirror, written in bright red lipstick was a message:

SAY I DO AND YOU DIE

Chapter 29

Siobhán sat next to Macdara in one of the back pews, her knee bouncing up and down. Forty minutes had passed since she'd tried to get Alice to stop the wedding. She'd told Macdara about the message on the mirror. She'd left out the rumor about his mam asking Colm Cahill for a loan. Even if it was true, Macdara had nothing to do with the murder, and now was not the time to discuss why he had never mentioned it.

And there was always the possibility that Paul was lying.

O'Brien had subtly placed extra guards inside the church as well as outside. Guests were politely searched for weapons. None were found. Father Kearney was giving the Mass without the bride present, which wasn't something he'd do under normal circumstances. But even he seemed to want to get this wedding done and dusted. Everyone was just looking forward to drinking and dancing. Heads kept turning to the back of the church. Paul finally entered, and nodded. "She's ready." Macdara slipped up to the front, and Paul took his place waiting for his bride. Paul appeared to be breathing heavily, and sweat dappled his forehead. Cold feet? Guilt?

Siobhán's mind returned to the message on the mirror. Next she replayed the image of Susan Cahill bursting into the room. Her lipstick was an exact color match for the message on the mirror, not to mention the windshield of Macdara's car. Siobhán strongly disagreed with the decision to go on with the wedding. She'd even begged O'Brien to somehow put a stop to it. She thought the revelation about Margaret finding the diamond ring under Paul's pillow would do the trick. But no. O'Brien had made her swear up and down she wouldn't tell a soul, even Macdara. So here she was, keeping secrets from him. O'Brien was using the wedding to suss out the killer. Waiting for him to make a move. Siobhán had had the same idea earlier, but now she had a bad feeling. It was too risky.

Organ music filled the air. Nancy Flannery played beautifully, her hands floating across the keys as the notes swelled. Ann and Gráinne paraded up the aisle, gently tossing rose petals out of little baskets tied with white ribbon. Bridie's touch, no doubt. Gráinne caught Siobhán's eye and stuck the tip of her tongue out and rolled her eyes. Siobhán didn't think anything could make her laugh right now, but she had to slap her hand over her mouth and look away. All this stress had put her close to hysterics. Getting her brood into the act must have been a last-minute development. Paul, standing next to the priest with Macdara by his side, looked terrified as he watched the procession come closer. Siobhán's eyes drifted to the first pew, where Susan Cahill sat, crying into a handkerchief.

Crocodile tears?

Next Ciarán came tripping up the aisle, grinning and holding a pillow with rings. *All but the diamond engagement ring.* He waved at Siobhán and almost tipped over, rings and all.

"Eejit," Eoin whispered behind her.

Siobhán swatted his knee, then kissed his cheek. "Settle."

Once more, heads turned to the back doors, this time awaiting the bride and her father.

"Psst." Brenna opened the door to the church, letting in a hideous flash of yellow. She hissed and motioned for Siobhán.

Jaysus, what now? Siobhán hurried over. "What is it?"

"The father of the bride has gone missing."

This was just like him. A rush of anger overtook Siobhán. She was beginning to think Alice was right. Her wedding was cursed. Or at least she was cursed with a nasty family. Colm had been unable to stop the wedding, so he was going to throw a fit. She could suddenly empathize with Alice and Paul for wanting to go ahead. Now even she wanted the wedding to go on. Nobody liked a bully. "What does Alice want to do?"

"Ask Martin if he'll be willing to step in."

"Of course." Well, that was one way to stick it to her father.

Brian hurried to the back with his iPad. "What's going on?"

"The father of the bride is missing," Siobhán said.

Brian's hawk-like eyes scanned the patrons of the church. "I'm also missing a bottle of champagne, in addition to Macdara's flute."

"Well, there you are," Siobhán said. Was Colm off somewhere with a bottle of bubbly, drinking out of Macdara's flute?

"Are we delaying?" Brian's voice went up a notch.

"No. Alice is going to ask Martin Donnelly to walk her down the aisle."

Brian gasped. "Colm will take that as a sign of war."

"I believe he fired the first shot," Siobhán said, going along with the metaphor and then quickly regretting it as Brian paled. She turned and headed up the aisle, keeping a smile pasted to her face as all the guests stared at her. She grabbed Martin, and amid murmurs they made their way back to the foyer of the church, where Alice stood, bouquet in hand, frozen smile on her face.

"Are you okay?" Siobhán asked gently.

Alice took Martin's arm and nodded to Siobhán. Siobhán stepped back into the church and signaled to Nancy. Once again the wedding march began to play. Siobhán slid back into her pew. She was poised on the edge of the bench, wound up like a tightened violin.

The minute Alice and Martin entered, the bride took one look at her groom and started to beam. Paul smiled back, and for the two of them the rest of the room disappeared. Soon they stood face-to-face, clasping each other's hands.

Father Kearney wasted no time in getting to the vows, and the audience was on the edge of their seats.

Siobhán wondered if Colm was watching from somewhere. If he was, it was too late to stop it.

"I do," Paul Donnelly said loud and clear. Anyone could see the fierce love in his eyes for Alice.

"I do." Alice's voice was just as strong and steady. They turned to face the guests. Alice had tears streaming down her face. The audience rose and began to clap. They'd done it. They were married. Ronan was crouched in front of them, photographing every second.

Alice's gaze was on the back of the church. "Daddy!" she cried out. All heads turned. The door to the church swung shut. Someone had just been there. "He came," Alice said, clutching Paul's hand. "He saw."

"We'll make it work," Paul said. As the bride and groom hit the door, the guests scrambled after them, haphazardly throwing bird seed.

—

The bride and groom paraded through town with the guests, townsfolk, and a few guards in their wake. They made their way down Sarsfield Street, passed the colorful façades of homes, shops, and pubs, working their way toward the abbey. Before reaching the field, the townsfolk parted and waved good-bye. It was only a matter of common sense that Chef Antoine had not made enough to feed an entire village. It was sufficient for them to witness the ceremony and see the happy couple off.

"Out with it," Macdara said as Siobhán hurried toward the abbey, unable to shake the feeling that this had been a terrible mistake.

"I'm convinced that Colm either tried to kill Paul, or Paul tried to kill Colm." She hurried through the news, hoping it would make it easier to handle.

"A dozen suspects, and you think you've narrowed it down to two?"

"Two hard and two soft."

"Are we talking about suspects, or have ye moved on to eggs?"

"Paul and Colm are my two hard. Susan and Val are my two soft."

"You're just guessing. That's not how this works."

"Susan was wearing the same red lipstick as the message on the mirror."

Macdara stopped. "What message on the mirror?"

Shoot. She was starting to forget who knew what. She sighed. O'Brien was going to kill her. She brought her

281

mobile out of her handbag and showed Macdara the photo she'd snapped of the mirror.

"When did this happen?" Macdara was practically shouting.

"Just before the nuptials. I told O'Brien. He made me swear not to tell anyone."

Macdara digested that. "Do you think the writing looks the same as the message on my car?"

Siobhán nodded. They had both been written in red, although the message on the car looked more like paint, and the letters were larger. "We need to examine them side by side. Do you have the photo from the car?"

Macdara took her hand. "I turned it over to the guards. We need to let them do their job."

"Nobody's been stopping them, and look where that's gotten us," Siobhán said.

Macdara sighed. "At least Alice and Paul had their wedding. Maybe the killer has no reason to strike again now."

"Colm, Paul, and you are the only three men besides Kevin who could have been the intended target."

"Me?"

"You're the right height, and you had on the tracksuit. But only one man had declared he was going to walk to the peak of the hill every morning."

"Colm."

"Yes, Colm. The man who is currently missing."

"He's off pouting somewhere," Macdara said. "Licking his wounds that he didn't get his way for once."

"I hope so," Siobhán said. But she had a bad feeling. A very bad feeling.

"Susan has the strongest motive."

"And she has the lipstick."

Just as they passed the Kilbane Inn, Margaret came hobbling out on her cane. "Did ye tell him?" she shouted. "Where are the guards? I don't want that t'ing near me any longer."

Siobhán froze. Macdara almost ran into her. With all the distractions, she'd almost forgotten about the diamond ring. Macdara was staring at her, waiting for an explanation he wasn't going to like. She gave it to him. She was right. He didn't like it.

"Let me have a look," he said to Margaret. He threw a look over his shoulder at Siobhán. "It's not Paul," he said. "Paul could never murder a man."

Siobhán opened her mouth.

"Not a word," he said. "It's not Paul."

"Okay," Siobhán said. *Blind spot.*

"I'll meet you at the abbey," Macdara said. Siobhán leaned forward to kiss him. He stepped away from it, then turned to follow Margaret back to the inn. Siobhán felt the sting of rejection, followed by a hot flash of shame. It wasn't her fault. If his best friend was a killer, that was not Siobhán's fault. Everybody had a blind spot. Paul was in Macdara's blind spot.

Chapter 30

The transformation of the abbey into a wedding reception venue was stunning. Bridie had done an amazing job with little more than ribbons and flowers. Nature was the main decoration. The creek that ran through the abbey, the green fields, the remains of the stone monastery and bell tower, and even the Irish blue sky added to the ambience. It was on the cool side, but the rain had held off, and guests were mingling with glasses of champagne. A makeshift curtain made out of linen sheets was hung between the main area and the Tomb of the White Knight. They had fastened the sheet to the stone walls on either side with stones and tape. Beyond the curtain was where Pio's band would set up and the cake would be cut. Siobhán wondered why on earth they'd want to add any more mystery to today, but after all her hard work, Bridie wanted the cake to be revealed in a dramatic fashion, and everyone was respecting her wishes and steering clear of the tomb for now.

Tables were set up to serve the food buffet style, and Chef Antoine was bent over, extremely focused on presenting each dish just so. There would even be a carving station for delectable prime rib, turkey, and ham. Siobhán's mouth watered just upon seeing the station set up, and she realized she hadn't eaten much the past few days. It was so easy to eat while she was working in the

284

bistro, but things had been so crazy she hadn't had time. If one wanted to lose his or her appetite, investigating a murder seemed the way to go.

Alice and Paul were having their photographs taken in the bell tower. Ronan was perched on top of a stone wall, aiming the camera down on them. Siobhán had to hand it to him: he seemed willing to assume whatever position was necessary to get the best picture. Susan was pacing in front of the buffet table. Brian was darting back and forth between stations. Brenna was standing with a glass of champagne in hand, flirting with Val. Faye and Nancy were holding cups of tea and huddling together as if trying to keep each other warm. Martin Donnelly was standing in the field near the creek, smoking a cigarette. Siobhán crossed through the open rooms of the abbey and made her way to the creek to join Martin.

"What brand?"

"Pardon?"

"What brand are you smoking?" He reached into his pocket and brought out the packet as if he'd forgotten. Newtons. The same as the ones she'd found in the woods. Val hadn't been lying. "Don't bother giving me a lecture; that's what me wife is for."

"Someone dropped a pack in the woods," Siobhán said. "I saw them on my way to the crime scene."

"Are ye going to arrest me for littering?"

"No. But I would like to know when you were in the woods and if you saw anything?"

Martin sighed. "I was the first one up that morning. Since the accident, the doctor recommended daily walking to build my muscles back up. I guess I've taken a liking to it. Especially that time of day between day and night, when everyone else is asleep and it's like you get the world to yourself."

"What time was this?"

"It was half four."

"And where did you go first?"

"Went into the woods. Planned to go to the top of the hill for a smoke, but my packet of fags was missing, so I turned back. Guess you solved that for me."

"And no one else was around?"

"Just me and the birds."

"And then what?"

"Then I headed back down to the road. I'd read about Kilbane's medieval walls, and I wanted to check them out for m'self."

"And did you see anyone?"

Martin's eyes darted left and right. "You're not a guard."

He had seen someone. And he didn't want to tell her. Up until now he had been very chatty. There was only one person she could think of who would make him clam up like this. She decided to take a gamble.

"Paul told me he ran into you," she said.

Martin lifted his eyebrow, then laughed. "My son had a right to be up to a little mischief on one of his last days of freedom."

Paul had missed the morning walk with Alice. Said he overslept. Said he was locked in his room. So he'd lied. Lie upon lie. Siobhán had disliked Colm Cahill so much that she hadn't given anything he said much thought. But what if Colm had been right about Paul? What if he knew something about his nature and that's why he'd been so adamant about stopping the wedding? And if that was the case and he had something on Paul, then why hadn't he just come out and said it?

She had to find Colm Cahill. After all this, he hadn't even shown up for his own daughter's wedding. Alarm bells started ringing in Siobhán's ears.

"Did you and Paul stop for a chat?"

Martin stiffened. "What did he tell you?"

"Pardon?"

"You said Paul told you we ran into each other," Martin said. "I'm sure you got your answers from him."

"I can't keep everyone's stories straight."

"And why should you? Like I said. You're not a guard."

"Right then. Well, congratulations." She turned and started to walk away.

"For what?"

Siobhán turned back. "Your son just got married."

"Ah," he said. "Right." He sighed, blowing out smoke that drifted into the air and then disappeared.

—

As Siobhán was crossing back into the abbey, she almost bumped into Susan, who was hurrying out.

"Have you seen your husband?"

"He has some nerve!" She didn't even try to disguise her anger.

"You won't have to put up with him much longer, will you?" Siobhán hadn't meant to say it, but Susan was off-kilter. Throwing her even more off-kilter was the best way Siobhán could think of to get some results.

"What do you mean?" Susan began to blink, rapidly.

"Don't worry, I won't breathe a word," Siobhán said. "It's a family matter." A sense of shame washed over

Siobhán. It was bad form to talk about Susan's divorce in the middle of her daughter's wedding.

"I suppose you want money," Susan said.

"Of course not," Siobhán said.

"Why not? Everyone else does."

"I just want to know where your husband is."

"That makes two of us." Susan started to head off again, and Siobhán crossed in front of her.

"May I see your tube of red lipstick?"

Susan looked horrified. She clutched her handbag. "No."

"Has it been out of your sight?"

"What on earth is your problem?"

"Why does your husband dislike Paul?"

"Because nobody is good enough for his Alice."

"No other reason?"

Susan's eyebrow arched up even further. "Like what?"

"Did he have certain information on Paul?"

"Again. Like what?" Susan sounded sincerely curious. Maybe Siobhán shouldn't have opened her gob.

The ring had just been found in Paul's room; perhaps he had married for money. Had he planned on selling it to help out his father? "I just need to find Colm," Siobhán said.

—

Chef Antoine was standing by the carving station, wiping his brow. "Have you seen Mr. Cahill?"

Chef Antoine looked peeved. "I see no one. I see prime rib, and turkey, and bacon." She moved on. Brian was by the makeshift bar counting flute glasses. "Did you find Macdara's champagne flute?" He almost jumped five feet in the air.

"No. It's still missing."

"Have you seen Colm Cahill?"

"Not since just before the wedding."

Siobhán sighed. Looks like he was actually going to skip out on his own daughter's wedding. There had to be a reason.

—

Siobhán was standing by the Tomb of the White Knight when a breeze blew through, sending the untethered bottom of the sheet swinging up like the wind lifting a woman's skirt. It only stayed up for a second, but that was long enough for Siobhán to get a glimpse of a man's shoes. Was someone behind the curtain? She looked around. Nobody else noticed it. Before Brian could scold her, she slipped in.

The shoes were pointing straight into the air. They were attached to long legs, in a gray suit. Colm Cahill was lying on the ground. His eyes were closed as if he was just taking a nap. His mouth was slightly open. He was as rigid as the tomb. Next to his hand was a spilled glass of champagne. And lying in the puddle of the champagne was a dead bird. A frightful scream rang out, and it took several seconds before Siobhán realized it was her. She was screaming. She didn't even realize she was moving, physically backing up, until she slammed into someone. She whirled around to find Brian and his piercing dark eyes staring at her. He only looked at her for a second before his eyes landed on the horror on the ground.

"Is he?" Brian stammered.

Siobhán wrung her hands. "I think so," she said. "But I'm not sure." But she was. She was sure. Colm was way too still. She'd been staring at him for any little sign that he was just unconscious, but every bone in her body knew. She ran over and placed her hand on his neck. It was cold to the touch. She gently pressed but couldn't find a pulse. She tried his wrist. It was like cold rubber, and once again she couldn't find a pulse. Should she try CPR? The thought brought her gaze to his lips. They were blue and foam trickled from the edges. It was too late. He was gone. She threw a desperate look over her shoulder and shook her head. Brian screamed, and this time everyone came running.

Chef Antoine was the first to burst through. "Mais non!" He followed it with swearing and something that Siobhán assumed meant "Not again!"

Susan Cahill was in next. "Oh my God. Is this a joke? Get up!" she screamed at the body. Siobhán had to hold her back. "Keep Alice away!"

"Keep me away from what?" The bride and groom came running in. Alice pushed through the crowd. Soon the rest barreled in, and it was déjà vu, the first murder all over again, with shocked guests frozen in place.

"Daddy!" Alice flew over to the body, knelt down.

She probably shouldn't be touching the body, but Siobhán wasn't going to keep her from him. The crowd backed up and gave her some room.

"Is that the bird that's been dive-bombing me?" Brian whispered, pointing to the dead bird.

Siobhán nodded. "I'd say that's yer man."

"And yer missing flute," Brenna said.

"Who cares at a time like this?" Susan said.

Paul lifted Alice off the ground. "What happened?" Alice cried, hands still reaching for her father's lifeless body. "What happened?"

"Poison," Siobhán whispered. The clues were there. The spilled glass. The dead bird. The foam at the corners of the poor man's mouth.

"Poison?" Alice cried. She looked at the dead bird and then the glass. "Why was he even here, drinking champagne?"

Why indeed.

"Let's all move out of the area," Siobhán said. At her urging, everyone stepped out, backing up slowly. Alice began to weep.

Siobhán turned to Brian. "Gather all open bottles of champagne." He immediately nodded and flew over to the cart. He was the type who needed to have a task to keep calm. Siobhán was hurrying to where she'd stashed her mobile when Macdara strode in. He was smiling until he saw the ashen faces of the group. His eyes quickly fell to Colm.

"Oh, God, no."

"We just found him," Siobhán said. "I was about to ring ye."

"Who did this? Who?" Alice yelled.

"Susan was trying to divorce him," Faye suddenly piped up, pointing at the mother of the bride. "But he told her the prenup was ironclad. That the only way she would get any of his money was over his dead body."

"What?" Alice whirled on her mother. "Divorce?" Shock was stamped on her face.

"That has nothing to do with this," Susan stammered. "We both wanted it."

"You both wanted to keep all of the money too," Faye said.

Susan whirled on Faye. "He was having an affair, so I would have inherited."

Alice stepped forward. "He was having an affair?" This was definitely not the wedding day she had imagined.

Susan nodded. "You might as well know. Your father was unfaithful, and Paul has the proof." After dropping the bombshell on her daughter, Susan shook her fist at Faye. "You're going to be disbarred. That was lawyer–client confidentiality."

"What does she mean 'You have the proof?'" Alice said to Paul.

"I don't have it. I swear." Paul held his hands up.

"She's the one who done it." Faye shuddered, crossed herself, and pointed at Susan. Rosary beads came out of her handbag, and she began to rub them. "She set him up. Her own husband."

Susan towered over Faye. "You were the one who blackmailed me into switching champagne suppliers so that Martin's Transport could deliver it."

"What's that got to do with the price of tea in China?" Faye said. Her frightened demeanor was gone. She stopped rubbing her rosary beads.

"Obviously the champagne was poisoned," Susan said. "Maybe that's why you arranged for a new shipment in the first place."

Faye gasped. "What quarrel would I have with your husband?"

"Maybe you have the photo," Susan said. "Maybe you've had it all along."

"Why I never!" Faye said. "You're the one who profits from his death."

"Only with the photo, you silly cow. And I don't have it!"

"Mother!" Alice said.

"Mother," Paul said.

Alice gripped Paul's arm. She was shaking. "What did she mean 'You have the proof?'"

Ronan edged in. "I knew it," he said, pointing at Paul. "You took my camera card. Where is it?"

"You lied to me," Martin said to Faye. "You said it was Mrs. Cahill's idea to switch suppliers."

Faye gave a wry laugh. "Mrs. Cahill. As if she's beneath ye. That woman wouldn't give up an extra word without incentive."

"I did not murder your father," Susan said to Alice. "Don't ye think I would have done it by now?"

"But you weren't divorcing him until now," Alice said. Everyone was yelling over each other. It was impossible to follow who was saying what. Siobhán had possibly just incited a mob.

"I found an open bottle right here," Brian said, pointing to a champagne bottle leaning against the wall. He was about to pick it up.

"Don't touch it," Siobhán said.

"Bottle?" Macdara said.

"There's a spilled glass of champagne next to the body. And a dead bird lying in the pool of liquid. We believe it's been poisoned."

"Just like the brown bread," Brenna said.

"My stolen flute?" Macdara guessed. Siobhán nodded. "Great." It was going to make him a suspect. Again.

"It *is* Macdara's missing flute," Brian said. He pointed at Macdara. "How do you explain that?"

Macdara shook his head. "Obviously Colm grabbed a glass and didn't stop to care whose name was on it."

"Are there any other glasses missing?" Siobhán asked. It seemed strange that he would be drinking champagne alone. They were interrupted by a click.

Paul grabbed the camera out of Ronan's hands. "I'm sick of your despicable behavior."

"Give that back."

"Like hell I will. No more pictures."

"I'll sue."

"There's no point suing me," Paul said.

"Get used to it," Susan said. "You're rich now. Everybody sues."

Siobhán glanced at Macdara. Secrets were starting to come out, and there was still one that was being held back. "Did you get Alice's ring?"

All heads snapped to Macdara. He glared at Siobhán. But she had to do it. Emotions were raw. The killer was one of them. This was the time to get everything out in the open and see if it split open a clue.

"We'll talk later," Macdara said.

"The ring?" Paul said. "You found her ring?"

"Under your mattress," Alice said. "At the Kilbane Inn." Siobhán had to hand it to her; Alice wasn't shy when it came to confrontation. "See? You can't even deny it."

"Darling," Paul said, "it's not what you think."

"So you did take the ring?" Alice said.

"I wanted it to be a surprise."

"It's a surprise alright. The man I love is a thief and a liar."

Paul looked crestfallen. He reached into his pocket and pulled out a small box. "I didn't want you to have that ring. I wanted you to have this one." He opened the box, revealing an impressive diamond, slightly smaller than her grandmother's diamond ring, but beautiful and sparkly. "I was going to put it on your finger during the ceremony, but one look at you coming down the aisle knocked every thought clear out of me head."

Alice put her hand over her mouth. She reached for the ring, then retracted it. "Wait. So you broke into my parents' room and ransacked it?"

"I didn't mean to. At first. After Kevin's body was discovered, we only had a few minutes to clear out. That's when I snuck into your parents' room. I couldn't find the ring. By the time I did, the place was a mess. I thought if you thought the ring was stolen, you'd be more open to wearing this one."

"I see."

"I'm so sorry. I love you."

"Anything else?"

"Pardon?"

"Any. Other. Lies?"

Paul sighed. His shoulders slumped. He snapped the ring box shut and shoved it back into his pocket. "I knew your parents were getting a divorce."

Alice whirled on her mother. "Did you kill him? Did you kill my father?"

Susan gasped. "Take that back."

"Did you write that message on my mirror?"

"What message?"

Macdara stepped between mother and daughter. Alice looked ready to pounce. She was sweating and gulping air. "Let's just wait for the guards. They're on the way."

"I'm telling them everything." She glanced at Susan. "I'm telling them about your divorce." She glanced at Paul. "I'm telling them about the ring."

"They already know," said Macdara. "Please. Let's keep our heads on."

Paul dropped to his knees in front of Alice. "I'm sorry. I'm sorry."

"Please," she said. "Not here."

But Paul remained kneeling at her feet. "I was so sick of your father saying that I wasn't spending a pound of my own money. I wanted to get you something special. Don't you like it? I really thought you'd like it."

"My father is gone. How can you ask me to care about such frivolous things in this moment?"

"You're right," Paul said. "I'm sorry. I'm sorry." Paul's handsome face was filled with anguish. "Tell me you know I didn't kill Kevin." He stared at Alice. She swallowed.

"I know you didn't kill Kevin," she said.

He rushed forward and took her hands. "And I certainly didn't kill your father. I was terrified of him. Everyone was."

"You did fight with him right before the wedding," Brenna said.

Macdara hauled Paul to his feet and patted his back. "Everyone fought with him right before the wedding," Paul said as Macdara pulled him away from Alice.

"I believe Colm was the intended target all along," Siobhán said. "Kevin was mistaken for him the morning of his death."

A gasp rose from the crowd. Macdara grabbed her wrist and pulled her toward him. "What are you doing?"

"They're cracking like eggs on the cooker," Siobhán whispered. "We have to turn up the heat."

"Right before the wedding, Colm came into the abbey," Brian said. "I was setting up."

"What time was this?" Siobhán asked.

"Twenty minutes before the ceremony?"

"Did you speak with him?"

Brian looked at the ground. "He asked me to leave. Said he had a meeting."

"A meeting," Siobhán said. "Here?"

"Those were his exact words," Brian said.

A meeting with a killer.

"That's not unusual," Susan said. "Everything to him is a meeting. *Was* a meeting." Susan's voice wobbled, and then she too began to cry. Alice flew to her side and held her. "It was me," Susan said. There was another gasp from the crowd. "It was me," Susan said again, wailing. "It was me."

Chapter 31

Alice stepped back from her mother, her face turning to stone. "What was you?"

Susan seemed to shrink before their very eyes. She gripped a handkerchief. "The meeting was with me."

"Go on," Alice said. Her voice was ice.

"We argued. I told him that even without the proof of his infidelity I was going through with the divorce."

"What is this proof?" Alice cried out. "Somebody tell me."

Susan stuck her chin up. "The night before Kevin was killed, your father was in the pub making out with another woman. A full-figured woman with too much makeup, no less. A local."

Siobhán cringed, knowing Annmarie would strangle the woman for describing her in such an unflattering light.

"Let's tell the whole truth," Paul said. Alice looked from her mother to Paul. Susan shrugged. "Your mother paid this local to come on to your father so that Ronan could snap a picture and she could get out of the prenup."

"Oh my God," Alice said. She grabbed her mother. "Kevin knocked the camera out of Ronan's hands. Did he get the camera card?"

"I don't know," Susan said.

"Did you kill Kevin?"

"No," Susan said. "I don't know who has the camera card."

"What happened during your meeting with Colm?" Siobhán asked.

"Nothing. He was thrilled that I couldn't get around the prenup. That's all that happened. I swear. When I stormed away, your father was still very much alive." She shivered and turned her head.

Alice looked like she wanted to pounce again, but Siobhán cut her off. "Which way did you exit the abbey?"

Susan indicated the west entrance. Macdara sidled up to Siobhán. "What are you thinking?"

"I'm thinking the killer entered with the champagne and flutes while Susan was making her exit. With the poison in the flute with your name on it."

"But why my flute? And how did the killer even get him to drink champagne? Before the wedding?"

"I think your flute was stolen to divert attention from the real killer. Just like your cap."

"Why me?"

"I don't know. But I'm getting close. I have to talk to Eoin and Ciarán." Thankfully her brood had opted to go back to the bistro. Chef Antoine had made them extras and left the food in the kitchen.

"Eoin and Ciarán?" Macdara said.

"I'll be back," Siobhán said. "Can you keep them from killing each other until then?"

Macdara raised an eyebrow. "I'll do me best," he said. "But I can't guarantee it."

—

The bistro was jammers. It seemed as if everyone in town was in for a late brunch and eager to pore over the details of the wedding. Chef Antoine had made extra goodies for everyone. Ham and roast were piled on nearly every plate. Siobhán immediately checked underneath the register. *The Big Book of Poisons* wasn't there. Ciarán and Eoin were in the kitchen. Siobhán quickly herded them to the back garden.

"What's the story?" Eoin asked.

"Do either of you know where *The Big Book of Poisons* went?"

They shook their heads simultaneously. "When's the last time you saw it?"

"When you took it from me," Ciarán said.

"When we were back here with Chef Antoine," Eoin said.

"Then what did you do with it?"

"I put it back where I found it, on the shelf under the register."

"It's not there." Siobhán began to pace. "Remember when Antoine was teaching us about all the poisonous herbs?" Eoin's eyes went wide. He swallowed and nodded. "Did you tell anyone?"

"Why are you asking me?"

"I just need to know. Who did you tell?"

"A few lads. Bridie. James. Macdara. Alice and Paul."

Alice and Paul. Of course he was trying to impress Alice. "I'm going to need you to speak with the guards and tell them every single person who might have heard you talking."

"Why?" Eoin said. "What happened?"

Siobhán gently pushed Ciarán toward the door. "Why don't you go in and have a slice of cake?"

"I want to stay," Ciarán said.

"Two slices," Siobhán said.

Ciarán cocked his head, then ran for the door and disappeared inside. Eoin waited.

"Somebody might have put poison in a flute of champagne," Siobhán said.

"Is everyone okay?"

Siobhán shook her head. "Colm Cahill drank it. I'm afraid he's no longer with us."

Eoin dropped his head. "It's my fault, isn't it? For telling everyone about that book."

"Oh, petal, no." Siobhán grasped Eoin's hands. They were clammy. She held on anyway. "It's not your fault at all."

Eoin nodded, then sniffed. "Chef Antoine couldn't have done it, could he?"

Siobhán glanced toward the window that looked into the dining room. "How long has he been in the kitchen?"

"All day. He's been here all day."

"I'd say that should clear him. Was Brian in here with any of the champagne bottles?"

"No."

"Or did you see any of the champagne flutes around?"

"I didn't. I swear."

"No worries, luv. I believe you."

"I thought it was so cool. *The Big Book of Poisons.* But it's not. It's really not."

"There's nothing wrong with being curious. Or imaginative. You did nothing wrong."

"Is Alice okay?"

"She's okay, luv." She pulled him close. "Let's tell the guards what we know."

"I'm afraid to eat or drink anything now."

She was too. "Nothing to worry about. We'll just make sure we only eat and drink what we make ourselves until this whole business is sorted."

"Will it be sorted? Will it?"

"It will," she said. "Of course it will." She could only pray she was right.

–

By the time she got back to the abbey with Eoin and Chef Antoine, the guards were there, and everyone was standing by the river, lined up, facing the guards.

"What's going on?" Siobhán whispered to Macdara.

"They're taking them all into the station for questioning," Macdara said.

"Eoin and Chef Antoine might be able to help. We think the killer stole Ciarán's *Big Book of Poisons*."

"I'll bring them along then."

"How long will they be able to hold all the wedding guests at the station?"

Macdara flicked his eyes over her. "Why?"

"I'm close to figuring this out," Siobhán said. "I'm so close."

Macdara sighed. "I could probably bury them in paperwork for a few hours."

"Thank you," Siobhán said. "Thank you." Macdara nodded. She hurried over to O'Brien. "I'm going to need your help."

O'Brien, to her surprise, agreed. "Anything," he said. "Anything you need."

–

Siobhán had a specific list of questions, and she knew she had to start at the beginning. She had to start with the Huntsmans. And then she needed to ask Brenna a very important question. Fact-check something with Susan, and if she couldn't answer it, maybe Faye could.

Ask the guards another very important question, and double-check it with Val. She turned to Macdara once more as the guests began walking toward the station. "I need your help."

"Finally."

"Do not let Alice or Paul out of your sight. Not even for a second."

"You think they're in danger?"

Siobhán nodded. "I do," she said. "I do."

—

Carol Huntsman reluctantly took the call, which Siobhán placed from the reception desk of the castle. Siobhán made it quick. She only had five questions. "Who took the fax?" She kept her voice stern, letting Carol know that she wasn't messing. Her hand trembled as she wrote down the name she didn't want to hear.

When Carol spoke next, her voice trembled. "Alice was so furious with me."

"How do you mean?"

"The tracksuits. Because of the tracksuits nobody knew what or who they saw that morning. If they weren't wearing them, maybe someone could have identified the killer. Or cleared an innocent. We left town before the guards blamed us too. How was I to know someone would be murdered on our property?"

Siobhán glanced at her fourth question. "Did you tell the guests that someone in Kilbane was robbing folks?"

Once again Carol vehemently denied that accusation. Siobhán expected as much. "Does the castle have a secret passage that can be accessed from the outside?"

"How did you know?" Carol asked.

"Who did you show it to?" Siobhán asked. She underlined the name already written in her notebook. When she was finished with the phone call, she went to the back of the castle and finally found the little wooden door in the patio. She lifted it. Stairs led down to the passage. The killer had used this very passage to sneak into the castle and push Siobhán down the stairs. There was no need to go down and make the journey. It was enough to see how it was done. Next she collected some soil from the lavish gardens, and finally a guard showed her the exact spot along the wall where the killer had buried Kevin's belongings.

–

As soon as she completed her business at the castle, Siobhán ran back to the bistro and collected the item she needed out of Gráinne and Ann's room.

Next she asked O'Brien for the envelope of alibis. "None of them are missing," O'Brien pointed out as he handed it over. Siobhán knew that. But one of them had been altered. Brian's. And Siobhán thought she knew why. She got permission to speak with him and watched as he read his alibi. "I left out an item," he said, sounding thoroughly perplexed.

"No, you didn't," Siobhán said. "It was deleted."

"By who?" Brian asked. "And why?" Siobhán disappeared before he could badger her any further. She would ask O'Brien to find out if anyone in the police station had allowed the killer to use one of their computers and printer. Susan Cahill was next on Siobhán's list.

Susan was all too happy to be let out of the guard station to talk to Siobhán. "Yes," she finally admitted, "my red lipstick has gone missing. Why do you care?" Siobhán asked her second question. "Of course he threatened it. He threatened it all the time." Siobhán wrote something down. "It means nothing," Susan said. "If that was the reason, he would have been killed before we even got to this godforsaken village."

"Don't assume you know where I'm going with this," Siobhán said. "And if you breathe a word of our discussion, you will be arrested straightaway. There's no Armani in a Cork City jail." Siobhán was bluffing, but Susan's eyes grew wide, and she clamped her lips shut.

She talked to Faye next. "Of course it wasn't me. I was already representing his wife."

Siobhán nodded. It was hardly a mystery that Colm had his own solicitors. She would have to find out who all he employed and have the guards start making calls.

Next Siobhán questioned all the guards who had been on duty Friday afternoon until one admitted his transgressions. From the tone of his voice, it was clear that he was ashamed he had broken the rules. "It was a rather special occasion."

"Of course," Siobhán said. "Of course."

She spoke with Brian about who had access to the champagne flutes. She remembered Chef Antoine's words about wolf's bane. The snap of his finger. "Massive heart attack. Like that."

–

She found Annmarie in her shop. A suitcase was by the counter. Annmarie was shoving money from the cash register into her purse. She froze when Siobhán came in.

"I thought I locked it."

"Going somewhere?" Siobhán asked.

"Spain," Annmarie cried out. "My mother was right. Kilbane isn't safe anymore."

"So this has nothing to do with the fact that you were kissing Colm Cahill a few nights ago and now he's been murdered?"

"Kissing is a far cry from killing," Annmarie said. She didn't do it for the money, she insisted. She found him to be a very attractive man. "He wasn't a killer," she said as Siobhán was leaving. "He was with me Thursday morning. He snuck out to see me. There, that's everything. Now go, will ye? I have a plane to catch."

Siobhán remained standing. "Where's the USB card, Annmarie?"

"I don't know what you're talking about."

"Yes, you do. Listen to me very carefully. You're not a suspect. But you're holding a very important piece of evidence. If you don't come clean, the killer might slip away. Is that what you want?"

Annmarie shook her head, tears filling her eyes. She turned and unlocked a safe behind the counter, reached in, and took out the USB card.

"As soon as the picture was snapped, I realized I'd been a pawn in that sick woman's game," Annmarie said. "I saw my opportunity when the lads were fighting and the camera fell to the ground. Kevin tried to snatch it, but he was way too drunk."

"And you were going to use it to extort Colm Cahill."

"He's a businessman, isn't he?" Annmarie said. "It wasn't extortion. I had something for sale that he wanted to buy."

"That's why he came to you that morning, isn't it?"

Annmarie nodded. "I knew he wasn't the killer. Because he was with me. We were negotiating the terms of the sale."

"If you sold him the photo, then why do you still have it?"

Annmarie scoffed. "Rich people don't carry money on them. He was having it wired. I was waiting for it."

"He bought you that red dress you wore to the wedding, didn't he?"

Tears spilled down Annmarie's cheeks. "I don't care what anybody else says. He was a generous man."

-

Finally, the guards handed over all of Ronan's photographs. Some of them were quite stunning. But Siobhán wasn't interested in the artistry, nor did she need to look at all the photos. She was only interested in two occasions. Right before Kevin's murder, and right before Colm's murder. And it was as she thought. Circumstantial, of course, but not when you put it together with everything else. Last, she talked to all the townsfolk who had come to the wedding. Finally, she found the one she was looking for.

"Yes," Peter admitted. "I was late for the wedding. When I poked my head in, they were walking down the aisle, hand in hand, man and wife."

That was the last bit she needed. And if she played the game right, it would be enough to elicit a confession.

None of it would matter without the confession. And she only had one chance to get it.

If only Siobhán had had time to warn Colm that he had been the intended victim all along. And finally she organized a search. If she could find that bit of evidence, the guards would have a case, even without the confession. With the confession it would be the last nail in the coffin. The guards would dig by the abbey wall. Murderers, after all, were people first. And as the killer well knew, people were creatures of habit.

Chapter 32

They stood out in the back garden of the bistro, Siobhán and Macdara with the bride and groom. Siobhán had sent the young ones to Bridie's. Trigger was darting in and out; every time Siobhán thought she had a handle on him, he would run away again, barking indignantly at her attempts to scoop him up.

"It's such a relief," Alice said, "that everyone has gone home."

"I'm shocked," Paul said. "A traveler, you say?"

"Brenna was right all along," Siobhán said. "There was a robber in Kilbane. I wish I would have believed her."

"Have they arrested him yet?" Alice asked.

"Yes. He'll not see the light of day again." Siobhán didn't dare look at Macdara. He hadn't been on board for this, and he didn't even know all the details. Siobhán knew he had to see it for himself or might not ever believe it. Not to mention it involved tricking one party to get the other to reveal him or herself. Siobhán wished there was another way.

Alice was sitting on a bench, long legs crossed. Trigger jumped on her lap and began licking her hand. Paul was leaning against the back wall of the bistro. Macdara stood, hands folded, by the door. "But you know what's funny?" Siobhán tried to keep her voice light, but it wobbled a bit.

"What's that?" Paul said.

"The Huntsmans insisted they didn't start that robbery rumor."

"That is odd," Paul said. "And yet it turned out to be true."

"I know. I just don't like it when things don't fit. So I went back to Brenna to ask why she said it."

"She's always been a liar," Alice said.

"And yet you chose her as your maid of honor."

"She was a childhood friend. I didn't realize how much she had changed."

"I know what you mean," Macdara said, with a glance at Paul.

"It still doesn't make sense," Siobhán said. "Brenna was lying about something that turned out to be the truth?"

"I suppose stranger things have happened," Paul said.

"I spoke with Carol Huntsman yesterday."

Paul looked at Siobhán, then Macdara, and finally he looked at Alice. "Whatever for?"

Alice set her teacup down. "I have to use the jacks."

"I wouldn't do that if I were you," Siobhán said. Alice froze.

"Do what?" Paul said. "Use the restroom?"

"No," Siobhán said. "Do a runner."

Paul stepped forward. "What is going on?"

"I accused Macdara of having a blind spot," Siobhán said, "when all this time it was me."

Paul looked at Macdara. "What's she on about?"

"But I'm seeing clearly now," Siobhán said.

Alice took a step forward "What on earth are you talking about?"

"You," Siobhán said. "I'm talking about you."

Alice clung to Paul. "She's accusing me of murder," she cried.

Paul stuck his chest out. "I did it," he said. "I'm the one."

"You did what?" Alice looked between the three of them.

"A traveler didn't kill Kevin or your father. I did."

"Don't be ridiculous."

"I'm going to make a full confession." He took Alice's hand. "Don't worry about a thing, darling. We'll hire the best solicitor money can buy."

"Stop saying that. This isn't funny."

"I didn't mean to kill Kevin," Paul stammered.

"You didn't kill Kevin," Alice insisted.

"I didn't mean to. I thought he was your father." Paul truly sounded as if he was guilty.

"No. No." Alice's pretty head shook from side to side.

"It was barely light out, and those tracksuits," Paul stammered. "Your father is the one that was supposed to be up there."

"He snuck out to meet Annmarie instead," Siobhán said. "It saved his life." *But not for long.*

Alice whirled on Siobhán and Macdara. "You had better not believe a word of this. We're not at a gardai station. This is not a confession. Not one word."

"It's done," Paul cried. "I've confessed."

"Did you know Ronan loved taking photographs of Alice?" Siobhán said to Paul.

"Everyone loves taking photographs of Alice," Paul said.

"We were able to look through all of his photos," Siobhán said.

"So?" Alice said. "So?"

"I've confessed," Paul said. "Now take me to the gardai station."

Macdara clamped a hand on Paul's shoulder.

Siobhán continued. "Ronan never stopped taking pictures. And there were only three occasions when Alice wasn't in them." Siobhán held up a finger. "The night everyone went to the pubs. Everyone but Alice."

Alice stayed quiet. No doubt she was remembering how she had used that time. To find the perfect rock. To put it in the perfect spot.

"How could he take her picture when she wasn't there?" Paul said.

"Do you want to hear the other two times there were absolutely no photos of Alice?"

Paul flicked his eyes nervously to Alice. She stared straight ahead. "The morning of Kevin's murder, and right before Colm's murder."

"I don't see—"

"She wasn't around to be photographed. Or he would have been photographing her."

"That's circumstantial!" Alice cried.

"Yes," Siobhán said. "'Tis."

"Why are you doing this to me?" Alice said, whirling on Siobhán. "They said they arrested a traveler."

"I've confessed," Paul said. "Didn't you hear me?"

"We don't accept your confession," Macdara said.

"What are you doing?" Alice cried.

"I couldn't let an innocent man go to jail for me," Paul said. "I have to do this."

"No," Alice said. "No."

"The guards are digging around the abbey wall as we speak," Siobhán said. "They're going to find Colm's will."

Paul's head snapped toward Siobhán. "His will?"

"He had a new will faxed to the castle. One that cut Alice out completely if she married you."

"He was always threatening that," Paul said.

"But this was more than a threat. This was the actual will. Only someone took it before he could sign it."

"Circumstantial," Alice said.

"Do you want to know what should have been my first clue?" Siobhán said. Alice didn't blink, move, or breathe. "You got sick *before* Chef Antoine came sprinting out with the news of Kevin's murder." That was the first clue. Siobhán had missed it because she'd been too upset over Brenna saying the brown bread had been poisoned and rumors that Alice might be pregnant. Colm strode onto the lawn, and Alice promptly got sick.

"So?" Alice thrust her chin up.

"You got sick because you thought you saw a ghost."

"A ghost?" Paul said.

"Her father. He was leading the group across the lawn. She thought she'd just bashed him over the head with a rock." Siobhán turned to Alice. "That was the moment you realized you killed the wrong man."

Alice clenched her fists. She was thinking of those darned tracksuits, no doubt. Poor Carol Huntsman had only tried to be nice. Alice had really laid into her after the murder, blaming her for the case of mistaken identity. She'd scared them so much they'd fled from the castle. No doubt Carol also realized that Alice had stolen the fax. And no doubt she knew the fax was Colm Cahill changing his will. No wonder they fled.

Paul's eyes narrowed. He jabbed his finger at Siobhán. "I want to talk to the detective sergeant. Tell him I want to make a full confession."

"And then there was the black soot on the note that Kevin thought was summoning him to the hill. Black

313

soot that came from the gardens. There's a photo of Alice kneeling by them."

"So?" Alice said. "Anyone could have done that."

"But they'll be your fingerprints they find on the note, won't they? Along with Kevin's gold watch and chain. First, you buried everything along the wall. This is when the tracksuit actually helped you out. Chef Antoine saw you digging over there and from a distance assumed it was Val. He only saw the back of you hunched over. You buried Kevin's things, and then you started the rumor about the robbery. Not the Huntsmans. Not Brenna. You. Then, when Chef Antoine told you he thought he saw Val digging near your burying spot, you had to go back and see for yourself. That's what you were doing when Val came upon you. And then I arrived to find you wrestling with the poor lad, at which point you pretended he had been attacking you. But we know now that it was the other way around. Because it was you Chef Antoine saw digging, not Val."

"The Huntmans told us about the robberies!" Paul said. He was still trying to protect his bride.

"That's what Alice told you," Siobhán said. "She couldn't let the rumor be traced back to her."

"You won't find any hard evidence. It's all circumstantial!"

"Oh, Alice. Don't be confused by the circumstantial. Because strung together, the evidence is almost insurmountable."

"I won't hear of it," Paul said. "She didn't do it."

Siobhán pressed on. "A guard will testify that he let Alice go to Limerick on wedding errands on Friday afternoon."

Paul stole a glance at Alice. "I thought you were napping."

"You wrote the message on Macdara's car. Just like you wrote the message on the mirror. I'm sure the handwriting will match your signature on the magazine you signed for me. The guards are comparing and analyzing them right now." That was a little white lie. O'Brien was probably using the magazine to prop up his wobbly table.

"I hate you," Alice cried. "You could have just let this go."

"You poisoned your father before the wedding. You brought the champagne flutes and bottle of bubbly, then told him you were calling off the wedding. That certainly called for a toast, didn't it?"

Tears came into Alice's eyes and spilled down her cheeks. "He just wouldn't stop," she said.

"You took Ciarán's *Big Book of Poisons* and went on a little search. I don't know which one you used. But I'm sure the toxicology report will tell us."

Alice began to blink rapidly.

Paul turned to his bride. "Don't say another word." His complexion was taking on a sickly shade of green.

He was still trying to protect her. He was still in denial. Siobhán found that kind of sweet and utterly heartbreaking.

"Peter Hennessey admitted that he was the one who poked his head into the church when the nuptials were over. You saw the door open and pretended it was your father."

"That's right," Macdara said. "I forgot about that."

"No one could have mistaken the five-foot Peter for Colm Cahill. Especially not his lovely daughter. And your father was already lying dead in the Tomb of the White Knight."

A strangled sob escaped Alice.

"No," Paul said. "This can't be." He had been protecting her, even confessing because he vehemently believed in her innocence. The illusion was starting to crack.

"We'll pay you," Alice said. "I'll pay you. You can go to college. Get out of this bistro. This godforsaken village!"

"Tell the truth," Siobhán said. "That's the only choice you have left."

"We're all friends," Alice said with a forced smile. "We can work this out. How would you like for your siblings to be taken care of for the rest of their lives? I heard you only rented this place. How would you like to own this bistro outright?"

"You're offering her a bribe in front of a guard," Macdara said.

Alice's eyes flicked over Macdara. "I could send your mother money too. She'd like that, wouldn't she?" Alice snapped. He clenched his jaw. Alice produced a flask from her handbag. "How about we all have a stiff drink?" She started to put the flask to her lips. Siobhán grabbed it. Alice cried out.

Paul stared at the flask. "You think that's poison, don't you?" he asked Siobhán. His voice was low and dark.

"Don't listen to any of this," Alice said.

Paul grabbed the flask. He put it to his own lips. Alice shrieked and lunged for him. She knocked it out of his hands. It toppled to the ground, where the liquid snaked out along the patio.

"Oh, God," Paul said.

Alice broke down and sobbed. "I tried to protect you," she said. "I even locked you in your room so they wouldn't suspect you."

"That was you?" Paul said.

Tears spilled over Alice's cheeks. "I didn't want you to be a suspect. I stole a key from the front desk so I could lock you in. You could have opened it from your side with your key, but I took the chance that you'd be too hungover to figure that out."

Siobhán thought of something. She turned to Paul. "But you couldn't have been locked in. Your father saw you out walking early that morning."

Paul hung his head. "I told you I was locked in. What I didn't tell you was that I discovered it way before sunrise and Carol let me out. When Alice was upset that I missed the photo shoot, I simply used that as the excuse."

"Why were you up so early then?" Siobhán asked.

"Does it really matter now?" Macdara said.

Siobhán sighed. "I just hate loose ends."

Paul put his face in his hands. "I heard Kevin stumbling out. That's what woke me. I was going to see what he was up to. By the time I got out of the room, he was nowhere to be seen. I was already out and about, so I went for a walk."

While they were talking, Alice had started to sneak away. Macdara caught her arm just as she was about to make a run for the back gate.

"You're not going anywhere," he said.

"I can't go to jail." Alice yanked out of Macdara's grip with surprising strength. "You should have just let me die."

"Darling, why?" Grief oozed from Paul. In two strides he crossed the patio and held his bride. "Anyone would have wanted that man dead." Paul looked at Macdara as if pleading with him. "Anyone."

"He was always bullying me," Alice said. "My whole life."

"You never thought he would do it," Siobhán said. "Actually write you out of the will."

They would find the will buried near the abbey wall, close to where Alice had buried Kevin's things. Even criminals were consistent.

"What else, Garda Siobhán?" Alice said sarcastically. "I want to hear everything the girl genius figured out."

"You used the secret passageway to sneak into the castle while I was there to collect your things. You shoved me down the stairs and grabbed the alibis. It was Brian's alibi that you took. Because he noted seeing the fax, then running into you outside just a few minutes later."

"She shoved you down the stairs?" Macdara said.

"I should have killed you," Alice said. "It's a pity I didn't shove you harder."

"Alice," Paul said, breaking away from her. The reality of who he had married was starting to sink in.

"How did you catch me?" Alice said, her eyes narrowing. "A common girl like you."

"Maybe I am common. Or maybe you just didn't plan the perfect murder. Although you were clever. Throwing blame on everyone but you."

"What do you mean?" Macdara asked.

"She told me Paul had dirt underneath his fingernails when she saw him that morning—"

"Me?" Paul said.

"She used her mother's lipstick to write the nasty notes—first on the car, then on the mirror. She placed your garda cap under Kevin's hands—"

"Someone had dropped it on the grounds," Alice said. "They should have immediately arrested him for the murder."

"You even tried to blame Val for stealing. Yet you were the one Chef Antoine saw digging by the wall, scrunched over in the dirt by Val's post. He simply assumed it was Val."

"I would do it all over again," Alice said. "Just to be free of my father. You can't imagine what it was like to live under his thumb."

"Poor Kevin," Paul said. The veil was lifting. He was finally starting to see what the love of his life was really like.

"I didn't mean to kill him. He wasn't supposed to be up there!"

"You did it for the inheritance," Macdara said. "Paul would have married you either way, you silly woman. Don't you know that?"

"You're the one who doesn't know anything. You can't just stop being rich."

"For money? You did this all for money?"

"Paul, don't listen to them. I stopped you from drinking poison, didn't I?"

Paul broke away from Alice, shaken. "I wish you hadn't," he said. "I wish you hadn't."

Alice suddenly fixated on something lying near the herb patch. Before anyone knew what was happening, she swooped something off the ground and held it up. The silver blade of a large chef's knife gleamed. Once again Chef Antoine had been careless with his tools, no doubt beleaguered by the wedding preparations. And now Alice was holding up a very large, very sharp knife. "I'm going

319

to walk out of here," she said. "If one of you makes a single move, I'm going to slice that person, and then cut my own throat in front of your very eyes."

Chapter 33

Once the threat was delivered, Alice turned and ran. She escaped through the back fence to the alley behind the bistro.

"I'll get the car," Macdara said.

"I'm coming with you," Paul said.

"Stay here," Macdara said to Siobhán.

The minute Macdara and Paul jumped into the car, Siobhán jumped onto her scooter. Macdara would be furious with her, but she had to go. *Stay here.* As if. Besides, she was pretty sure she knew exactly where Alice was going. Back to a secret hiding place.

Siobhán reached the castle, turned off her engine, and pulled her scooter to the side of the road. Macdara would spot it straightaway. She texted him the location of the secret passage as she was running toward it. Alice was in there; she was sure of it. She had already tried to drink poison, and there was no telling what she would do with the knife. She was going to have to face justice, but that didn't mean she deserved to die. Alice was a cornered animal now, and chances were good that she was going to hurt herself. Siobhán couldn't have that on her conscience. She hurried along the woods and then cut to the back of the property. The trapdoor to the passageway was flung open. Alice hadn't even bothered to close it.

Siobhán slipped down the stone steps and into the dark tunnel.

It was pitch-black and smelled like mold. She could hear water dripping in the distance. She listened for more. And then, there it was, the sound of heels echoing down the passage. Siobhán took off her shoes. Once again in her bare stockings, and they would get wet, but at least she could sneak up on Alice. As she hurried down the passage, she could see there was a light somewhere in the middle. It was coming from a bulb by the second set of stairs, this one leading up into the castle.

Siobhán infused her run with the most speed she could muster, flew past Alice, and plastered herself against the door. The knife was still in Alice's hands.

"It's over," Siobhán said. "You need help."

Alice cried out, startled to see her. Then she shook her head. In the dim light, her pretty face looked tortured. "Why?" she cried. "Why couldn't you just let it go?"

"I'm going to let it go," Siobhán said. "Just put down the knife, and let's get out of here."

"You should have at least let me drink the poison, wretched woman that you think I am."

"I don't think you're wretched," Siobhán said. "Come on. Paul is waiting for you."

"Wolf's bane. Chef was right. It's very fast acting. My father didn't suffer. He never even knew what I had done. His last thought was that once again his little girl was doing his bidding."

"Put the knife down."

"Or I could kill you," Alice said. "We could die together."

In the distance, voices and footsteps drew closer.

"That will be the guards surrounding the grounds," Siobhán said. "I left the trapdoor open. They'll find us."

Siobhán needed to open the door she was leaning against. But she knew better than to turn her back on Alice. Just as she was reaching behind her to try and feel for the latch, Alice reached forward and grabbed Siobhán's hair. Siobhán screamed as Alice dragged her down to the ground.

Siobhán had only been in one fight in her life. A bully in grade five. She'd lost. Afterward her father had coached her. How to poke someone in the eye. How to protect one's face. Siobhán put her hands up to do just that, and at the same time tried to get to her feet. She had just about made it when Alice grabbed onto her ankles, sending her crashing down once again. This time Alice leapt on top of her. She straddled her, holding the knife aloft in her right hand. When Siobhán looked into her eyes, she saw a madwoman. She reached up with both hands and dug her nails into Alice's right wrist. Alice screamed, and the knife clattered to the ground. But before Siobhán could push her off, Alice's strong hands found Siobhán's neck, and she began to squeeze. Footsteps pounded down the passageway.

"Stop!" It was Macdara.

"Alice, don't!" Followed by Paul.

At the sound of Paul's voice, Alice stopped squeezing. Siobhán sank her teeth into one of Alice's fingers. Alice screeched and finally let go of Siobhán's neck. This time, Siobhán didn't hesitate. She shoved her off and rolled out from underneath her. Alice lay facedown in the passageway, sobbing. Siobhán scrambled to her feet, kicked the knife far out of the way, and ran for Macdara. He swept her into his arms and held her tight. When he finally let go, she saw concern stamped all over his face as he eyed the red marks on her neck.

"I'm okay," she said.

"The thought of losing you." Macdara's voice choked.

"Let's get out of here." Macdara kept a tight grip on Siobhán's hand as he led her out of the passage and onto the castle lawn. Then he turned to help Paul, who was wrestling with Alice. The minute they hauled her out of the passageway and onto the grounds, she collapsed in a heap, wailing. Pity seized Siobhán's heart. Despite everything, it was so easy to love her.

"Don't leave me," she implored Paul. "Don't leave me."

Paul sank next to her.

"Boss?" Macdara said.

"Just give us a minute," Paul said. "For old time's sake." He took Alice's hand. "Come on, my darling wife. Don't cry. It's such a beautiful day."

Epilogue

Siobhán and Macdara stood at the counter in Naomi's Bistro. Macdara was holding the stack of university catalogs.

"Promise me," he said, "that you'll go back to school, and never investigate another murder ever again." He set the catalogs on the counter. Only a day had passed since Alice had confessed and been arrested. This was not the time to tell Macdara she didn't think she wanted to go to college. She had something else in mind. "I couldn't bear it," he said. "I couldn't bear if anything like this ever happened again."

"Would you like a cappuccino?" Siobhán asked.

"You could take evening or weekend courses," Macdara said. "I can drive you into Limerick myself, or you could commute to Charleville on your scooter and then take the train in."

"I'll look into all my options," Siobhán said softly.

"Swear to me."

"I swear." She wasn't lying. She would carefully consider everything. That she promised. But there was another promise she couldn't keep. That he would like what she chose.

He leaned in, kissed her. "I've got to go. We'll be jammed with paperwork."

She watched him go, his broad shoulders disappearing down the street. She sighed, gently shoved the catalogs away, and made herself a cappuccino. She took the mug of heaven to the chair by the fireplace and plopped down. She reached down and picked up her laptop, which she'd stashed near the chair. She opened it and stared at the search bar. She typed in her query:

How do I join An Garda Síochána?

Just reading the query made her tingle with excitement. Could she do it? Could she become a guard, and one day a real detective? As she stared at the page, Trigger jumped into her lap and curled into a ball of love. Ciarán had been right all along. A few treats and the mutt loved her. She massaged his little head and glanced at the clock. Thirty minutes before her brood would come home, to tell her all about their first day of school. Thirty minutes until the bistro was filled with the sounds of young ones arguing and shoes stamping up and down the stairs, and arguments over what would be for supper. Thirty minutes until the best part of Siobhán O'Sullivan's day. She hit enter and, heart in throat, waited.

Acknowledgments

Thank you to my agent, Evan Marshall, my editor, John Scognamiglio, and all the hardworking staff at Kensington from copy editors to publicists, to cover artists. Many thanks to friends, family, and readers.